W9-AAB-150

FLORA NWAPA

♦

Efuru

HEINEMANN

Heinemann International Literature and Textbooks
a division of Heinemann Educational Books Ltd
Halley Court, Jordan Hill, Oxford OX2 8EJ

Heinemann Educational Books Inc
361 Hanover Street, Portsmouth, New Hampshire, 03801, USA

Heinemann Educational Books (Nigeria) Ltd
PMB 5205, Ibadan
Heinemann Educational Boleswa
PO Box 10103, Village Post Office, Gaborone, Botswana

LONDON   EDINBURGH   MELBOURNE   PARIS
SYDNEY   AUCKLAND   SINGAPORE
MADRID   ATHENS   TOKYO   BOLOGNA

ISBN 0 435 9026 9

© Flora Nwapa 1966
First published 1966
First published in *African Writers Series* 1966
Reprinted six times
Reset 1978

Printed and bound in Great Britain by
Cox & Wyman Ltd, Reading, Berkshire

92 93 94 95 10 9 8 7 6 5

To the memory of
A. C. Nwapa

CHAPTER ONE

They saw each other fairly often and after a fortnight's courting she agreed to marry him. But the man had no money for the dowry. He had just a few pounds for the farm and could not part with that. When the woman saw that he was unable to pay anything, she told him not to bother about the dowry. They were going to proclaim themselves married and that was that.

Efuru was her name. She was a remarkable woman. It was not only that she came from a distinguished family. She was distinguished herself. Her husband was not known and people wondered why she married him.

It was after the festival in which young men and young women looked for wives and husbands that Efuru first met Adizua. Adizua asked her to marry him and she agreed.

One moonlit night, they went out. They talked of a number of things, their life and their happiness. Efuru told him that she would drown herself in the lake if he did not marry her. Adizua told her he loved her very much and that even the dust she trod on meant something to him.

'But what about the dowry?' the woman asked.

'You will come to me on Nkwo day. Every place will be quiet that day being market day. Take a few clothes with you and come to me. We shall talk about the dowry after.' Efuru agreed and went home feeling very happy and light.

'It's late, Efuru, where are you coming from?' one of her cousins asked her as she was opening the gate of the compound.

'Don't you see the moon?'

'Is that the reason why you should come home so late? I shall tell your father. A young woman like you should not be out so late.'

'I don't care whom you tell.'

The next morning the cousin went to Efuru's father and told him that he had seen Efuru at a very late hour last night and

7

when he asked her why she was so late, she was rude to him.

'My brother, help me to talk. I am tired of talking. I don't know what is wrong with young women of these days. I noticed that Efuru has been coming home late for quite some time. I asked her whom she was seeing so late and she said nothing. If her mother were alive, she would have known how to handle her.'

'Do you think there is a man in her life?'

'I think so, my brother. If the man wants to marry her, there is nothing wrong about that. The man should come and fulfil the customs of our people and marry her. But as it seems now I don't think the man in question wants to marry her. And that is dangerous. What if she gets pregnant? Who will look after her, now that her mother is dead?'

'I shall do my best to be of any help to you. I shall investigate.'

On Nkwo day when everybody had gone to the market, Efuru prepared herself. She had her bath very early in the stream. She took great care that morning over her appearance. Her father was now not at home. She took a few of her belongings and went to her lover's house.

The mother of the young man went to the market; when she returned she was surprised to see Efuru's clothes and and a few other possessions in her son's room. The young man was quick to explain. He told his mother that Efuru was his wife. 'I have no money for the dowry yet. Efuru herself understands this. We have agreed to be husband and wife and that is all that matters.' The young man's mother was excited for her son had indeed made a good choice.

'You are welcome, my daughter. But your father, what will you say to him?'

'Leave that to me, I shall settle it myself.'

Efuru's father returned from the market and did not see his daughter. 'Perhaps she went to the stream,' he said to himself.

But Efuru did not return. Just when he was about to go to bed, he heard a knock at the door.

'Who is that?'

'It's a man. Open the door.'

'Oh, is that you, my brother? Did you see Efuru?'

'Efuru has run away to a young man. It is a shame. Our

8

enemies will glory in this. This young man is nobody. His family is not known. Efuru has brought shame on us. Something must be done immediately to get her back.'

'What are we going to do, my brother?'

'We shall send our young men to go to the man's house. Efuru will be asked to come home with them. That's all.'

On the appointed day, the young men went to bring back their daughter who had brought so much disgrace to them. Immediately Efuru saw the men, she came out and greeted them.

'Welcome, my brothers. What good wind brings you here today. I hope all is well?'

'All is well, our daughter,' the men said.

'We have come for a business,' the spokesman added.

'We shall have kola before the business. It is a pity my husband is not at home. He went to the farm.'

Efuru brought two big kola-nuts. They were fit only for kings. She put them before the men, with some alligator pepper. The spokesman took one kola nut and blessed it. Then he broke it and gave the men.

Meanwhile, Efuru brought out a bottle of home-made gin – a very good one that had been in a kerosene tin for nearly six months.

'I am sure you will like this gin. Nwabuzo had it buried in the ground last year when there was rumour that policemen were sent to search her house. When the policemen left, finding nothing, Nwabuzo was still afraid and left it in the ground. A week later, she fell ill and was rushed to the hospital where she remained for six months. She came back only a week ago. So the gin is a very good one.'

The men enjoyed the drink very much. They finished the bottle and some of them were even tipsy.

'We shall go, our daughter,' the spokesman said. 'You seem to be happy here and we wonder why your father wants us to bring you back. We shall tell him what we have seen. But your husband must fulfil the customs of our people. It is very important. Our enemies will laugh at us. Tell your husband, he must see your father. Let him not be afraid.'

Efuru knelt down and thanked the men. 'Tell my father that I shall be the last person to bring shame on him. Since my

9

mother died five years ago, I have been a good daughter to him. My husband is not rich. In fact he is poor. But the dowry must be paid. I must see that this is done.'

The men thanked her and left. Efuru's father was not satisfied with what the men told him. He sent another batch of young men from his village. But nothing came out of it. So he gave up his daughter as lost.

Efuru refused to go to the farm with her husband. 'If you like,' she said to her husband, 'go to the farm. I am not cut out for farm work. I am going to trade.' That year the man went to the farm while his wife remained in the town.

The farm was far away from the town. You must paddle a canoe for ten hours before you get there. Life there was very hard and there were plenty of mosquitoes. In the evenings, the farm people went to the bush to collect leaves to drive away mosquitoes. Efuru's husband went with them. When they came back they spread the leaves round their bamboo beds. Sometimes when there were not many mosquitoes they could sleep. But during the rainy season, the mosquitoes came in hundreds. They did not only bite, they sang in men's ears teasing them, trying their patience.

The young husband felt his work on the farm irksome now that he was married. It had not mattered before but now it was different. He had a lovely wife; so the least thing sent him home to her.

Efuru welcomed him

'How are you?' she would ask him. 'How is everything in the farm? What did you bring me from the farm?'

'I brought you some vegetables and fish. We caught plenty a week ago. I dried them for you. And here you are.' He brought out the fish from his bag. They were well dried on sticks.

'Thank you, my husband. Now go and have your bath while I prepare some food for you to eat.'

The husband went off to have his bath in the stream. Efuru went to the kitchen to cook. She used plenty of fish and cooked delicious nsala soup for her dear husband. When her husband came back from the stream she welcomed him and put the food before him. When he finished, Efuru asked him if he would go out to see his friends.

'No, not today. I shall see them some other time. I am tired and must go to bed early.'

Efuru's husband stayed in town for two days before he went back to the farm. One day, Efuru's mother-in-law called her.

'My daughter,' she said to her. 'You have not had your bath.'

'No, my mother, I have not had my bath.'

'A young woman must have her bath before she has a baby.'

'I am not pregnant yet, mother.'

'I know, my daughter. I am not talking about that. A baby will come when God wills it. I want you to have your bath before there is a baby. It is better that way. It is safer really.'

'All right, mother. But my husband must be told and he will come from the farm before it is done.'

'Certainly, my daughter. I shall send for him.'

So the next day, Efuru's husband was sent for. He was very happy to come home. He was like a frog who wanted to go upstream and seeing no means was carried by a fast-flowing tide. In his excitement he forgot to tell any of the people in the farm. When he went, the other farmers gossiped.

'Why does Adizua go to the town so often?' one of the farmers asked.

'Don't you know that he has married a very beautiful woman. How the woman agreed to marry him still remains a mystery to everybody.'

'How? Is the woman from a very good family?'

'The daughter of Nwashike Ogene, the mighty man of valour. Ogene who, single handed, fought against the Aros when they came to molest us. Nwashike himself proved himself the son of his father. He was a great fisherman. When he went fishing, he caught only asa and aja. His yams were the fattest in the whole town. And what is more, no man has ever seen his back on the ground. Ogworo azu ngwere eru ani.'

'So that's the man whose daughter that imbecile married?'

'Yes. The amazing thing is that the father has done nothing about it. He has sent some young men to fetch his daughter, but she did not go with them. And since then he had done nothing about it. If it were in his youthful days, Nwashike would have taught that fool a lesson. Things are changing fast these days. These white people have imposed so much strain on our people. The least thing you do nowadays you are put into prison.'

'I don't envy him,' the other man said. But it was obvious that he was green with envy.

'I give them only three years. By then the woman will know her husband too well to want to stay with him longer. Why does she remain in town and not come to the farm with her husband?'

'She refused to go to the farm. She is trading instead. She said she was not cut out for farm work. And I don't blame her, she is so beautiful. You would think that the woman of the lake is her mother. Her mother died five years ago, she too was a very beautiful woman.'

'After seeing this type of woman,' the other man continued, 'one hisses when one sees one's wife.' The other laughed.

'You have a lovely wife yourself.'

'Yes, I know it but ... Well let's leave it at that.'

Efuru's husband returned home and was told about his wife's circumcision. 'It must be done now, my son,' his mother told him. 'And this is the time. Let's not leave it until she gets pregnant.' Adizua said it was all right. He could afford the expenses. But he was afraid of Efuru's father. 'Your father must be told, my wife. It won't be fair to have you have your bath without his knowledge. He must be told.'

'He won't be told. It will make him angrier. When we have enough money to pay the dowry, we shall approach elderly men who will help us beg him.'

So it was as Efuru said. Her mother-in-law got everything ready, the camwood, iziziani ufie awusa were bought on Nkwo day. She went to Onicha and bought home-made cloth for her daughter-in-law. When she came back she went to see the woman who would do the circumcision.

'Is that you, my friend?' the woman asked from within.

'Yes, Ugwunwa,' she greeted her.

'O o, and what is yours? I have forgotten it.'

'Omeifeaku.'

'Yes, Omeifeaku. And how is everybody in your home?'

'They are well, and yours?'

'We are well. It is only hunger troubling us.'

'It is good it is only hunger. It is better than ill-health.'

'That's what they say. Ill-health is worse.'

She came out from the room with a mat.

'Sit down here, my friend.' The two elderly women talked on general things for a while. 'I have no kola, please.'

'Don't worry about kola. It is very early. And besides this is Nkwo morning. Nobody gives kola to people on Nkwo morning. I have something important to tell you. You know my son has been married. His wife has not yet had her bath, so we want her to have her bath and that's why I have come. What day will suit you?'

'I am glad to hear this. Is your daughter-in-law pregnant?'

'I don't think so. She told me she was not.'

'Find out from her again. I don't want to do it if she is pregnant. It is risky. If she loses too much blood, it won't be good for her. So find out from her again and bring word tomorrow. Oh, what a pity I have no kola. Wait, let me see.'

She went into her room again. She came out with a bottle of home-made gin, and a ganashi.

'You will like the gin. My daughter cooks it in the farm. When she finishes, she puts it in a canoe in the dead of the night and paddles to town. When they come I hide them at the back of my house and no policeman will see it.'

She filled the ganashi and gave it to her visitor. Efuru's mother-in-law drank it in a gulp and made a noise with her mouth. The woman filled the same ganashi and drank the gin in a gulp also.

'It is a good gin. We shall continue cooking our gin. I don't see the difference between it and the gin sold in special bottles in the shops.'

Efuru's mother-in-law got up to go.

'Thank you very much. I am going.'

'You are going? Thank you. Come tomorrow, go well.'

Efuru's mother-in-law was at the woman's house the next day. She told her that her daughter-in-law was not pregnant.

'That's all right then. I shall come tomorrow morning after the cock crow. Get hot water ready.'

The next morning the woman was at Efuru's. She sat down and Efuru came out and greeted her.

'You are the young wife, my daughter. You are beautiful, my daughter. I will be gentle with you. Don't be afraid. It is painful no doubt, but the pain disappears like hunger. You know what?' and she turned to Efuru's mother-in-law. 'You know Nwakaego's daughter?'

'Yes, I know her.'

'She did not have her bath before she had that baby who died after that dreadful flood.'

'God forbid. Why?'

'Fear. She was afraid. Foolish girl. She had a foolish mother, their folly cost them a son, a good son.'

'How did you know?'

'They came to me early one morning and told me. They wanted it to be done in my house so that people will not know. The dibia had already told them that the baby died because she did not have her bath. I did it for them. She remained in my house for seven days. Is everything ready now?'

'Yes, come this way.'

The woman went to the back of the house and there it was done. Efuru screamed and screamed. It was so painful. Her mother-in-law consoled her. 'It will soon be over, my daughter don't cry.'

Meanwhile Efuru's husband was in his room. He felt all the pain. It seemed as if he was the one being circumcised. The neighbours wondered what was the matter. When they came to the house they saw that the back door was locked and they turned back.

'It's being done now,' one of the neighbours said to the other. 'Oh, yes, that's it, I saw the woman when she came. Efuru is having her bath. Poor girl, it's so painful.'

Efuru lay on her back with her feet apart. She was not crying any more. But it was still very painful.

The woman gave instructions. She prepared a black stuff and put it in a small calabash and left it outside the room where Efuru was lying. 'Sprinkle this on the feet of all the visitors before they come into the room. It will be infected if this is not done. Press it with hot water every morning, and night. If anything goes wrong send for me. Oh, where is my razor?'

Efuru's mother-in-law gave her the sharp razor that did the work. She wrapped it up and tied it at one end of her wrappa.

The next morning Ajanupu the sister of Efuru's mother-in-law came to the house. After eating kola, she cleared her throat.

'Ossai, you have done something. Why was I not told that Adizu's wife was going to have her bath. Why am I treated these days as if I am a stranger and not your sister? Adizua married a wife and you did not tell me. I heard it from outside. Again, Adizua's wife has washed and you have not told me either. What have I done to you?'

'Please, my sister, you have done nothing wrong. You have not offended me in any way. It is my fault and I am very sorry.'

'All right. I am happy I have told you. I don't want to bear any grudge against you. How is Efuru doing?'

'She is in the room: go in and see her.'

She saw the black stuff. There was a feather in it. She took the feather dipped it into the black stuff and sprinkled it on her two feet.

'How are you, my daughter?'

'I am well. Oh, you have come to see us today.'

'Nobody told me. I heard it from outside and so I came. Is it very painful?'

'It is much better now. It was dreadful the first day.'

'Gbonu, my daughter. It is what every woman undergoes. So don't worry.'

Efuru's mother-in-law saw to it that she was very well looked after. She was to eat the best food and she was to do no work. She was simply to eat and grow fat. And above all she was to look beautiful. The camwood was used in dyeing her cloth. She also rubbed it all over her body and the iziziani was used for her face.

She ate whatever she wanted to eat. She did not eat cassava in any form. Only yams were pounded for her. She ate the best fish from the market. It was said that she was feasting. On market days, her mother went to the market and bought her the best. When she prized something in the market other buyers gave her way and asked her how the feasting woman was getting on. She too rubbed some camwood on her hands and feet to tell people that her daughter has been circumcised.

As Efuru's mother-in-law was buying things in the market one day, she heard someone calling:

'Mother of a feasting girl; mother of feasting girl.' She turned and saw that it was her sister, Ajanupu.

'How is she now?'

'She is well, my sister.'

'Has it healed?'

'Yes, it has healed. She had good body.'

'That's very good. The woman who did it has good hands, too. She never has any trouble with all her cases. Unlike Mgbokworo.'

'No, Mgbokworo is not good. She has not actually learnt the operation.'

'What are you buying for your daughter-in-law? Let's see your basin. You have bought so much. By the way is she a good daughter-in-law?'

'You cannot see two like her. She is such a nice girl. I like her very much; I am glad my son married her.'

'I am happy to hear this. I heard something about the dowry. Tell me all about it.'

'Well, my son cannot afford the dowry now. We hope that after the harvest we shall pay it.'

'It must be done my sister. Take this fish to your daughter and also the ground-nuts. Tell her I shall come and see her on Eke day. I am going home now. My son is not well.'

'Nnoro?'

'Yes, Nnoro. I don't know what he wants me to do, that boy. There is no dibia I have not been to. He had a convulsion yesterday.'

'Convulsion? How did it happen?'

'I was lucky it happened in my face, if not he would have died. One day he felt unwell so I gave him some tablets I got from the dispensary. Then just as I was about to leave for Abatu village to collect a debt, I heard a shout. I dropped what I had and rushed to the next room. It was Nnoro. He was having a convulsion. I picked him up, got a spoon and put it between his teeth. Then I took kernel oil and emptied the whole contents on his body, head and face. I rubbed and rubbed. I put some in his eyes and made him drink some. Then I mixed some with mentholetum and put it in his anus – right into his anus. Then he passed out something on my hand. It was much better after that. I gave him some purgative medicine and today he was playing with the children outside before I left for the market.'

'I am sorry, my sister. Please look after him well. Because if an old woman falls twice, we count all she has in her basket.'

'Mother of a feasting girl, come and buy things for your daughter.'

Efuru's mother-in-law went to the direction of the call. She bought some oranges and bananas from the woman who called her.

'I hope she is doing well,' the woman asked her.

'Oh, she is doing very well. Thank you.'

Efuru's husband was still at home. He had not gone back to the farm yet. He too was being well looked after by his mother. When he played with his wife, she rubbed camwood on his singlet, and he went out without changing it. When his friends saw him, they knew at once that his wife had been circumcised and they teased him.

Efuru grew more beautiful every day. The camwood did a lot to make her already smooth body smoother. She looked very plump and appealing to the eyes. Now that the wound had healed, she went out with other women who were circumcised like her.

When they went out, they tied a wrappa dyed in camwood from their waist downwards. Then they had another one also dyed in camwood which they used in covering their breasts. Then they had an instrument used in playing which the people call nchakirikpo. They were objects of attraction; men, women and children stopped to watch and to admire them.

When people came to see Efuru, and many did come to see her, her mother-in-law gave them kola, ground-nuts and many other things to eat.

Efuru feasted for one month. Her mother-in-law wanted her to continue feasting for two months, but she refused saying that the life was a dull one. She wanted to be up and doing.

'Since you won't continue feasting, we shall talk about going to the market,' her mother-in-law told her one day. 'But if I were you, Efuru, I should continue for another one month. When I did mine, I feasted for three months. I know I cannot do for you all that my own mother did for me, but I will try.'

'No, mother. One month of confinement is enough. We have

not got much money, and I want to start trading. Again we have not paid the dowry yet. I shall go to the market on Nkwo day.'

'You are right, my daughter. I was only thinking of what people would say.'

'Never mind what people would say.'

So on Nkwo day, Efuru dressed gorgeously. She plaited her lovely hair very well, tied velvet to her waist and used aka stones for her neck. Her body was bare showing her beautiful breasts. No dress was worn when a young woman went to the market after the period of feasting. Her body was exposed so that the people saw how well her mother or her mother-in-law had cared for her. A woman who was not beautiful on that day, would never be beautiful in her life.

As Efuru was being dressed, a small girl of about eight years old was dressed in similar fashion. Just when the sun was going down Efuru took the girl to the market. They were followed from the house by a few women.

Efuru and the girl went round the market and were greeted by the people. As they were coming, some women asked 'whose daughter is that?'

'Don't you know her? She is the daughter of Nwashike Ogene.'

'She is very beautiful. I have never seen a woman so beautiful. Who is her husband?'

'Her husband is Adizua.'

'Who is Adizua? Who is his father? Is he known?'

'He is not known. And nobody knows why she ever married him, and besides, not a cowrie has been paid on her head.'

'What are you telling me?'

'It is true. The husband has not even gone with his people to Nwashike Ogene.'

'And what has the father done?'

'Nothing so far. What will he do now that he is getting old? If it were in his youth, his daughter would not have dared insult him in this way.'

As the two women were talking, Efuru came near. 'Wait, my daughter, take this,' and one of the women gave her some money.

'You are very beautiful my daughter: take this,' and another woman gave her some money also. Efuru thanked them and went on. When she had gone round the market, she went home without buying anything.

When she got home, she changed her cloth and the little girl changed hers also and they went back to the market, this time to buy little things like fruits, ground-nuts, kola-nuts and so on.

'Ahaa, this is a better cloth, the first one was rather old. This is nicer.' One woman said. Efuru heard this and laughed to herself. She went on buying things. This time her mother-in-law was in the market and she was being congratulated.

'Well done, Ossai. You have looked after her very well. Her cloth is gorgeous but the first one is better. Why, she should have tied the first one now.'

Efuru heard this also and smiled to herself.

'Who can please the world?' she asked herself. She knew that both cloths were very nice, and what was more they fitted the occasion. They were the cloths her mother left for her. She bought them many years ago and whenever there was a festival or the second burial of a relative, the cloths served very well. She knew that to buy some cloths in the market for the occasion would not do. The older the cloth the better. It showed that in the days gone by your mother could afford those cloths and so her prestige was enhanced, because her family was not among the newly rich, the wealth had been in it for years.

Efuru came home feeling very tired that evening. Many people came to the house to congratulate her and her mother-in-law.

'Everything went on well,' they told them.

'Your daughter's face is good,' they told her, meaning that she was popular with people.

'Your daughter has the face of people,' others told her, meaning the same thing.

'It is a good sign,' they agreed.

But underneath, something weighed Efuru down.

CHAPTER TWO

Life in the farm was becoming unbearable. Adizua no longer worked as hard as before. In the morning he slept while others went to work. When they had done more than two hours' work, he came to work, and left the farm before everybody else. He was so lazy that his neighbours gossiped.

'Why does Adizua's wife not work in the farm with her husband?' one asked.

'The farm is not meant for her. Have I not told you that she is so beautiful?'

'If I were Adizua, I would not stay in the farm. What's the point of dreaming about your wife. You can dream about a woman friend or another man's wife, but definitely not your own wife. Adizua is stupid. Every morning you see him sharpening his knife but he will not work.'

Adizua went to town very often. He had not the courage to tell his wife that she was responsible for his laziness. The young wife did not understand either. But when in a week he came to town twice, Efuru became apprehensive and asked him why he came home so frequently. Adizua told her. He told her he would like to stay in town with her and not go back to the farm. He told her that the people in the farm were unfriendly to him and that he did not want to farm any longer. He did not tell her that he thought of her so much that he no longer wished to be away from her.

'In that case,' she said to him, 'I would like you to leave the farm. But you have to wait until the harvest and after that you can come to town. Both of us can trade together.'

So, after the harvest Adizua left the farm for good. His harvest was of course very poor. His fellow-farmers laughed at him and said unkind words behind his back. He did not make any profit at all. But his wife consoled him. 'Never mind,' she said. 'What matters is health. Once you are healthy money will come.'

Efuru and her husband traded in yams. They would paddle a

canoe from their town to a tributary of the Great River, and thence to Agbor. There, they bought yams and other things rare in their town and sold them at a profit. When the yam trade was bad, they traded in dry fish and crayfish. It was in crayfish that they made their fortune.

They were the first to discover the trade that year. The place where they bought the crayfish was three days' journey on the Great River. It was a risky business. Thieves could waylay traders and rob them of their money. The river could be rough and when that happened their canoe could capsize.

When they got to the place, they bought crayfish in bags. Then they paddled back and sold the crayfish making a profit of over a hundred per cent.

Four trips gave Efuru and her husband a huge profit. The fifth trip was not so good. Many women had got to know about the business and had rushed into it and spoilt it. It was by sheer luck that Efuru and her husband recovered their capital.

'We won't go again,' she told her husband.

'Yes, we won't go again. But what are we going to do?'

'We are going to look for another trade. These women spoil trade so easily. When they see you making a profit in one trade they leave the trade they know and join yours and of course in no time it is no longer profitable. So we shall look for another thing to do, but we have to go to my father now that we have money. What day can we fix it?'

'Let's have it on Eke day. Today is Eke, in four days we shall go.'

'That is good. Now what about your people? Your father's brother is in the farm, somebody should be asked to go for him. You told me he is the eldest in the family.'

'Yes, he will be sent for,' Adizua said.

Efuru's father was happy when he was told that his daughter's husband was coming to see him. He called his people together and told them. 'We shall receive them very well,' one of the elders said. 'It is true that they have angered us.' Others spoke in this vein and they all agreed to receive them.

Meanwhile, Efuru and her mother-in-law went to the market and bought the best kola they could find. Then they went to the shops and bought six bottles of schnapps. Then they went to a woman near by and bought a big jar of home-made gin. The men were responsible for buying palm wine. So Adizua was in charge of that and he bought many kegs.

Before it was evening, Efuru went to her father's house, and waited for her husband's people to come. At night, Adizua and his people took all they had bought to Efuru's father's house. Many young men were there including Adizua's uncle. At Nwashike Ogene's house also young men from the family assembled. Adizua's uncle led the way. He went straight to the obi of Nwashike Ogene. 'Ochia, Mazi, Ogbukea', he greeted the people. And all in turn greeted, bowing their heads to the ground to Nwashike Ogene. They were asked to sit down. Kola was brought and, afterwards, Adizua's uncle stood up to tell them the object of their visit.

'Ochia, Mazi, Ogbukea. Our people, welcome to you. Nwashike Ogene we have come to see you this night. Our grandfathers said that he who disowns his daughter or his son is a fool. You can ask an adulterous wife to pack and go to her mother and she can pack and go and get married to someone else, who gives you back your dowry and thus the relation is severed.'

'It is true, it is true,' those present said.

'But Nwashike Ogene, you cannot disown your child, because for ever and for ever she will be your child. God has given it to you, your wife conceived her in her womb and therefore she is yours for ever.'

'It is true,' the others said.

'But, Nwashike Ogene, you have the right to be angry. Adizua's father would not have allowed this if he were alive. I was not in town when it happened. When I heard it, I came at once to town and there was nothing I could do about it. Adizua's mother was there, no doubt, but what can a woman do? When I came back from the farm, I told Adizua that he must do something about our custom; if not, our ancestors would be angry with us and cause ill to befall us. He told me his difficulty. Everybody experiences it at one time or the other. God has blessed the two young people. Your daughter has brought luck into our family.'

'That is what happened; that is how it happened,' the men said.

'Nwashike Ogene, your daughter is the best of women. She came to live with us just after the planting season; this is another planting season, since then we have never seen okasi leaves on her teeth. In short our people, she is a good woman. We have come to fulfil the customs of our people. Nwashike, don't be angry with the young people; they are young and youth intoxicates like our-home-made gin. Our people, thank you very much, Ochia, Mazi, Ogbukea.'

Efuru's father could not hide his happiness.

'Our people, welcome,' he began. 'I thank you for coming this night. I was angry when my daughter ran away from my house. Any father has a right to be angry, and I am no exception. I sent my people, but they did nothing. Efuru is my dear daughter. The only child of my favourite wife. As you know I inherited all the wives of my father. But Efuru's mother was my choice. I love her very much. After a long time she had Efuru. Then six years ago, she died. I was heart-broken. Efuru was my only source of happiness. To cut a long story short, I am glad you have come. Welcome.'

Somebody else wanted to speak. When he got up he said that Adizua was not going to be let off easily. He must pay a fine. Others agreed that he should pay a fine.

'You are to give Efuru's father a bottle of schnapps now,' Adizua's uncle said.

Adizua went out, and was making for home, when Efuru called him and gave him some money instead. So he gave the money to Efuru's father in place of the bottle of schnapps.

'We shall start now. There is no question now about asking Efuru whether we are to drink the wine or not, but we have to do what our people do,' the father said.

So Efuru was called.

'My daughter, this is the wine your husband's people have brought. Should we drink, or should we not drink?'

The people laughed. That question does not apply. Efuru had demonstrated to the world that she was very happy to marry Adizua.

The people drank. Schnapps was poured in a glass and given to Adizua to drink. Whilst he sipped it, Efuru was called. She was given the glass by her husband and when she was about to drink, the people shouted: 'Kneel down, kneel down, you are a woman.' Efuru quickly knelt down and drank and left immediately.

As they were drinking, the dowry was fixed and Adizua's people paid everything there. They drank and when the ceremony came to an end, Efuru's father called her and her husband and blessed them and gave them some words of advice.

They went home and for the first time since that fateful Nkwo day the two felt really married.

A year passed, and no child came. Efuru did not despair. 'I am still young, surely God cannot deny me the joy of motherhood,' she often said to herself. But her mother-in-law was becoming anxious. She loved her daughter-in-law very much. She defended her anywhere she heard people say unkind words about her. When Efuru was sad, she consoled her, told her that a child would come when God willed it. Neighbours talked as they were bound to talk. They did not see the reason why Adizua should not marry another woman since, according to them, two men do not live together. To them Efuru was a man since she could not reproduce.

Efuru was very worried in the second year of her marriage. 'My mother had only me,' she said one night to herself. 'My father told me so and also that she found it difficult to become pregnant. Am I going to be like my mother? But if I am going to be like her, then I too will have a daughter like her. But what if that is denied me? What if that also is denied me? What will I do? Oh, what will I do?' she wept.

Efuru did not sleep that night. Early in the morning before the cock crew she got up, dressed and went to her father. She opened her heart to her father. 'Something must be done, my daughter. It is not in our blood. Our women are productive. There must be a reason for this. We shall see a dibia.'

Efuru and her old father went to see a dibia. He was a very old and dirty man. He was almost blind and was unable to walk. His two grand-daughters lived with him and and ran errands for him. They were sent to the bush to collect some leaves or roots, to the market to buy things required for medicines and they cooked for him. It was understood that they would not live with him when they were over fourteen.

When Efuru and her father entered the compound, the dibia

shouted, 'Nwashike Ogene, I am happy you are coming today with your daughter. But I won't see you today because your daughter is menstruating. My medicines will be ineffective if she comes nearer. When she finishes bring her to me.' Efuru was spellbound.

'How did he know?' she asked her father.

'He is a dibia,' was the old man's reply.

'Oh, why did I not think of him all these years?' her father said half to himself.

Five days after, Efuru and her father went again to the dibia. 'Adobi,' the dibia called one of his grandchildren. 'Bring a mat for these people.' A mat was spread on a mud-bench in the room and the two visitors sat down. 'Njeri, bring kola.' The girl thus addressed went in and brought some kola in a saucer.

'Kola has come,' the dibia said.

'Kola is yours,' Efuru's father said.

The dibia took the kola and broke it. There were only three pieces. He looked at the pieces closely and shook his head.

'Njeri pass the kola to our visitors.'

'Didi, won't you have one first?' Njeri asked.

'You ignorant, foolish and stupid girl. A goat sucked your breasts. Don't you understand? Pass the kola to our visitors before I give you a slap equal to you.'

When they finished the kola the dibia cleared his throat. 'I am sorry about your daughter, Nwashike, but you have come in good time. Your daughter is not barren. She will have a baby next year if she will only do what I am going to ask her to do. Again she has not got many children in her womb. Some women are like that. It is not their fault. It is not God's fault either.'

Father and daughter were astonished.

'How did you know the object of our visit?' Efuru ventured to ask. The old man laughed.

'You are children. You cannot understand. You will not understand. Nwashike, this is what your daughter will do every Afo day. She is to sacrifice to the ancestors. It is not much, but she will have to do it regularly. Every Afo day, she is to buy uziza, alligator pepper, and kola from the market. Uziza must be bought every Nkwo day from a pregnant woman. Every Afo day before the sun goes down or when the sun is here,' and he pointed to the direction, 'she should put these things in a small calabash and go down to the lake; there she will leave the calabash to float away. So, go home young woman and be cheerful. Next year during the Owu festival if nothing happens to you, come back to me. Go in peace.'

'What is your charge?' Efuru's father asked.

'Charge?'

'Oh, yes. Charge.'

'All right if you want it that way. I want a head of tobacco. That's all I want, only a head. Don't bring two because I won't know what to do with two, my roof is leaking and rain will spoil the second one.'

Adizua was delighted to hear everything Efuru had to tell him when he returned from Agbor.

'I am happy that you went to see the man. But please don't think that it makes any difference to me whether you have a baby or not. You know I will be the last person to do anything that will hurt you, my wife. You know I cannot exchange you with a wife who would give me twenty sons.'

Efuru was happy because she had so much faith in what the dibia had told her, and did not worry so much about her state. But her mother-in-law was still worried and when she could bear it no longer, she went to her son.

'What are you going to do about Efuru's state?'

'Something is being done, my mother. We shall soon know the result.'

'I am glad to hear this. I was going to suggest you marry another woman. A woman who will give you children. It is going to be with the consent of Efuru, of course.'

About three months passed after Efuru's visit to the dibia, and nothing happened. She started to despair again. So one night she called her husband. 'It does not seem as if anything will happen before Owu festival. I am losing hope again. Don't you think it will be better if you begin to look around for a young girl for a wife.'

'Not yet, my wife. The Owu festival is still not come. Let us wait till it comes.'

The Owu festival at last and Efuru enjoyed it very much. She went out with other women and as they were watching the Owu dancing, she saw her mother-in-law's sister, Ajanupu.

26

'So this is your eyes, Efuru. Trade does not allow you to see anybody these days.'

'Aha, Ajanupu. Idenu.'

'O-o-o my daughter, Nwaononaku. How is your mother-in-law?'

'She is well, and your son?'

'My son is well now, but he had another attack of convulsion.'

'Thank God, he is well.'

'This year's Owu festival is not as interesting as last year's,' Ajanupu said.

'Yes, last year's was wonderful. I enjoyed every bit of it.'

'Look at that one dancing. He is dancing very well. I like his mask. He must belong to a wealthy man.'

'That's right. I know the owner. It is owned by Okam. He is the best. It is very refreshing to see really good ones.'

'When I was a young woman,' Ajanupu went on, 'Owu festival really used to be Owu festival. None of us young girls cooked for our mothers. We dressed gorgeously and watched the dancers till the end of the day.'

'Has your daughter-in-law told you anything?' Ajanupu asked her sister the following morning.

'No, she hasn't. What happened?'

'She has not mentioned anything to you about her health?'

'No she has not. Is anything wrong?'

'She does not know then. And you, haven't noticed anything yourself?'

'No, I have not.'

'You are just a woman for nothing. You can't see, you can't even hear smell. Your daughter-in-law is pregnant.'

'Efuru is pregnant? Orisha, thank you.' She raised her two hands to the sky, then knelt down and bowed her head, knocking it on the floor of the room, thanking Orisha, who is God.

'How did you know that, Ajanupu? Are you quite sure?'

'We watched the Owu dancing yesterday for nearly two hours. She was close to me and there is no mistake about it. I smelt it. She has missed her period. She may not know herself,' Ajanupu said confidently.

'God, thank you, thank you, God. My daughter will have a

baby at last. My daughter is not barren after all. My enemies will no longer rejoice. God, thank you.'

'I am going, Ossai. See your daughter when I am away. And look after her well.'

The next day, Efuru's mother-in-law called her. 'How are you feeling my daughter? Does your body communicate anything to you?'

'I don't understand, mother.'

'You children don't understand our language. All right. I shall say it in plain language. Have you missed your period?'

'No, it is not time yet.'

'Have you counted well?'

'Yes, I have counted well.'

'When will you see it then?'

'On Afo day.'

'All right come and tell me when you see it.'

On Afo day Efuru saw nothing. She told her mother-in-law who began to dance. 'God heard me. God has heard me. My daughter, you are pregnant. My sister Ajanupu told me.'

'But I saw her only on that festival for a few hours and I did not tell her anything.'

'Yes, you did not. But she knew it. She smelt it. I am so glad.'

They agreed not to tell Adizua until they were quite sure. Four months later, it was quite obvious that Efuru was expecting a baby. The neighbours knew it and talked of it. It was at this time that Adizua knew of it and asked Efuru, who confirmed it.

Efuru was very happy, She was even more beautiful now. She was fairer, robust and fresh. Many men envied her husband. Women were jealous of her beauty. Her mother-in-law delightfully spoilt her. She bought her delicacies on Nkwo days. She petted her. She did not want her to cook. She did all the cooking and the house-work herself.

One day, Ajanupu came to see them. They were eating ogbono soup.

'God forbid,' she shouted. 'Ossai, ignorance will kill you one day. Why do you allow your daughter-in-law to eat ogbono soup. Don't you know that ogbono is not good for an expectant mother?'

'Ajanupu, my sister, I did not know, and what about okra? Is it bad too for her health?'

'Yes, okra is not good. Snail is not good also. If she eats snails her baby will have plenty of saliva.'

Before Ajanupu went home, she listed all the dont's of a pregnant woman. She was not to go out alone at night. If she must go out, then somebody must go with her and she must carry a small knife. When she is sitting down, nobody must cross her leg.

Meanwhile, Efuru did all that the dibia had told her. Every Afo day, she bought the things she was told to buy and did as she was told.

At the seventh month, Efuru noticed that her legs were swollen. She told her mother-in-law who immediately told her sister. She came and looked at it and went away without saying anything. The next day, she brought some leaves and some palm wine. She also brought a new clay pot. She cooked the leaves adding a little palm wine. When she finished, she gave some to Efuru pouring some palm wine in it.

'Every morning and night, you warm it over a slow fire, put some palm wine in it and drink. When the palm wine is finished, buy another one from the market. Don't buy ngwo. You must buy nkwu.'

Efuru kept to the instructions religiously. The medicine worked. She discovered that she urinated more and that her legs and feet were no longer swollen.

She had no troubles after that. Her health was good and she went on with her trade though her husband told her not to exert herself. Then one day her mates came for her. They told her that one of their age-group was performing the ceremony of the second burial of her father and so they must go and dance with her. Efuru went with them. They danced all day. In the evening when she did not come back, her mother-in-law went in search of her. She saw her still dancing and begged her to go with her. Efuru did not want to go then, and told her mother so.

'No, my daughter, you have to come with me. Your husband is very angry with you.'

'Is it true? Then I must come home immediately.'

'Anama, Nwaononaku, Idenu,' she greeted them. 'I must go now. You can understand.'

'It is true. You must go,' the leader of the group said.

When Adizua returned and was told that his wife was not at home, he had his bath and went out. But when he came back again and saw that his wife was not home yet he became very angry. He sat on a stretcher outside thinking and shaking his legs.

As he was thinking of what he was going to do to Efuru when she came back, he heard a sweet voice from afar:

> 'My dear husband, don't sell me,
> My dear husband, don't kill me.
> Listen to me first before
> You pass your judgement.
>
> My dear husband, forgive me,
> My dear husband, don't kill me.
> Let me tell you how we danced,
> Let me tell you how we danced.
>
> My dear husband, my love is true.
> My dear husband, I am constant.
> My dear husband, don't be angry.
> I went to dance with my mates.'

Adizua was completely disarmed. By the time she finished she was near her husband. 'Oh, are you home already, Adizua— I must be very late. Did you miss me? Has my mother given you food to eat? Mother, have you given my husband something to eat?'

'I have eaten something. But where did you go?'

Efuru told him. He said nothing more.

That night Efuru did not sleep. She tossed in bed. Then she felt some pains. Very sharp pains. She woke her mother-in-law. Her husband was sleeping very soundly.

'I must go and call Ajanupu. I know nothing about these things,' the old woman said as she went to call her sister. Ajanupu came with her immediately.

'Lie down,' she commanded Efuru. Yes, that's it. That's the head. Good, thank God. Now you are to do exactly as I tell you. If you are afraid, you will have a weak and sickly baby. If you do exactly as I tell you, you will have a strong and healthy baby. All right. Now press very hard. Ossai, get some water boiling. She will soon have the baby. Good. You are a good child. Don't cry. Don't shout. If you cry or shout, you will continue crying and shouting each time you have your baby.'

Efuru was good. She was strong and she was not afraid. She did as she was told. In about half an hour she delivered her baby – a baby girl.

Single handed, Ajanupu attended to both mother and child. It was so easy for her. One would think that she was a trained midwife. She had eight children. One had died of convulsion. It was only the first and the second that she was helped to deliver. All the others she delivered herself. There was usually nobody around when she had her babies. She would have her baby all alone, wash it and wash herself before anybody knew what was happening. Neighbours only knew when a newly born baby began to cry.

So it was a joy to her delivering Efuru's baby. When the baby did not cry at once, she took hold of its two legs lifted it in the air and shook it until it cried. She washed and tidied everything.

'Now, Efuru, you put your legs together. Don't leave them apart, so that you will be able to walk properly in future.' She gave her a piece of chewing stick to chew. Efuru's mother-in-law was busy getting everything ready.

'Now, Ossai, she will be very hungry. Go and cook something for her to eat. Pounded yam and nsala soup will be all right. Put plenty of pepper for her stomach is cold. The soup must be steaming hot.'

Efuru lay there thinking of it all. 'Is this happening to me or someone I know. Is that baby mine or somebody else's? Is it really true that I have had a baby, that I am a woman after all. Perhaps I am dreaming. I shall soon wake up and discover that it is not real.'

As she was thinking those thoughts, she heard a knock on the door.

'Come in,' she said. It was her husband.

'It's a baby girl, Orisha has done well. I am so happy, Efuru.'

'I don't know whether it is real. Perhaps we are both dreaming.'

31

'You are not dreaming, don't you hear the cry of the baby?' He picked it up.

'Welcome, my daughter. Your name is Ogonim,' Efuru laughed.

'Tell me how it happened. I was fast asleep. It was just now I heard the cry of a newly-born baby.'

'When the pain started, I woke my mother and she went for Ajanupu.'

'She went all alone? Why did you not wake me?'

'We did not want to disturb you.'

'Go on then, what happened?'

'Ajanupu came and after a short time I had the baby. It was just like a child's play.'

'Wasn't it painful?'

'It was, but I don't remember it now that I can see my daughter in your arms. I think God has a way of making mothers forget the pains after the delivery of their babies. If it were not so, I am sure that very few women would want more babies after the first one.'

It was daybreak now. Neighbours saw Efuru's mother-in-law going to the stream, and asked her whether all was well.

'Yes, all is well. My daughter has had a baby.'

'Oh, Orisha, thank you. What did she have?'

'She had a baby girl.'

'Good, Orisha, thank you. Efuru is hot. It was only yesterday that she danced with her age-group and came back late. Whoever thought that she was going to have a baby in the night,' one of them said.

Every morning Ajanupu came and attended to the baby. She washed the baby with warm water. When she finished she would pick up one leg of the baby and say 'Uso, Uso, Uso'. She would pick up the other leg, lift it up in the air and say 'Uso, Uso, Uso'. She would do that to the two hands. Efuru was always afraid when she saw her doing this to her baby. One day she asked her why.

'You are children,' she said. 'If I don't do that to her, she won't grow strong and healthy.'

'But you can break her hands or legs by doing that. I am always afraid when you do it.'

'No, it is impossible for her legs or hands to be broken. Don't fear my daughter. I did all that to my children.'

'How many children have you, Ajanupu?'

'Hush, we don't ask people how many children they have. It is not done. Children are not goats or sheep or yams to be counted. I will tell you. I conceived eight times, one died of convulsion.'

When the baby was five days old, Ajanupu told her sister that it was time to put alligator pepper in her mouth so that her tongue will be free. If this was not done, Ajanupu said, the baby might be deaf and dumb. So early the next morning, some alligator pepper was brought and Ajanupu chewed it very well and then put it under the tongue of the baby. The baby yelled and yelled. She was quickly breast-fed, and she stopped crying.

'Ajanupu, my daughter will talk like you. I am afraid she will be very talkative.' Efuru's mother-in-law teased her sister.

'That is all right. Aren't you lucky that I am near to put alligator pepper in her mouth. Who wants to be quiet these days. Don't you know that if you don't lick your mouth the harmattan will lick it for you. You stay there and talk of being quiet these days.'

That evening, Efuru complained that her breasts were not full. In fact they were getting dry. She was afraid her baby might die of starvation if there was no milk in her breasts. Ajanupu was sent for at once.

'It is simple. When I had my first baby, the same thing happened to me. You have to drink plenty of palm wine, meanwhile I am going to treat you.' She chewed some palm kernels which she used in rubbing her breasts. 'This will help,' she told her kindly. 'If it has no effect, we shall call in a woman dibia. She is sure to help you.'

The woman dibia was not needed. Efuru was all right. Her breast was full. Both mother and baby were well. Her mother-in-law took great care of mother and child and was very proud of them.

Soon it was seven market days since Efuru's safe delivery. It was time for her to go out to market, and to visit friends. But before she went out, she had to go to the lake and put her feet in the water. On Nkwo day, she dressed gorgeously and went to the market.

When Efuru came back from the market, she told her husband that she would like to go to the dibia and tell him that she had had her baby and to thank him for everything.

'It would be a good idea,' her husband said.

'But as you know you never go empty-handed to play the masquerade.'

'Yes, I know. We have to take along with us some presents.'

'What are you going to give to the dibia?'

'We shall buy two heads of tobacco, kola-nuts and a fowl. Perhaps, we shall take some yams also.'

'These will do, when do we go?'

'On Eke day, after Nkwo when I shall buy all the things.'

On Eke day, the things were put in a basin and Efuru carried it. Her husband followed her with his walking-stick. Their mother looked after the baby. When they got to the gate, the dibia cleared his throat. 'The daughter of Nwashike Ogene, who is bringing you to my house today. And that's you, Adizua Ukachukwu. I saw you last the day your father died. You were a mere child then with mucous running down your nose. Come along and sit down, my children.'

Thus welcomed, Efuru and Adizua came in and sat down. Adizua helped her to put the load down.

'Njeri, my daughter, bring kola for us.' The girl brought some kola. The old dibia took it. 'Nwashike Ogene's daughter, to your health, Ogonim, to your health.' Efuru pinched her husband. 'Ukachukwu's son to your health. Our fathers, have some kola. I have been a dibia for more than thirty years. I have been upright.'

Efuru, Adizua and the two girls said 'Ise'.

'I have never caused any one to die.'

'Ise.'

'I have never prepared poison to kill anybody.'

'That's how it happened,' Adizua and Efuru said.

'I inherited all my medicines from my father, who inherited them from his father.'

'Ise,' they nodded.

'Our family is upright, and fear God. So God see to it that our enemies are crushed.'

'Ise.'

'Let Ogonim live long.'

34

'Ise.'

'Let Efuru have one baby, one baby until the house is full.'

'Ise.'

'Hear us, our fathers.'

'Ise.'

He broke the kola, and frowned with pain. 'Our fathers forbid, God forbid. God won't agree to this,' the old man said all in one breath. 'Why have I not seen this before? We have only two pieces of kola. It is not a good sign my children. Njeri, bring another kola.'

Njeri brought another kola. The old man started again.

'Our father, here is kola.'

'Ise.'

'I am upright.'

'Ise.'

'I have made people rich, though I am poor myself. It is the will of God that it should be so. In our family we are good, but poor. God has willed that it should be so. Our work is to make others rich and remain poor.'

The dibia broke the kola. Again, there were only two pieces. 'This is strange. My children come again on Eke day when the sun is here,' and he indicated the place he meant.

Efuru and Adizua understood the time he meant.

'We brought these to thank you, our father,' Efuru said. 'Last year my father and I came to see you, and now as you know I have a baby girl. "Agundu", thank you.'

'My wife and I have one voice, our father. Thank you, "Agundu". But we do not understand what is wrong now. We are blind though we have eyes to see. We are nothing at all.'

'Don't worry, my children. Thank you for your presents. Go home and come back on Eke day. I shall tell you all then.' Efuru and her husband went home.

'Something will go wrong. I can prevent it. But I must be given time. I have seen it, but not clearly yet. Our fathers will help me. I shall sacrifice to them. I shall ask their aid,' the dibia said slowly to himself, as Efuru and Adizua were leaving his hut.

On Nkwo day, a day to the appointed day, Efuru heard that the dibia was dead. He died in his sleep.

35

CHAPTER THREE

Adizua was not good at trading. It was Efuru who was the brain behind the business. He knew this very well, and so one night he spoke to Efuru. 'Efuru, I think it is time you should face your trade. Your baby is old enough to be left with a nurse. My mother will see that you get a good nurse. At this time, your baby can eat some mashed yam well prepared with palm oil. You have to think over this, my dear wife.'

'I have thought of it. You are right. I have to get a maid who will help me with Ogonim. We are not only making no profits, we are losing our capital. So we must do something about it. We have to put our heads together because our fathers say that if you don't think before you sleep, you break your head.'

Three market days passed. One of Efuru's friends came to see her. They talked on many things and about the baby.

'She is growing,' she said to Efuru.

'Yes, she is growing.'

'How old is she now?'

'She will be eight months next month.'

'She looks like a baby of one year. She is still breast-feeding, of course.'

'Yes, she is still breast-feeding, and she will continue till she is over a year. I shall stop when she is a year and a half or even two years,' Efuru said.

'That's good, my friend. My sister who went to school told me that her children, when she began to have them, would breast-feed for only six months. I told her she was mad. I wean my children when they are over a year.'

'Your sister should wait until she has her babies, then she can stop breast-feeding them when they are three months old. My mother told me that she found it difficult to stop breast-feeding me. When I was three years, I was still breast-feeding. She would go to market, remain for two or three days and when she came back, I would want her breast. She did everything to stop me, including rubbing bitter leaf on it. I would suck two

36

mouthfuls, spit them out and after that it wasn't bitter any more.

The two women laughed.

'What bothers me now is a maid. I want a maid to help me look after Ogonim while I trade with my husband.'

'A maid? You want a maid to look after your only child? She will kill her. I advise you not to have a maid. You will regret it.'

'I shall get a good one. I want to help my husband. We have been losing much money.'

'What is that to you? What is money? Can a bag of money go for an errand for you? Can a bag of money look after you in your old age? Can a bag of money mourn you when you are dead? A child is more valuable than money. So our fathers said.' As if these were not enough, Efuru's friend began to narrate all the atrocities of maids.

'You know Nwanta, don't you?'

'Yes.'

'You know that her first son is blind in one eye.'

'Yes.'

'A maid was responsible for it.'

'How?' Efuru asked in horror.

'The boy was playing with a stick. The maid saw him and did not take it away from him. So the stick went right into his eye and now the poor boy is blind in one eye.'

'Thank God it is only in one eye.'

'You know Nwanyuzo, don't you?'

'Yes, I know her very well.'

'You know that her daughter has a burnt face. And I don't know who is going to marry a girl with a burnt face. It was a maid who was responsible for it, too.'

Efuru did not ask her how that happened this time. It was not necessary.

'I have maids no doubt, but I know how to treat them. They cannot harm my children. I hold them with an iron hand. I do.'

When she went away, Efuru laughed at her. 'Who does she think she is fooling?' So the very next day, she told her mother-in-law to get her a maid to help her with Ogonim. A week later, Efuru's mother-in-law brought her a child of about ten years old.

'She is the daughter of my cousin, Nwosu. Her father lost all his yams in the flood, and the little yams that were left were not sold for one tenth of the money used for the farming. Only last week the court messengers came to his house demanding tax. His wife saw them in time and hid him in the innermost chamber of their house. When the court messengers were told that he was not in they left but told the wife that they were coming again. About thirty pounds debt is on his head now, through no fault of his own. He cannot find money to feed his children let alone pay tax. When the court messengers come again, they will take him and jail him. Then his children will die of starvation. There are five of them.

'The planting season is near. There is no money to buy yams to plant. There is no money for his wife to trade in cassava which is profitable now. He saw me this morning and when I told him that you wanted a maid, he was pleased. "Please ask her to take my daughter as her maid and give me ten pounds. At the end of the year we shall give her ten pounds plus four pounds interest and take our daughter," he told me. I promised him that I would see you and here is the child. If you don't want her, she will have to go back to her father.'

'Is it the flood that caused this?' Efuru asked.

'The flood, my daughter, the flood. The flood destroyed yams, houses and domestic animals. You and my son were lucky you decided to leave farming entirely alone and concentrate on trade. You would have been in the same predicament. Imagine working for a whole year and then just one day, the flood carries everything into the river. You lose everything and become a debtor in the bargain.'

'Mother, it is all right. I shall tell my husband tonight. Meanwhile the child can remain. I would like to see your cousin tomorrow.'

The next day Nwosu came to see Efuru and her husband on account of the child. His wife also came with him.

'Have you come? Welcome.'

'O-o, Nwaononaku, are you well?' Efuru's mother-in-law's cousin greeted.

'We are well,' Efuru replied. 'It is only hunger.'

'It is good that it is only hunger. Good health is what we pray for.'

'Please sit down here.'

38

Nwosu and his wife sat down. His wife had a baby in her arms. The baby was about six months old.

When they sat down she began to yell. Her mother quickly brought out her breast. She snatched at it and began to suck greedily.

'My mother-in-law told me about your daughter. My husband has just gone to the back of the house. He will soon be here. A woman has no say in these things.'

As they were waiting for Adizua, Efuru brought them kola and alligator pepper. 'Tell me what happened, Nwosu.' Efuru said.

'I don't know where to begin,' Nwosu said. 'It is very painful, Efuru, my daughter. It is very painful. I am known in our farm as a great farmer of yams. Two years ago, my yams were so big that when they were brought to the market for sale, one was priced five shillings and I refused. I was able to rebuild my house which was falling down and I paid all that I owed and even took a title. Then last year I worked very hard. I got workmen to help me. My yams were doing very well. Then just a few weeks before harvest, the floods came. It was earlier than usual. My wife sent for me for I went to the town. I came immediately and we started harvesting. It was too late. I worked as I had never worked before. The flood rushed in and made a mockery of all my efforts. The water reached my belly. It was no use. I gave up. I saw with my eyes the destruction of my sweat and labour.

'There was nothing we could do but to come home. My wife had a small farm of cassava and we dug up that and sold it three Nkwos ago. We had only two pounds. When the two pounds finish, we shall starve.

'I went to the man who lent me the money for my farm and told him everything. He did not cause the flood, he told me, so whatever happened, I should find his money and give it to him before the next planting season. He must look after his children. He and his family cannot starve because of the flood. So he told me.

'Just when I was bemoaning my misfortune, these court messengers came to demand tax. I told my wife to leave them while I loaded my gun. If they did not see my blood, I would see theirs. But my wife tricked me. While I was in the innermost chamber of my house loading my gun, she locked the door and told the court messengers that I was not in.

'My daughter, Efuru, if you do this thing for us, if you take my daughter Ogea and give us ten pounds, I shall for ever be grateful to you. We shall pay you at the end of the year, either in yams or money, whichever way you choose. This life is so miserable, one wishes to die and go and rest with one's ancestors.'

Adizua came and sat down quietly as Nwosu was narrating his misfortunes. When Nwosu finished, he greeted them and told them they were ready to help them. 'My wife will give you ten pounds, at the end of the year you will give us our ten pounds, you shall have your child. If anything happens and you cannot afford to give us this money at the end of the year, let us know.'

'Thank you very much, Adizua, and thank you so much Efuru. You do not know what you have done for us today. Only God will repay you.' His wife also thanked them very heartily. The money was counted and given to them.

That was how Ogea came to live with Efuru and her husband. She was a mere child, only ten years old. How could she look after a baby? Ogea cried and cried when her parents left her. She refused to eat and refused to do anything in the house. She was so unco-operative that Efuru did not know what to do with her. At first she was very soft with her. But when she saw that this did not work, she became very firm and flogged her when she was very naughty. Once or twice; she threatened to put pepper in her eyes.

It took the poor child a long time to settle down with Efuru. She did not know why her parents had brought her to the strange house, and this feeling of insecurity made her behave the way she did. Sometimes when she was given Ogonim and the child was crying she let her cry or she cried with her.

After about two months, Ogea was quite settled. She became part of the household and took great care of Efuru's daughter. She would take her to the sand and there play with other children. If any child made Ogonim cry, she would beat that child. When Efuru went to the market, Ogea took care of Ogonim, fed her and changed her dress. When she cried and her mother was long in coming home she sang this lullaby to her;

'My sister sleep and don't cry.
  Omerere, Omerere.

My sister sleep and don't cry.
  Omerere, Omerere.

Cows are in the yellow sand.
  Omerere, Omerere.

Pigs are in the sands of the river.
  Omerere, Omerere.

Your father went fishing.
  Omerere, Omerere.

Your mother went to the market.
  Omerere, Omerere.

Your father will come soon.
  Omerere, Omerere.

Your mother will return soon.
  Omerere, Omerere.

Your father will bring you fishes.
  Omerere, Omerere.

Your mother will buy you a nice pot.
  Omerere, Omerere.

My sister sleep and don't cry.
  Omerere, Omerere.'

When Efuru returned from the market, Ogea ran with
Ogonim strapped on her back shouting:

'Mama has come back,
  Ototo.

Mama has come back,
  Oyoyo.'

Then Efuru put down her basket and took her daughter from Ogea. 'How are you, my daughter? Ogea, bring me a piece of cloth for her nose. Did she eat well? Did she cry when I was away?'

Then Ogea opened her basket and brought out the things she had bought from the market. Sometimes, she bought them ground-nuts, oranges and pears. One day when she returned from the market, she gave Ogea a second-hand cloth she had bought for her.

'Here you are, my child, try this on. I bought it today for only two shillings.'

Ogea was very happy. She wore it and it fitted very well.

'You can have that instead of tying a wrappa always.'

When Efuru finished feeding her baby, she handed it to Ogea, then she took her pot and towel and went to the stream. By the time she came back from the stream, her husband was back and both of them ate.

'Ogea,' Efuru called. Ogea answered from within. 'Ogea, did you go to see Ajanupu today as I told you before I went to the market?'

'No. I forgot to go.'

'How many things do you have to remember? You will see her tomorrow, do you hear?' She turned to her husband, 'You know Ajanupu, she will think I don't want them to come.'

So the next day when Efuru was preparing for market, she prepared Ogea and the child for the visit. 'Take good care of her at Ajanupu's. Ajanupu's children are rough, so look after her well and don't let them push her. Don't take her to the stream, please.'

Ajanupu and her children were happy to see Ogea and Ogonim. 'Bring her here, Ogea. Ogonim, you have grown so big.' Ajanupu cleaned her nose and straightened her dress. Then she placed her on her lap and then . . .

'You naughty girl, you have urinated on my cloth. Your mother will wash my cloth for me. It is a good sign though. It shows you like me. Ogea, please bring me a piece of cloth to wipe this mess. Good. Now you don't urinate again, or I will beat you. Ogea, is she standing now?'

'She stands, but when she see her mother coming, she sits down again.'

'That's what they do. You are nearly a year now, my child. Don't be lame. You are so healthy and I don't see the reason why you should not walk before you are one. Now Ogea, you take that pot and go down to the stream quickly and fetch some water for me. That's your navel. Run.'

Ogea took the pot and ran as fast as her legs could carry her. She went straight to the stream, filled the pot and made for home. A child of about her age saw her coming and when she was near told her that her pot was not well balanced on her head.

'It is tilted to the right,' she told her.

Ogea tilted it to the left.

'It is now to the left,' the girl said.

When she tried to put it straight, she made a false move. The clay pot fell with all its might to the ground and broke into a hundred pieces. Ogea placed her hands on her head and yelled.

'Ewoo – Ajanupu will kill me today. Ewoo, I have broken Ajanupu's pot. I am done for. I am done for. I am dead. Ajanupu will kill me,' she wept.

Passers-by begged her to go home, but she refused and wept louder than before.

'Are you a fool?' a woman asked her. 'Go home quickly, your mother won't kill you. And besides she is waiting for you. Go home my child.'

'I won't go home, Ajanupu will beat me. She will kill me. I won't go home.'

When Ajanupu waited and Ogea did not come back, she sent one of her children to find out what was keeping Ogea from fetching the water. The child saw Ogea crying, and she, with some other children there, watched her as she cried. The girl quite forgot that she was sent by her mother to go and call Ogea.

Ajanupu waited and when there was no sign of Ogea and her child, she strapped Ogonim on her back and went angrily to the stream making sure that she had a whip with her.

At this time, Ogea was collecting the pieces of the broken pot together. She did not know that Ajanupu was coming.

'Foolish girl, have this, and this,' she gave Ogea two strokes of the whip. Ogea jumped up in the air and ran. She could have run to the end of the world at that moment.

'Foolish child, stupid child,' Ajanupu went on. 'To break my pot and refuse to come home. What was she carrying with it? Such a small pot. It is an old one. I have had it for a long time and now that fool of a girl has broken it. You wait until you come home. And you, have this, and this,' she turned to her child whom she sent to find out about Ogea.

'You have the audacity to stay here and stare at me when you were sent to fetch Ogea.'

The little girl ran home yelling. Ajanupu picked up the whip jerked Ogonim in position and walked homeward still very angry.

'What is the matter?' a woman asked her.

'It is that fool of a girl who does not know her right from her left. That girl who has been in the farm since she was born and is so bush. She broke my water-pot. The water-pot I have had for many years.'

'Never mind. Children of these days are no use. What was she carrying with it? The pot is not a heavy one.'

'I don't know what she was carrying with it, my sister. The water-pot is not heavy.'

Ajanupu went on. Ogonim was becoming uncomfortable and started to cry. 'You remain where you are or ...' and she jerked her angrily. Ogonim kept quiet as if she heard Ajanupu's threats.

Somebody fetched some water for Ajanupu and she began to prepare some food. Her eldest daughter who was about fourteen was in school. The little ones were too small to be of much use. So Ajanupu did all the cooking with Ogonim on her back. She finished cooking and gave Ogonim some to eat. After eating, she fell asleep.

Ogea came back when Ajanupu was pounding the fufu and hid at the back of the house. When she saw that Ogonim was asleep and Ajanupu was about to eat she appeared.

'Have you finished running you fool? Now go to the kitchen and wash up.'

Ogea went to the kitchen and began to wash up. Ajanupu came to the kitchen. 'The mortar is not properly washed. And wash the whole length of the pestle. When you finish, sweep the floor. And be quick about it.'

When Ogea finished, she began to sweep the floor. 'Bend

44

down properly, you are a girl and will one day marry. Bend down and sweep like a woman,' Ajanupu commanded.

When she finished sweeping, she began to eat. 'You don't sit like that when you are eating. Put your legs together and sit like a woman.'

Ogea did as she was told and continued eating. She ate some fish in the soup and Ajanupu came along again. 'You eat your fish last. I wonder what Efuru has been teaching you. I must tell her to handle you better. Children eat their fish last. You will steal at this rate. Efuru will have to bring you here for a few weeks.'

When Ajanupu saw Efuru in the evening she told her about Ogea. 'You are spoiling Ogea. You just leave her to do what she likes. Remember she is a girl and she will marry one day. If you don't bring her up well, nobody will marry her. By the way, can she cook now?'

'She can boil yam for Ogonim. That's all she can do.'

'You mean she does not know how to pound fufu?'

'No, she does not pound fufu, I do that myself.'

'A girl of her age should know how to cook everything. You are to blame.'

'I am so busy, Ajanupu. Our trade is bad. People don't pay their debts, and so when I return from the market I go to collect these debts and have no time for anything else. Do you know what? Nwabuzo has not paid that money she borrowed a year ago.'

'What did she tell you today when you went to her house?'

'She asked me to come on Eke day.'

'You will not go. I shall go to her. Leave it to me. She will have to vomit out that money. You don't know how to collect debts. You remember that woman who borrowed ten pounds from my husband. For two years she did not want to pay. So one day, I collected my four children. We went there and sat down. She was the only person in their compound that day. We did not allow her to cook. If she made fire, I would ask one of my children to scatter the fire. If she wanted to go to the stream, we would take the water-pot from her. When it was too much for her, she begged us to go that she would bring me the money. I refused to go. All I wanted was my money. I did not want a part of it, I told her. I wanted everything. She knew

45

I was determined. She had insulted me and the people I sent to her previously, I had no sympathy for her. Then she said somebody owed her some money in the farm and she had promised to pay the next day could I go and she would bring me the money the next day. I refused. I was not leaving her house until my ten pounds was counted and given to me. It was not that she had no money. She had money because she and her husband were building a house, and wanted to build with my ten pounds. You need to see the cloth she had on during the Owu festival and also the trinkets. All these made me refuse to go. Finally, she went in and brought five pounds. I told her it was not correct, I was not going until she gave me the remaining five pounds.

'It was at this stage that people came in and intervened. 'She has tried,' they said to me. 'Take your money and go. Don't be obstinate.'

'Then you are the right person to go,' Efuru said to Ajanupu. 'It is only five pounds. If you collect it, I shall give you ten shillings out of it.'

Ajanupu went the next day. She was told that Nwabuzo, the debtor was not in. She sat down and waited. She did not have to wait for long when Nwabuzo came in, water-pot on her head. Ajanupu helped her put the pot down.

'Is it well today that you have come to my house?' Nwabuzo asked.

'It is well but not very well,' Ajanupu replied.

Nwabuzo went in and brought some kola. When they finished the kola, Ajanupu started, 'Efuru sent me to you. She said the five pounds is now overdue and that she will go to Akiri soon. She wants her money urgently and besides you asked her to come today which is Eke day.'

'It is true I said that. But I am sorry I have no money today. I know it has taken a long time since she lent me the money, but I have no money today. My husband and I went to the Great River to trade in ground-nuts. As we were returning our canoe capsized and we lost all our ground-nuts. I nearly lost my own life, but for my husband. When we lost everything, we came home and collected all the money we could find and went off again, this time to buy gari because we were told that gari trade was very profitable at the time. We bought our gari all

46

right and put them in bags ready to be taken down to the Great River for the homeward journey. My husband went for carriers and I watched the gari. Then suddenly, it seemed as if the heavens were opened and rain poured down in bucketfuls.

'Ajanupu, I was helpless. I could do nothing. I saw our gari soak and there was nothing I could do. I could not lift a bag. I wept and called passers-by to help me. Good people, they came and helped with a few bags before my husband came. The next day, the gari was put out to dry. Much of it was bad. We then took it to the market to sell, but nobody will buy it. Then someboy in uniform came along and kicked our gari, a basin-ful emptied on the ground. My husband was selling his in a bag. He ran away with his. 'If you are not careful,' the man in uniform told us, 'I shall hand you over to the police.' We returned home. The gari is still here. We have tried to sell it but who will buy such gari. Please have patience, let's see what we can do next Nkwo.'

'You are talking rubbish,' Ajanupu said. 'I have heard these stories before. You go to the room and bring me five pounds. That's all I want. I won't go until you have given me that amount. I am not leaving your house if you give me four pounds, nineteen shillings, eleven pence half-penny. Do you hear?'

Ajanupu sat down on the mat and stretched her legs. She was determined to stay there till doomsday. Nwabuzo did not know what to do. If there was money, she would have given it to Ajanupu. But there was no money. Nwabuzo called an elderly woman on the compound. When she came, she begged Ajanupu to go and come back the following day.

'I will not go, Nwabuzo will give me Efuru's money today. I will not go without it. So don't worry yourself begging me.'

The woman went away. When Nwabuzo saw that Ajanupu was deaf to all entreaties, she went into her room, untied her wrappa and brought out a very long bag which she used also in tying her wrappa. She counted some shillings. Then she opened her box and brought out a piece of cloth about six yards long which she had not sewn and gave the money and the cloth to Ajanupu.

'This is one pound. The piece of cloth cost me four pounds. Take it and when I have four pounds, I shall claim it.'

Ajanupu took the money and the cloth. 'Thank you, I am going. We shall find out whether the piece of cloth is worth four pounds.'

'Has she gone?' a woman on the compound asked.

'She has gone. I gave her a pound and a piece of cloth which cost me four pounds. Thank God I could give her those.'

'God forbid. What is all this about? What swells Ajanupu's head? Ajanupu's mother could not afford a good piece of cloth to tie round her waist. Her grand-mother died of hunger. Her father took no title. What is it that intoxicates her now?'

'That's how the newly rich behave. They have never seen money. When they see it, they lose their heads.'

'But she is not rich by any standard.'

'Well, she is. Don't you know she is building a house?'

'And so what? If she is building a house, she is building it for herself and I have nothing to do with it.'

When Ajanupu got home she cursed herself for not going directly to Efuru, a woman was waiting for her. She was sitting down comfortably on the mat. It was obvious that she had been there for a long time. Ajanupu said nothing to her when she came in. She opened her door, went in and came out again, locked the door and was walking away. The woman got up.

'Ajanupu, I have come to your house. There is no need to behave like that, or pretend that you don't know me. I want my money. I am tired of coming to your house. And besides I won't be in town for some time. Please give it to me.'

'How much do I owe you?'

'It is only five shillings,' the woman replied.

'All right, come tomorrow. I have no money today.'

'You have told me that several times. I won't come tomorrow, I want my money today. I am leaving town early tomorrow morning.'

'I say, come tomorrow I have no money today.'

'I said that I cannot come tomorrow.'

'You stay there then, I am going out.'

'Ho, you cannot go. You have money. Please give it to me.'

'Nonsense, what is wrong with you? How much do I owe you that you won't let me go about my business? Aren't you the daughter of Ijeoma who died of the white disease? Aren't you the daughter of Nwakaego who stole in the market and was killed by the juju?'

'You are a liar,' the woman replied. 'My father did not die of the white disease. My mother died a natural death. But you, your mother died of hunger on her way from Akiri. Your father was so poor that he could not bring her corpse home to be buried. So she was buried in a strange land. Shame on you. Your mother was buried in a strange land. You must give me my money today.'

Many people came around.

'What is the matter?' they asked.

'It is Ajanupu,' the woman said. 'It is Ajanupu, the newly rich, who has forgotten the poverty of her mother and father. She bought some yams from me three months ago. She gave me one pound and asked me to come the next day for five shillings. I have gone to her house nearly every day for the money but she refused to pay. Today, I told her that she must give me the money because I would be going to trade very early tomorrow morning. But she still insisted that I should come tomorrow. Then she told me my father died of the white disease and my mother died of juju. As if everybody in this town did not know that Ajanupu's mother died of starvation and her miserable father could not afford to bring back the corpse to be buried at home.'

'You don't have to quarrel,' one of the spectators said. 'Ajanupu,' she continued, 'if you have money, give her her money. There is no need to quarrel. The world is not good.'

'It is true,' another woman said. 'Ajanupu don't quarrel. Give her her money. And don't say bad words to each other.'

Ajanupu hissed. She went gingerly into the room and when she came out she handed five shillings to her creditor.

'It is because of these people,' Ajanupu said angrily to her creditor. 'If not you wouldn't have got this money.'

'Thank you very much, Ajanupu. A man asked his friend to cut up some meat for him. When the friend finished, he asked whether it was properly cut, the man told him that if he called him again to do the same job he would know whether he did it well or not.'

Ajanupu had banged her door by the time the woman finished this tedious proverb.

CHAPTER FOUR

At this time Adizua was missing many meals. He would return from the market, have his bath and disappear. Efuru would wait for him and when he did not return, she would eat without relish. Then she would go to bed very sad. At midnight, Adizua would come back and knock, Efuru would get up quickly and open the door. 'Have you returned my husband?'

'Yes.'

'Shall I bring food to you?'

'No, I am not hungry.'

Efuru would then go to bed and think. 'What is wrong?' she would ask herself. 'How have I offended my husband? What am I going to do to win him back. Has he found another woman?'

These thoughts kept her awake all night. In the morning, she was very weak but she got up early all the same, did her housework and went to market to buy and to sell.

She decided to take her mother-in-law into confidence. So one evening, she went to her: 'I want to tell you something,' she began.

'Is it all right with you and your husband?' her mother-in-law asked.

'It is bad, but not very bad,' Efuru said and hissed. 'My husband is not happy with me,' she continued. 'I don't know what is wrong. He comes home very late and won't eat my food. I don't know what to do.'

'You are sure you have not offended him in any way?' Efuru's mother-in-law asked.

'I am sure I have not offended him in any way. I have not even quarrelled with him for not eating my food. For a long time now we have not lived as husband and wife. If he wants to marry a wife I shall be only to happy. In fact, I have been thinking of it for some time for I have not had a second baby, and now I wonder whether a second one will ever come.'

'God forbid. Our fathers forbid. You will have babies. Don't wish yourself evil. Our ancestors will not allow this. I am sorry about what you have told me. I have not noticed anything. I shall see my son tonight.'

When Efuru went away her mother-in-law was very sorrowful. 'The son of a gorilla must dance like the father gorilla. Our elders were quite right when they said this. Adizua is every inch like his father. God, please don't let him be like his father. Efuru is such a beautiful and good wife. How she agreed to marry him is what I cannot understand. If Efuru leaves, that will be the end of me. I cease to live the day Efuru leaves my son.'

Adizua returned from the market, had his bath quickly and went out. He said nothing to anybody. His mother waited for him to come back and when it was midnight and there was no sign of him, she went to sleep. But she could not sleep. She thought about her son and what would become of her if Efuru left him.

When the cock crew, she went to Efuru's door and knocked.

'Did he return?' she asked.

'Oh, it is you, Omeifeaku,' Efuru greeted her mother-in-law.

'O-o-o my daughter, Nwaononaku. Did he return last night?' Ossai asked again.

'You mean Adizua, my husband,' and she laughed but without mirth. 'My husband did not return last night. I waited till about midnight and when I did not see him I went to bed, but I did not sleep a wink.'

'Has he been doing this for long?'

'He had been doing this for weeks now. What beats me is that I have not offended him. If I had offended him, I would render an apology easily.'

'Have patience, my daughter. Don't be in a hurry. Everything will be all right. Don't mind my son. It is only youth that is worrying him and nothing else. He will soon realize what a fool he has been, and will come crawling to you. Look after your daughter and your trade. Your husband will come back to you after all his wanderings. Men are always like that.'

Efuru took her mother-in-law's advice. She went about her business cheerfully. But many nights her husband was not home and most of his meals were not eaten. So Efuru refused to cook any more meals. One night, he returned and demanded his food.

'I did not cook anything for you. For weeks now you have not asked for your food, and tonight you have returned demanding your food. There is no food. I have wasted a lot of money cooking food that you never ate.'

'I want my food tonight,' Adizua said quietly and went to his room.

Efuru went to the kitchen and prepared something for her husband. When it was ready, Adizua was called, and when there was no reply from his room, Ogea was sent. The room was empty. Efuru left the food on a tray and went to bed.

That night Efuru did not sleep. She relived all her life from the time her mother died, to the day she ran away from her father's house to Adizua's house. She thought of the tactful way in which she handled her relatives sent by her father to persuade her to leave Adizua's house. She remembered the day she and her father went to the dibia and what the sage told her. And above all, she remembered the first day she felt in her womb that she was expecting Adizua's baby and also the day she had the baby. All these were great events in her life, and she wept.

When she returned from the stream in the morning, she heard some sounds in Adizua's room and knew that he was in. She went straight in. 'Where did you go last night?' she asked very quietly. She was surprised to notice that despite all her anger the night before, she was quite composed and far from losing her temper. Adizua did not answer. He was busy examining a blunt knife. It was Adizua's silence and indifference that made her mad. 'Don't you hear me?' she raised her voice. 'Adizua, don't you hear me? Where did you go last night and why did you get me up from bed to cook for you only to go out before I finished cooking?'

Adizua made no reply.

'Adizua, are you deaf? Why don't you answer me?'

Adizua was still busy examining the blunt knife. He was looking at it as if his whole life depended on the result of this examination.

'You are deaf and dumb then. I wish you will continue being

52

deaf and dumb. And I tell you, you are going to be sorry for this behaviour.' Efuru left the room. What can a woman do to a man who has bluntly refused to quarrel.

Did Adizua do this because he wanted to avoid an early morning quarrel with his wife or did he do it because his wife was not worth quarrelling with? Efuru thought of this all day and was convinced that Adizua's indifference was not due to anything but lack of love. She said nothing more to her mother-in-law. She complained to no one and she stopped cooking for her husband and her husband in turn did not notice that his wife had stopped cooking for him.

One morning, Adizua knocked at Efuru's door. It had been a long time since he knocked at his wife's door so early.

'I am going to Ndoni this morning,' Adizua said indifferently. 'I hear ground-nuts are profitable now.'

'Really,' Efuru said. 'Go well and buy things for us.'

Adizua left the room. In about an hour he was gone. He did not even say anything to his mother.

When Adizua left the room, Efuru sat down on her bed and began to think. 'Adizua is not going to Ndoni alone,' she said to herself. 'I am quite sure a woman is in this. His every movement suggests this. Adizua must be in the influence of some woman. And what's more this woman must be well to do. He is still pleasing to my eyes, but I am not pleasing to his own eyes any more, and I cannot explain it. How long will this last? How long will I continue to tolerate him. There is a limit to human endurance. I am a human being. I am not a piece of wood. Perhaps he wants to marry this woman. What is wrong in his marrying a second wife. It is only a bad woman who wants her husband all to herself. I don't object to his marrying a second wife, but I do object to being relegated to the background. I want to keep my position as the first wife, for it is my right.

'And my daughter is nearly two years old now,' Efuru continued in her thought. 'And there is no sign that I am going to have another baby. But how can I have another baby when for nearly six months my husband has not slept with me. How then can I be pregnant when I am and always will be a faithful wife. Oh, if only I could know how and when I offended him, I shall ask people to beg him. I shall try all in my power to win his

53

love. If I fail in this attempt, then I will have no other course than to leave him.

'Perhaps there is no woman in my husband's life after all. He is just behaving queerly. No. It is not possible. Men behave this way when women are in their lives and she is so influential that they cannot but bow to her whims and will. No, I was right. There is a woman behind this indifference. A woman whose personality is greater than mine. Yes, greater than mine; I must face facts. This woman's personality is greater than mine. If mine were greater he would not have left me. Perhaps she is very beautiful and has long hair like mine. Is she fair or dark? Are her teeth as white as mine? Is she as stately as I am. She is an ugly woman. But how do I know that she is not as beautiful as I am? It is mere wishful thinking.'

Efuru found it difficult to build a picture of her rival in her mind's eye. It was painful to her to think of her as a beautiful woman, so she refused to imagine her as such. But then she must be remarkable to be able to steal her husband.

When it was time to go to the market, Efuru went. She sold her things quietly and sadly. One of her customers asked her why she was so sad and she told her to mind her business. It was obvious that she was not very interested in what she was selling. She did not care whether her customers bought from her or not. She did not call them to buy from her. Occasionally a woman would ask her if she had any change to give her. If she had some change she would give her without saying a word.

'What is the matter?' the woman would ask her.

'Nothing,' Efuru would reply.

'But you don't look yourself today. Is Ogonim ill?'

'No, Ogonim is not ill.'

'What is wrong then?' the woman would insist.

'There is nothing wrong, believe me,' Efuru would lie.

As she was selling in the market one day, Efuru listened to a conversation between two elderly women who were about the age of her husband's mother. She was not in fact eavesdropping. She was compelled to listen.

'You were telling me about your daughter when we were interrupted.'

'Yes, my daughter went to Ndoni about a week ago. She left very early and she did not tell me whom she was going with.'

'Well, you never can understand young women of these days, but what about her husband?' the other woman asked.

'Her husband?' she repeated. 'You are the only person who has not known that story. She has left her husband.'

'She has left her husband? Why did she leave her husband and what about her children?'

'Why she left her husband is a long story which I cannot tell now. She had two children, one died and the other one is with me. She is about three years old. When the husband came for his child, she told him in his face that the child was not his. That when the child grew up she was going to give her to the real father.'

'This is an abomination. What is wrong with these children nowadays. When we were young, we dared not do this. You mean that she was committing adultery in her husband's house? Oh, our poor ancestors are wronged no wonder things are not smooth for us, and what did your husband say to her?'

'He threatened to kill her, and she ran away and hid in a friend's house. She is a bad daughter, my friend. She is a bad daughter. She won't listen to me. She won't listen to anybody. I am fed up with her. She simply brought her daughter to me the morning she was leaving for Ndoni, without making adequate provision for her. The child's body is full of yaws. Yesterday, I took her to the stream and scrubbed it with a sponge. She cried and cried and called me all sorts of names.'

'And you say that she has gone to Ndoni? When is she coming back?'

'How do I know? She did not tell me.'

'You do not even know whom she had gone with?'

'No, I don't know.'

Efuru listened to this conversation attentively. This must be the woman who went with Adizua to Ndoni. She found this impossible not to believe.

'Who is this woman?' Efuru began to think again. 'Adizua must have been seeing her for a long time and both have gone to trade together. I am now certain that Adizua left me for another woman. What are Adizua's plans about this woman? Does he intend to marry her? Or are they only friends? But why is he so secretive about it? He is the lord and master, if he wants to marry her, I cannot stop him.'

55

Efuru packed her things and went home. Her mother-in-law was in, Ogonim and Ogea were in also. She picked Ogonim up and wiped her face. 'How are you, my daughter?' she asked her. And the little one showed her eight white teeth and was busy pulling at Efuru's buba to breast-feed.

'I must be serious about weaning you. Mother, how am I going to stop her?' Efuru turned to her mother-in-law.

'I don't think she has had enough. If I were you I will continue to give her for another month or two. It is only at night that she breast-feeds, so let her have it for another month or two.'

'All right, mother.'

Efuru went about her business normally. She did not appear sorrowful as she was a day or two ago. When she had tidied her room and had given Ogonim and Ogea what she bought for them from the market, she took her water-pot and as she was about to place it on her head, she heard Ajanupu's voice.

'Ossai, are you in?' Ajanupu asked in a most unfriendly manner.

'Yes, I am in,' Ossai replied. 'Is that you Ajanupu, come in. Idenu.'

'Omeifeaku,' Ajanupu greeted her sister. 'Is Efuru in?'

'She is in.'

'Ajanupu, Idenu, welcome. I am in. I heard your voice.'

'How are you, my daughter. Is everything well with you, my daughter, and Ogonim, is she well?'

'Ogonim is well. I am trying to stop breast-feeding her.'

'Stop breast-feeding her? Who will feed on your breast if you stop breast-feeding her? What has gone wrong with you?' Ajanupu looked at Efuru for some time without talking. 'Oh, what a fool I are. Are you pregnant?'

'No, I am not pregnant Ajanupu.'

'I thought so. If you are pregnant I will know. Leave Ogonim to breast-feed for another month or two before you stop her. I shall teach you the best way to stop her, the best and the easiest way.'

When they had had kola, Efuru's mother-in-law went to the stream and Efuru and Ajanupu talked generally. After an hour or so, Ajanupu suddenly said, 'Efuru, I came to your house.'

'Ewuu, is it well?' Efuru exclaimed.

'It is well, but not very well. It is said that an elderly person cannot watch a goat being entrapped and do nothing. That is why I have come to you. Your mother-in-law and I are sisters. Our mother had us and two others, both of them men. If anything happens to my sister today, it will be my responsibility to look after you. So I am your mother-in-law today. When I see or hear anything that would affect you adversely, it is my place to come and tell you. I do not like the footsteps of your husband. I do not like it at all. There is a rumour that he is going to marry another woman soon. But I don't quarrel with that. Only a bad woman would like to be married alone by her husband. I had to recommend a girl for my husband when I saw that I was too busy to look after him and my children, and at the same time carry on with my trade. So there is nothing wrong in his wanting to marry a second wife. But he must go about in an open and noble way. And I want to tell you this . . . But by the way, where is he now?'

Efuru did not answer. Ajanupu looked at her and saw tears flowing freely down her cheeks. She made no attempt to stop the tears. Ajanupu was full of pity.

'Don't take it that way, my child. No, please don't take it that way. Why are you weeping? Wipe your tears my child. It is not as bad as all that. Wipe your tears and tell me everything. Take me into confidence and I shall give you all the help I can.'

'Adizua has left me. Before he left, he told me he was going to Ndoni and today in the market I overheard two women conversing. I am sure now that Adizua went to Ndoni with a woman. I gathered that this woman had left her husband.'

'Oh, you know already about this woman, the daughter of a beach, a worthless woman that cannot meet you anywhere and dare look at you in the face.'

'Yes, I knew about this woman only in the market today, though nobody told me her name neither was my husband's name mentioned, yet I knew by intuition immediately I heard the conversation, that my husband ran away with her. For months, Ajanupu, my husband came home late every night. Some nights he did not come home at all. He did not eat my food and when I stopped cooking for him, he did not notice. Then one night he came back earlier than usual and asked for his food. I told him I did not cook anything because for weeks

57

he had refused to eat my food. He insisted on eating that night and went to his room. I went to the kitchen and cooked something for him. When I finished and sent Ogea to call him, he was not in his room. Ajanupu, I am fed up with this. I don't know how I can go on tolerating this. God in heaven knows that since I married Adizua I have been faithful to him. Our ancestors know that since I ran away from my father's house to Adizua's that nobody, no man has seen my nakedness. But Adizua has treated me shabbily. He has treated me the way that only slaves are treated. God in heaven will judge us.'

'Don't say that, my child. Don't call on our God's name. Adizua will not see the light of day tomorrow if you call on our God's name to judge him. Everybody in our town my child, knows that you have been a faithful wife. Everybody knows that you are a good woman and what is more they love and respect you. As I was telling you, there is a rumour that Adizua wants to marry this woman. She is not a good woman. But she is a good trader and like you, her hands make money. Her mother and father are not well known and I hear from a reliable source that her father died of the 'small cough'. The woman is well known among her age-group where she lords it over them. My advice is this my dear child: be patient and wait. It is only the patient man that drinks good water. Some men are not fit to be called men. They have no sense. They are like dogs that do not know who feeds them. Leave Adizua with this woman. He will soon be tired of her and you will resume your position again. This is all I have come to tell you. When Ossai comes, tell her I have gone. All right then. I am going.'

'Go well and greet your children for me.'

Efuru remained seated, and stared into space. 'So that's it. All I suspected have now been proved correct. I was not just imagining things. It is true that Adizua went to Ndoni with a woman. And who is this woman? I don't know her and Ajanupu did not even mention her name. So that is the woman who is responsible for all my misery. But why is Adizua so queer about her. If he wants to marry her, he only has to say so. I cannot stop him. If Adizua does not love me any more, I too will try to learn not to love him any more. It will be a difficult task but it is not impossible.'

When Efuru's mother-in-law came back, Efuru went to her

and told her what Ajanupu had told her and also the conversation she overheard in the market. Her mother-in-law was very sad. She beat her chest and cracked her fingers many times in wonder.

'My daughter, I cannot doubt what you have said. My son has neglected you. But as my sister Ajanupu has advised you wisely, be patient. It pays to be patient. I have been patient myself all my life. You don't know what my life had been. I have not told you my life-story with Adizua's father. No woman of today can suffer as I have suffered. Adizua's father married me as a woman was married in our day. He paid the dowry in full and performed all the customs of our people. After two years of my marriage I had Adizua. He was exactly like his father. We were in the farm when he was born. There was no mat, so we used the leaves of plantain tree. We had so many plantain trees in our farm. Adizua grew like a plantain tree, and for a long time, we were in the farm. Life in the farm was so different from life in the town and I felt like a fish out of water each time I went to the town, so I preferred to remain in the farm.

'When Adizua was five years old, he was very ill. We went to a dibia and he told us to go to town and sacrifice to our ancestors. He said that our ancestors were angry with us because we had not taken Adizua to town. That was how we went to the town. In the town, Adizua was timid and shy. Town life was so different from the life in the farm. He felt very unsafe, but I was always on his side when other children teased him and said unkind things about him. Adizua's father was in the farm looking after the yams.

'Harvest came,' continued Efuru's mother-in-law, 'everybody returned to the town to sell their yams, but Adizua's father did not return. Some people told me that he had not yet harvested his yams. Others told me that he was going to Abonema to sell his yams. For a long time I heard nothing from him and we almost begged for food. My sister, Ajanupu, and my mother gave me some money and I started a small trade in fish.

'Then news came from him. He was in Abonema. He had sold all his yams and left the money under his pillow. At night a thief came, lifted his head and took away all the money. I wept bitterly when I heard this. But Ajanupu and my mother had no sympathy for me. They told me that my husband was lying and that the money was not stolen. He must have used the money on a woman or he gambled it away. But I was on the side of my husband. I told them were unkind and heartless.

'My husband refused to return. I sent messages upon messages but he refused to return. When Adizua was nearly ten years old, we heard that he was at Ibeocha. I went to Ibeocha and for days I searched for him in the streets. Nobody could give me any information about him. I returned home in distress. My mother asked me to leave my husband's house, but I refused. I still had faith in him. I was so confident that he would come back to me and to Adizua. As for Ajanupu, she was so disgusted with me that she refused to see me.

'Just exactly six years after he had gone to Abonema to sell his yams, we heard that he was at Abor and was married to a very wealthy woman. I did not doubt this because my husband was a very handsome man. You can see this in Adizua. Adizua is exactly like him – the height and everything.

'When I heard this, I made up my mind to go and find him. My mother thought I was mad in wanting to go. It was very far away. It would mean paddling our canoe for about three days in the Great River. But I did not care about the hardship involved. Immediately I could afford the journey I took my son to Abor. Again nobody gave us information. We walked from lane to lane, from one village to the other, but did not see him nor did we see anybody who had seen him. That was the last time I went out in search of him.

'When I came home, I was ill and Adizua was ill too. But for my mother, I would have died of that illness. She took me home and nursed me. But when I was well I went back to my husband's house. Many men came to marry me but I refused to have anything to do with any of them. My mother talked and talked, but I refused to say yes to any of them. I was through with marriage, I said. Ajanupu scolded me, told me I was a weakling that I was wasting my life, but I did not heed her.

'Three harvests after, my husband came home without any warning. I welcomed him, I embraced him and wept for joy. He begged me to forgive him and promised that he would be faithful to me. I took him for his word. We lived together. He could not go to the farm any more. His life had changed completely and he brooded most of the time. One Nkwo day he disappeared.

'Ajanupu came to the house and poured words into my ears. She knew all along that my husband did not come to stay. I was a fool to think that that man cared for me and my son. I did not say a word to her. Then six months later my husband came back. This time he was very ill. He had contracted a disease and had come to me to cure him. I took him to a dibia. The dibia said he had annoyed the ancestors and the gods of the land and therefore he must receive his punishment. It was a bad disease that killed his soul. I went to the market on Nkwo day to buy the things the dibia had asked me to buy and before I came back, Adizua's father was dead. I mourned for him for three years. His brother wanted to marry me but I refused. I am still in my husband's house till today.

'My daughter, I can only solicit patience. Have patience. You may not wait as long as I did. I gained nothing from my long suffering, so the world would think, but I am proud that I was and still am true to the only man I loved.'

Efuru did not say a word. She left Adizua's mother and went to her room. Adizua's mother watched her as she left for her room. 'She will leave my son,' she said again. 'She is so young and I will be surprised if she waits for him. But I do not blame her. Poor child, what will she do? Perhaps I shouldn't have told her about my married life, and my sorrows. Why did I tell her? I shouldn't have told her. She now knows that Adizua is doing exactly what his father did and it will be of no use to stay and hope. Oh, why did I tell her?'

Efuru's mother-in-law sat down in her room with bowed head, and wept. Meanwhile Efuru was in her room deep in thought. 'So it is in the family. There is no point staying then. Adizua's waywardness is in his blood and you can do nothing about it. And my mother-in-law, poor woman. She does look as if she had seen many sad days, and the behaviour of her son has reminded her of all she suffered in her younger days. Perhaps self-imposed suffering appeals to her. It does not appeal to me. I know I am capable of suffering for greater things. But to suffer for a truant husband, an irresponsible husband like Adizua is to debase suffering. My own suffering will be noble. When Adizua comes back, I shall leave him. And what about my daughter?' she asked herself. 'I can leave a man, but I cannot leave my daughter. Of course, I shall take my daughter with me. I shall go back to my father's house. Thank God he is still alive.'

The next day Efuru went to see her father. She had Ogonim on her back. Her father was not feeling very well. He was sitting down in his obi – the sitting-room where he received guests. Before Efuru stepped into the sitting-room, she greeted her father.

'Agundu,' she greeted.

'Yes, my daughter, Nwaonoaku; sit down here. It is a long time since I saw you last. Is everything well with you?'

'All is well, my father. Ogonim come down and greet your grandfather.' Ogonim walked unsteadily to her grandfather, but she stopped before she reached him.

'Come along, don't be afraid,' her grandfather encouraged. She made one unsteady step again and stood still. She did not know whether to go back to her mother or to go forward to her grandfather.

'You don't want to come? Come,' her grandfather stretched his hands to her encouragingly. 'Come, my dear daughter. I have some fish for you.'

Ogonim turned and ran to her mother and buried her face on her mother's lap. Then she lifted her head, looked at her grandfather and buried her face again on her mother's lap, laughing.

'So you have refused to come to me?' her grandfather asked her. 'All right then, I won't give you fish.'

Ogonim shook her head and then went to her grandfather. 'That's right, my dear daughter. Now I can give you fish. Who is there?'

Somebody answered from within.

'Please bring some fish for Ogonim.' Some dried fish was brought and it was deposited into the hands of Ogonim and she began to eat greedily.

'I don't see your husband these days, is he well?'

'He went to Ndoni.'

'Did you not go with him this time? You always went together to trade in the Great River.'

Efuru made no reply. Her father saw that she was not happy.

'I came to see you, father, about Adizua,' Efuru said in a quiet voice. 'If he ill-treats me further I shall leave him.'

'What is the matter? Did he beat you? Did he bring a woman into the house?'

Efuru shook her head. 'He did not do any of these, father.'

'What then?'

'For months now, father, my husband has come home very late. Some nights, he has not come home at all. Sometimes he has refused to eat my food. And now I have heard that he wants to marry a woman who has just left her husband. This woman had gone to Ndoni with him, father. And what will become of me? Oh, my God, my life is ruined.'

'God forbid. Your life is not ruined my daughter. Our ancestors will not agree. It does not matter my daughter if Adizua wants to marry another woman. It is only a bad woman who wants to have a man all to herself.'

'No father, I don't object to his marrying a second wife. I don't object to it at all. Even before I had Ogonim, I was thinking of marrying a wife for Adizua. But our ancestors were kind enough to bless me with a daughter and the joy of having a baby, the realization that I was not barren filled me with happiness that I did not think of getting a wife for him any more. But I have not abandoned the idea completely. So I don't mind if he marries another wife. But rumour has it that this woman is a bad woman. So, father, that is why I am unhappy.'

'I can understand you, my daughter. But have patience. Wait until he returns from Ndoni. I shall see him then. Meanwhile go home and be a good mother to your daughter.'

Efuru pondered this advice. She thought of a conspiracy of all these three that she had sought advice from: Ajanupu, her mother-in-law, and now her father. She did not want to disobey these people. They had been important in her life. 'But when Adizua comes home,' she said aloud, 'it is going to be a straightforward business, cut and dried and no nonsense. Does it not occur to my mother-in-law, Ajanupu and my father that Adizua is quite satisfied with this woman and does not want me any more? Need I to stay until he says: "Efuru I don't want you any more. Return to your father's house, and when you marry again I shall come for my dowry?" Our ancestors forbid that I should wait for a man to drive me out of his house. This is done to women who cannot stand by themselves, women who have no good homes, and not to me the daughter of Nwashike Ogene. And besides, my face is not burnt, I am still a beautiful woman.'

Efuru returned from the market one day and, as usual, she picked Ogonim from the ground where she was playing and gave her things she bought for her. She saw that her body was warm.

'Ogea,' Efuru called, 'Ogonim's body is warm, did you notice it?'

'Yes, I did. Her body was warm this morning so I did not give her a bath. I cleaned her body with a wet towel as you taught me and rubbed kernel oil on her body and head.'

'That's good. But her head is still warm. Did she eat anything?'

'She did not eat much, and she has not passed anything since morning.'

'Is it true? Something should be done then. Ajanupu told me that if a child does not pass anything it is dangerous, and that you have to force her to pass something. So Ogea, you go and get me some mentholetum.'

Efuru gave Ogonim a hot bath and put some mentholetum in her anus. She then rubbed kernel oil all over her body putting it in every opening of the body. She tried to breast-feed her, but she refused it. Efuru put her on her back and in no time she was asleep. She brought her out again and put her on the bed. 'Now stay with her Ogea, while I go to Ajanupu.'

Efuru walked as fast as she could, occasionally breaking into a run. Ajanupu was in. 'My daughter is ill,' she told Ajanupu before she sat down. 'She has a fever and she has lost her appetite. I have rubbed her with kernel oil.'

'When did this start?' Ajanupu asked like a young medical practitioner who is at a loss what to ask next.

'Only this morning,' Ajanupu thought for a while. 'Has she passed anything today?'

'No, she has not.'

'That's the trouble. We must make her pass something; if not she will have a convulsion.' She went into the room, took her cloth and came out again. 'Let's go,' she said to Efuru. Both women walked briskly to Efuru's house.

Ogonim was on Ogea's back when they arrived.

'When did she wake up?'

'Immediately you left.'

'Bring her and go and ask mother to come. She went to the stream.'

Ajanupu took Ogonim and began to examine her. Her temperature was rising. Her eyes were not normal.

'If we don't take care,' Ajanupu said, 'she will have a convulsion. It is obvious, look at her eyes. But first of all let's make her pass something.' Ogonim had an enema but she did not pass much. Ajanupu then rubbed more kernel oil on her this time mixed with some leaves, and covered her up. Then she sent Efuru home to get some medicine. Efuru came back with the medicine and some was given to Ogonim to drink.

'That's all I know,' Ajanupu said. 'This is all I give to my children when they have fever to prevent them from having a convulsion. Watch her in the night. I shall come again tomorrow morning.'

Ogonim was restless all night. She cried and tossed in bed. Her temperature would rise suddenly and then fall again. When it rose, she shuddered. She did this for a while and when Efuru could bear it no longer, she asked her mother-in-law to go for Ajanupu. When Ajanupu came, she took Ogonim and looked at her, as before. Then she heard Ogea whimpering at a corner. 'You good for nothing child. Why are you crying? Don't frighten anybody with your crocodile tears. Go to the kitchen at once and boil some water.'

Ajanupu had brought with her a bottle full of roots of different plants. She wanted it warmed.

'It is obvious she is going to have a convulsion. Our task is to prevent her from having it. Go to the kitchen at once Efuru, and warm this yourself.' She gave her the bottle.

When Efuru got to the kitchen, she was surprised to see that Ogea had made the fire already. The medicine was warmed and some was given to Ogonim. 'Drink it, my daughter,' Ajanupu said. 'Drink all of it, don't throw it out. Drink all of it. That's good. That's a good girl. Give me some water, Ogea.' Ogea brought some water and Ajanupu washed her hands. 'Now take her Efuru, and breast-feed her.'

Ogonim fed for a little while and stopped. She felt sick and before anything could be done she vomited out everything and began to cry. Efuru removed her clothes and used them in wiping her mouth and legs. Ogea went quickly and brought another dress for Ogonim. It was a thick one that would prevent cold.

'We won't give her another dose of medicine. Let's watch her and see how she gets on. Ogea, give me a mat.' Ogea brought Ajanupu a mat, spread it on the floor of the room and Ajanupu lay down. She was unable to sleep. None of the women slept that night.

In the morning Ogonim was better. Efuru was happy, but she did not go to the market. This was the first time Ogonim had given her an anxious time. Hitherto she has been a very healthy child.

'What will I do if I lose her?' she thought. 'If she dies, that will mean the end of me.' It was then that she remembered what the dibia told her and Adizua when they went to him after the birth of Ogonim. The dibia after breaking the kola saw that something was wrong. He was not sure what it was. He had asked them to come again on Eke day and before that day, they heard that he was dead. 'What did he see?' Efuru asked herself. It was only now that Efuru thought seriously of what the dibia told her and her husband more than a year ago. And she was very frightened. She had wanted to tell her father what the dibia said, but she was afraid of the unknown. And of course, she was so full of her baby then that anything which made her unhappy was quickly forgotten. Now, Ogonim was ill. The day she and Adizua went to see the man came back vividly to her. She saw herself walking behind her husband with their presents for the dibia on her head. She remembered how the dibia greeted them. Then the kola-nuts!

'What was revealed to him in those kola-nuts?' Efuru asked herself. 'Would it be of any use if I went to another dibia? Will another dibia tell me the truth? And what is the truth?' Efuru was not quite taken in about dibias. She knew that many of them were quacks. There were some good ones who knew medicines and how to administer them. Her father had told her that the only good dibia they had in the town was the dead one. So she discarded the idea of going to any of them.

Ajanupu slept on the floor all night and in the morning she

went home, but came back almost immediately. She took Ogonim from Ogea and examined her closely. 'She is getting better. Let's give her the medicine again.' Ogonim took the medicine. Ajanupu rubbed some kernel oil on her again, and put her on Ogea's back. 'I am going home,' Ajanupu told Efuru. 'Send for me if there are some adverse developments.'

Efuru went to the stream to wash a few clothes soiled by Ogonim at night. As she was rinsing the last cloth she looked up and saw Ogea running down the stream. Efuru's heart jumped into her mouth. She left all the clothes on the stone used for washing and ran to Ogea. 'Come, come quickly. Somebody has gone for Ajanupu.'

Efuru ran home. Her mother-in-law was holding Ogonim firmly. She was shaking convulsively. She took her from her mother-in-law. 'Give me a spoon, a small spoon quick.' Her mother-in-law gave her a spoon. She put the spoon in Ogonim's mouth, between her upper and lower teeth.

'Mother, bring kernel oil.' A bottle of kernel oil was brought and Efuru nearly emptied the contents of the bottle on the sick child's head and body. The Ajanupu arrived.

'Evil forces leave my child, evil forces leave my daughter. It will not happen. It cannot happen in my presence. Our ancestors fight against them. Our ancestors fight against death, don't let death defeat you. Give her to me. Give her to me quickly. God forbid that anything should happen to you. Give her to me at once.'

Ogonim was still having the convulsion. She stretched and began to shake again. 'Let's go to the kitchen. Put some alligator pepper in the fire. Put ordinary pepper in the fire also. Hold her legs Ossai, while I hold her head. Yes over the fire. Over the fire, I say,' Now Ogonim was still, everybody thought she was dead. Ajanupu shook her and felt her chest. 'Her heart is beating. She is alive. Put more pepper in the fire.' When this was done, Ogonim sneezed. 'Yes, sneeze my child. We are stronger than they are.'

At last the convulsion left her. She began to cry softly. 'Don't cry. You are all right. Don't cry, my daughter, my only child. You are not going to leave me for the other world. Our ancestors will not allow it.'

Efuru put the sick child on her back, and walked to and fro.

If she stopped walking, Ogonim yelled as if she had yaws and you accidentally touched it. So she walked from one end of the compound to the other.

Efuru's mother-in-law was busy preparing something for Ogonim to eat – some mashed yam with palm oil. When she finished, Ogonim refused to eat, and started crying. 'All right, all right. You don't eat it. Nobody wants to force you to eat it, my dear child,' Efuru told her. So all day long Ogonim did not eat anything. It was only water she agreed to drink. All day long she was on Efuru's back. When she dozed off and Efuru tried to put her to bed, she yelled as loud as her strength would let her.

Ogonim had a quiet night and Efuru had some hope of her recovery, but early in the morning when the cock crew, her temperature rose again. Kernel oil was used to put down the fever, but her temperature continued to rise. She had another attack of convulsion and before Ajanupu arrived, she was dead.

CHAPTER FIVE

Ajanupu took the dead child in her arms and looked at it
closely. Tears rolled down her cheeks. Up to the time Ajanupu
arrived, Efuru did not know exactly what had happened. Then
she saw tears on Ajanupu's cheeks and she realized that her
only child was dead. She threw herself on the floor of the room
and wept hysterically.

Ogea ran out, put her two hands in both ears and shouted:
'Our people come, come: Ogonim is dead. Ogonim the only
child of Efuru is dead.' Neighbours ran to Efuru's house. Ajanupu was still holding the dead child. Tears were still rolling
down her cheeks. Efuru was rolling on the floor. The first
woman to arrive took the child from Ajanupu.

'Why, she is not dead. Don't you see that her body is warm.
She is still alive.'

Ajanupu hissed:

'Give her to me. Don't you see? Have you eyes and you don't
see? Don't you see that she is dead?' Ajanupu snatched the dead
child from the woman. She put her on her lap again and began
to look at her as before. 'Ogonim, so you have gone. So you
refused to stay with us. You are a foolish child to leave all the
wealth and riches for the land of the dead. You are ungrateful
for leaving your good mother. A mother who is more than all
mothers. A good mother in the real sense of goodness. You saw
the wealth, the riches, good home and you chose the life in the
other world. You have not done well, my daughter.'

Ogea wept in her corner. She went to her mistress and placed
her hands on her lap. 'Mama, Ogonim has wronged us. Ogonim
has not done well. What will you do? What am I going to do?
Who am I going to look after? Oh, Ogonim, why did you treat
us like this?'

Efuru's mother-in-law wept softly at her corner. There were
no tears. She was not given to much talk. Throughout her life,
she had been to herself a symbol of suffering. These self-imposed sufferings had sobered her. Now, nothing excited her.

She even found it difficult to produce tears from her eyes. She had shed so many tears that it did not seem as if there were any more tears for her to shed. But watching her in her corner, anybody could see that she was in great grief.

Efuru was still rolling on the floor. Sometimes she would would take Ogonim from Ajanupu, look at her, shake her head and hand her back to Ajanupu. She called on the gods to bear witness. She raised her hands and asked the gods and her ancestors where and when she offended them that they should allow her only child to be snatched by death.

'Let's not sit down doing nothing,' Ajanupu said, getting up from the floor. 'Ogonim's father must be sent for, the corpse will be buried and there are sympathizers to be looked after. Ossai, get up and be useful. This is early morning. Go down to the stream and see if there are people going to Ndoni and give them a message for Adizua. Be quick, please. You will find many people going to Ndoni today being Eke day.'

'But will his "wife" allow him to come home?' Ajanupu thought. 'Men are such queer people. They are so weak that when they are under the thumb of a woman, she does whatever she likes with them. And that woman? That devil in the form of a woman, she won't allow him to come home and bury his only child. I can see the subtle way she would do it. I can imagine her now saying that she is expecting a baby, and pretending to be very ill, and Adizua putting off homecoming every day until it is too late to come home. But why think about this now, when there is so much to be done?' she thought.

Efuru was too tired and confused to be of much use. Ogea had the corpse now, she was still weeping but this time very softly. She was so grown up now. 'Ogea, put her down on the bare floor. The floor is cool and the coolness will preserve the corpse. Now go and get some water from the stream. When you return, leave it at the back of the house.' Ajanupu said.

When Ogea went to the stream, Ajanupu swept the floor. She carried the bed from the bedroom to the sitting-room and spread a beautiful velvet cloth on it. She went to the mud wardrobe and brought out some mats with beautiful designs and spread them on the mud-benches for sympathizers. 'Now Efuru, tie your cloth well and come out and sit down in the

70

sitting-room. You cannot stay in the room for you will faint for want of air. Get up, my daughter, and come with me.' Ajanupu supported Efuru as she left the bedroom for the sitting-room. Now sit down at this corner. You will be able to recognize sympathizers when they come. Now be brave about it. Don't weep too much for you will be ill afterwards. Remember that Ogonim has gone and gone for ever. No amount of weeping will bring her back to life.'

Neighbours and sympathizers were now arriving. Mats were spread outside for them to sit down. Ajanupu went to the back of the house and there she washed Ogonim thoroughly. Ogea brought out a new dress for the corpse, and showed it to Ajanupu.

'Show it to her mother first,' Ajanupu said.

When Ogea showed it to Efuru, she shook her head and beckoned Ogea to come nearer. Then Ogea went to the mud wardrobe – the room in a room, very dark both in the daytime and at night. The mud wardrobe was used for storing valuable things – boxes of clothes, jars, ornaments, iron pots and jewellery. If the house caught fire, the things in the mud wardrobe would not have been burnt. The top of the mud wardrobe was used as a shelf for odd things like mats, cooking-pots, soups, boxes and broom. When policemen came to search for home-made gin it was hidden away in the mud wardrobe for policemen did not know there were such things as mud wardrobes.

In this wardrobe, Efuru put her most valuable things of all, like the ornaments she had inherited from her mother and rich clothes of different kinds. Ogea entered the mud wardrobe and struggled out with a heavy box. She put it down, opened it and brought out a dress made of damask material. 'This is the one Ogonim's mother wants her to wear,' she told Ajanupu. Ajanupu took it from her and put it on the dead child. Then she powdered her face and sprinkled some perfume on her. After this, she carried her reverently to the bed which she had already prepared. Then she moved a step backwards and surveyed the corpse, the little body lying in state. It was a human being that was full of life only three days ago, now it was a corpse. If it was not buried by the time the sun went down, it would stink, and sympathizers would flee from the place. As

71

she looked at the little body, Ajanupu began to weep all over again. 'You wanted to leave us, and you have left us. So good-bye, my child.'

Efuru's mother-in-law came in. She was surprised to see that Ajanupu had washed the corpse and dressed it. She tapped Ajanupu on the shoulder. She turned and followed her into the room.

'I have sent messages through different people going to Ndoni. In two days' time, our message will reach Ndoni and Adizua should arrive in four days' time.'

'That's all right. Let's perform the sacrifices expected of us, and let the gods take any blame.'

'You are right, my sister,' Efuru's mother-in-law said to her sister. 'You are perfectly right. We must do our bit so that we are not accused of negligence.'

Sympathizers poured in in great numbers and wept on the feet of Efuru one after the other. The sitting-room was full and mats were spread outside for them to sit down. A distant relation of Efuru came and fell on her feet. 'Efuru,' she began very slowly. 'I am very sorry. I am indeed very sorry. So all your sufferings have come to naught. Efuru, in what ways have you offended our ancestors? What is the reason for this – a child who was more than two years old. You were married and for a long time you did not have a child. Then our gods and the ancestors opened your womb and you had a baby girl. We all rejoiced for you. A girl is something, though we would have preferred a boy. You looked after your child very well, feeding her and nursing her. And now, that only child is dead. And you have suffered for nothing. So you have come to the world to suffer?

'As if all this is not enough for a child like you to bear,' the woman went on. 'I hear your husband has run away with that worthless woman, the daughter of a bitch. He has left you to bear the burden alone. The world is strange. Adizua who was nobody before you married him. Adizua whose father roamed the length and breadth of the Great River and later on died of a bad disease. And you the daughter of Nwashike Ogene, a man of noble parentage. A man who is upright and whose ancestors were upright and just.

'Leave everything to the gods and our ancestors, my daughter. God will heal your wounds and our gods will visit Adizua and the woman who . . .'

'That will do,' Ajanupu shouted from the room. 'That will do, I say. What nonsense. Nwasobi, if you don't know how to sympathize with a woman whose only child has died, say you are sorry and leave her in peace, and don't stay there enumerating all her misfortunes in a tone that suggests that you enjoy these misfortunes.'

'Ajanupu, you are right,' said a woman. 'I have never seen anything like that before. Nwasobi, don't talk like that any more. When you go, Efuru will think of all you have said and will be more miserable.'

The woman was embarrassed, she got up. 'I am sorry, my daughter. Please pardon me. We are old women and therefore know nothing.'

Efuru was quiet. She did not say a word to anybody. She did not even hear Nwasobi when she was blabbing like a woman possessed. When the woman said she was sorry, she simply nodded. Ajanupu watched her all the time. She saw that she was thinking very much and that was bad for her health. And what was more more she was not crying any more. It was better to shed tears than to restrain them from flowing freely. One feels better after shedding tears, for tears sometimes have a soothing effect.

'My daughter,' Ajanupu said to Efuru placing her hands on her shoulders. 'My daughter, please weep, weep, my daughter, weeping will do you good. Don't stay like that without weeping. Weep! Let your tears flow freely. If you don't weep, your heart will be injured.'

'I cannot weep any more, Ajanupu. My grief is the kind of grief that allows no tears. It is a dry grief. Wet grief is better but I cannot weep.'

'No, my child, try and weep. Tears wash away sorrows. Your burden is made lighter if you weep. Women weep easily and that is why they do not feel sorrows as keenly as men do.'

'Ajanupu, my daughter has killed me. Ogonim has killed me. My only child has killed me. Why should I live? I should be dead too and lie in state beside my daughter. Oh, my chi, why have you dealt with me in this way?' When Efuru said this tears rolled down her cheeks.

73

'That's better, my child. Weep,' Ajanupu encouraged.

There was a shout from a distance.

'My people, come and see me, come round and see my friend Efuru and her only child. I am lost. I am done for. What am I hearing?' The shout of this new sympathizer cut through the silence of that serene morning, the morning that brought doom and darkness to Efuru.

'Who can that be?' Ajanupu asked irritatingly. 'She is not going to say nonsense here like that other woman.'

The new sympathizer was one of Efuru's friends, the woman who had painted fearsome pictures of nursemaids and had advised Efuru not to have anything to do with them.

'Efuru, my friend,' she said and fell on her feet. 'Efuru, sorry, I am very sorry. I saw Ogonim hale and hearty only three days ago. She and Ogea were returning from Ajanupu's place. She had a banana and when I asked her to give me the banana she gave it to me. I thanked her and gave her back the banana and she smiled at me. It was such a sweet smile. What killed that healthy child? A child whose other name was life itself, how did death get at her? Sorry my dear friend. Have heart and don't worry. God knows best.'

When she finished, she went to the little corpse and began to talk to her.

'Ogonim, the daughter of my friend, the daughter of Efuru and Adizua. Why have you treated my friend in this way? Did we not treat you well? Why have you left us? Where are you going? Is it as good as this place?'

She got up and went and sat at a corner. A fairly elderly woman got up from her corner and went to Efuru. 'Efuru I am going. Nobody owns this world. Death does not know how to kill. Death visits everybody, the rich, the poor, the blind and the lame. When it visits us, it seems as if our own grief and loss are more than our neighbours'. I conceived eight times. All died before they were six months old. The last one was a girl and when she did not die after six months, I killed a white fowl for my chi. I named her Ibiakwa – Have you come again? After a year and she did not die I called her Nkem – My own. She was a beautiful girl, she shone like the sun and twinkled like the stars in the sky. I never lost sight of her.

'Then I returned from the market one day and saw that she

74

was shivering with cold. I was afraid. My daughter had a fever. I rubbed kernel oil on her and wrapped her up. In the night she developed a convulsion and died.'

'Ewo-o-o,' the people cried. 'So it happened,' some who knew the woman said.

'My only child died,' the woman went on. 'The world was in darkness for me. I wept like a human being, I wept like an animal. I threatened to jump into the grave and be buried alive with my only child. But I am still alive today. I have not had another baby since then. Have heart, my daughter. You are still young. It is still morning for you. So have heart. We cannot explain the mysteries of life, because we are mere human beings. Only God knows. I am going.'

'That's it,' Ajanupu said. 'That's how to sympathize with a woman who has lost her only child. There are words of wisdom and encouragement. Efuru, you have heard what she said. So please have heart.'

Efuru nodded in assent.

Outside, people talked in whispers.

'Do you say that he is not home?' said one of the women.

'Don't you hear? He went to Ndoni with another woman and since then he has not come back. His mother has sent for him, but it will take two days for the message to get to him. If he comes home immediately, he will be here in four days.'

'Poor Efuru,' the other said. 'We all were surprised when she married the fool. And now see how shabbily she has been treated.'

'Do you think she is going to leave him?'

'You mean if Efuru would leave Adizua?'

'Yes.'

'I can't say. Efuru loves him very much and you know how we women love blindly. If he comes back to Efuru, I think she will forgive him. The problem is not that Efuru would not forgive him, it is that Adizua might not come back to her. It is in the family. Adizua's mother suffered at the hands of her husband just as Efuru is suffering.'

'It is a great pity, when I look at her, she does not know why I am looking at her. She has beauty, wealth and good breeding. Why should any man treat her like this?'

75

Meanwhile young men in the village were sent to go and dig the grave in the graveyard.

Ajanupu was still in control of everything. She went to Efuru and whispered something into her ears. She got up and sympathizers held her on either side. She went to take the last look of her only child. Ajanupu beckoned to the men and they brought in the little coffin. As soon as Ogea saw the coffin, she began to weep again.

'Please don't put her in that coffin,' she wept. 'Please don't put her in that wretched coffin, put me instead. Oh, Ogonim you have killed me. Oh, Ogonim why did you decide to leave me. Did I not look after you well? In what way did I offend you Ogonim? You have killed me.' Sympathizers hissed and shook their heads. Ogea was led away.

Efuru watched the men as they lowered her only child into the coffin. She stood there like a statue with tears running down her cheeks.

The men began to nail the lid of the little coffin.

'Please don't nail it,' Ogea shouted from the room as she heard the men's hammer. 'Please don't nail it, Ogonim is not dead, you know she is not dead.' She went nearer. 'Ogonim will be afraid when she wakes up and sees herself in a coffin. Please don't nail it. Put me in there and nail the coffin.'

As she was talking in this way, not knowing what she was saying, one of the men carried the coffin on his head, and walked away. Others followed him. The mourners rose and went to their respective homes.

The men placed the coffin in a canoe and about six of them paddled the canoe to the graveyard where they buried it.

Ajanupu went home after telling her sister what to do. That was the first time she had been home since she had been sent for by her sister. She sat down on one of the mud-benches in her sitting-room quite exhausted. One of her children came to her and asked her about Ogonim.

'She has been buried,' she told him.

'So we won't see her again?' the child asked.

'No, we won't see her again.'

'Why did she die, mother?' the innocent child asked.

'We don't know why she died, but we know the cause of her death.'

'Won't she be afraid in the coffin?'

'No, she won't be afraid, my child. She knows no fear now. Now ask Adiewere to give me water and soap.'

The boy went off. Water and soap were brought to Ajanupu. She washed her hands thoroughly as if she was having a ritual cleansing.

'Why do you take so long in washing your hands?' Ajanupu's child asked.

'I washed Ogonima's corpse and dressed her before the burial. If I don't wash my hands very well I shan't forget things easily.'

Meanwhile Efuru's age-group took her to the stream to have her body thoroughly cleansed after weeping for her dead daughter. Efuru was given a new sponge and new soap, and she scrubbed her body well. While she was washing, one of the members of her age-group washed her clothes. Then the head of the age-group took her to her house, there she was given something to eat which she could not manage to eat. She rested there and many sympathizers poured in.

'Efuru, I was just returning from the farm when I was told about the death of your child. When did Ogonim take ill? What do these young babies mean by treating us in this way? Sorry. Have heart, there is God, he understands everything.'

Towards evening, Efuru was taken home by the members of her age-group who had brought Kola-nuts, home made gin and palm wine for the entertainment of sympathizers. Those who were unable to go to the market brought money.

Efuru was well known in the town and so she had many sympathizers. She herself had given generously to her friends who were bereaved so these friends also gave to her generously. When sympathizers left Efuru's house, they said good things about Efuru.

'Good child,' they said. 'A good woman who has good words for everybody. A good woman who greeted you twenty times if she saw you twenty times in a day. A woman with a clean heart, and who respects her elders. God, please give her strength to bear this heavy loss.'

Four days passed and Adizua did not return. Efuru's mother-in-law had waited for this fourth day with fear and anxiety.

She knew that Efuru was a good woman. She knew that her son could not have made a better choice. But she knew also that Efuru's patience could not be tried. Her kind of suffering did not appeal to her. She was not meant to suffer at all. Life for her meant living it fully. She did not want merely to exist. She wanted to live and use the world to her advantage.

Efuru's mother-in-law knew also that her daughter-in-law was self-willed. She tolerated Adizua because she loved him. As days passed and she saw no sign of her son, she began to despair. 'Did I not say that Adizua was going to take the footsteps of his father? What have I done to deserve this? Why is everything against me? Have I not sacrificed to my chi and the ancestors? Why do I find no favour in their eyes?'

She watched her daughter-in-law every day, but she dared not mention Adizua to her. Efuru on the other hand refused to discuss him with anybody. Conversations that could easily have led to the discussion of Adizua's whereabouts were tactfully avoided. But she waited. She anxiously waited for the day her husband would return. But each day brought her misery and unhappiness.

One day Efuru's father sent for her. The old man had wept when he heard about the death of Ogonim. He could not come because a corpse was taboo for him. So he sent people to represent him. It was now more than a month since Ogonim died, and Efuru's father wanted to know the position of things. After the usual greetings he asked her, 'Have you heard the voice of your husband?'

'No, I have not heard.'

'What are you going to do?'

'Nothing. Perhaps I shall continue to wait. I don't know. I have not made up my mind. Once it is made up, there is no coming back.'

'Well, I thought you heard about him because some of our people who returned yesterday from the Great River told me they saw him and the woman at Ibeocha.'

'True, so they are there now.'

'He is not thinking of coming home. Perhaps you can consider going there yourself.'

'I shall think about it,' Efuru replied.

'In case you decide on going, I shall give you some people to

78

go with you. Or if you don't want to go yourself, our people will go for you.'

Efuru thanked her father and went home. She changed her clothes and went to the stream. Ajanupu came while she was away feeling angry with everybody. 'Where is Ossai?' she asked Ogea roughly. Ogea who dreaded her after the broken pot episode, moved a step backwards, opened her mouth and closed it again without saying a word. 'Where is Ossai? You timid child, haven't your bush ways left you yet? You came here bush, you want to leave here bush. Good for nothing girl, where is Ossai?'

Ossai heard Ajanupu from within and came out.

'What is the matter? Why are you quarrelling?' Ossai asked.

'Who is quarrelling with whom. Who am I quarrelling with? With Ogea? Eh? With Ogea? Sometimes, Ossai, you want, rather you need, someone to talk to you seriously. 'You want someone to be downright frank, brutally frank with you.'

Ossai had always been a good younger sister. She was not impudent as younger sisters sometimes are. She did not have that fighting spirit which Ajanupu possessed in abundance. So when her misfortune came, instead of fighting against it, as Ajanupu would have done, she succumbed to it. She surrendered everything to fate. Ajanupu would have interfered with fate. She would have played her own tune and invited fate to dance to it. Not Ossai. When Ajanupu and her mother wanted her to do something after her husband had left her, she did nothing. She merely folded her hands and waited for her truant husband to come back to her.

On this occasion, Ossai said nothing. That was her way. She let Ajanupu talk, and Ajanupu used this silence to her own ends.

'Didn't my mother and I tell you to leave that wretched husband of yours? You would have married a better husband and had children. Instead you remained in your husband's house and shut yourself out from the world. You wanted to be called a good wife, good wife when you were eating sand, good wife when you were eating nails. That was the kind of goodness that appealed to you. How could you be suffering for a person who did not appreciate your suffering, the person who despised you. It was not virtue, it was plain stupidity. You

79

merely wanted to suffer for the fun of it, as if there was any virtue in suffering for a worthless man.'

Ossai said nothing. She simply let Ajanupu talk.

'And now,' Ajanupu went on, 'your son, where is he now? Your son who was married to such a woman. Let me tell you the truth, for it is when you are angry that you say the truth. I was one of those people who wondered what Efuru saw in that son of yours. I did not say anything then. I was up in arms against those who criticized the marriage because Adizua was my sister's son, and not because he was a good match for Efuru.

'Now, your son, instead of settling down with Efuru and working hard to rebuild the family which your husband left in such a mess, did exactly what his father did – this time your son ran away with a woman who had left her husband. And you stay here doing nothing. You stay here watching that innocent woman pining away. Why don't you go in search of your son?' Ajanupu raised her voice. 'Why don't you, as you went in search of your husband many years ago. You are the cause of your child's bad ways. You never scolded him because he was an only child. You delightfully spoilt him and failed to make him responsible. You failed to make him stand on his own so that now he leans on these rich women not because he loves them, but because they are rich.

'And here is Efuru. She is suffering, she is taking it well now, but I tell you, there is a limit to human endurance. She is not meant to suffer, she will leave your son if nothing is done and done very quickly. You can't even see it. You have eyes but don't see. I tell you she will leave you. This is where it has been written.' As she said this, she drew a line on the mud wall.

Ossai said nothing. It was no use, but she was thinking deeply. Then she heard Ajanupu shout at Ogea.

'Where is Efuru?'

'She went to the stream,' Ogea answered immediately. Her inability to answer at once before had been disastrous for her. 'Why don't you allow me to finish before you answer, you goat? When did she go, and won't she return? Did she go to "Ose Oru" that she cannot return soon. Give me a mat to sit down. I shall wait for her.'

Ogea brought a mat and spread it on the mud-bench in the sitting-room. Ajanupu sat down and stretched her legs in front of her. Then she crossed them. She waited. Sometimes she folded her arms on her bosom and at other times she left them between her thighs.

'Ogea,' she shouted. 'Give me some water to drink.' Ogea washed a glass and filled it with water from the water-pot and gave it to Ajanupu. She looked at the glass for some time and when she was satisfied, she began to drink. She drank all the water.

'Shall I bring you kola?' Ogea asked Ajanupu. She was feeling more confident in herself now.

'You have kola?'

'Yes, we have kola, shall I bring it?'

'All right.'

Ogea brought a big piece from the bowl where Efuru put her kola, she also brought a knife for the kola. Ajanupu broke the kola and ate a piece, then tied the other pieces at one end of her wrappa, and got up.

'Ogea,' she called. 'Tell Efuru when she comes back that I waited for her a long time, but she did not return from the stream. Tell her I want to see her today. Let nothing prevent her from coming to see me today. And that ... Now listen I have not finished, where are you going? You children, why can't you stand still for a while. Now don't forget. If you like stay there and continue nodding like a lizard. If you forget, I shall crack your head. Ossai, are you there?' Ajanupu called her sister. 'I am going, Ogea offered me some kola. Thank you.'

That evening Efuru went to Ajanupu's house. Ajanupu asked her to come into the bedroom.

'Ogea is learning, so she remembered to tell,' Ajanupu said.

'Oh, yes, she told me you wanted to see me. Ogea does try. You know she was very raw when she came.'

'What do you expect from a girl who had lived all her life in the farm? I am glad she is improving. Knock out all those crude farm ways out of her.'

'Yes I am trying. It is a difficult task. But Ogea is responsive. She is willing to learn.'

'That's good.'

'Efuru, I came to see you yesterday,' Ajanupu began unnecessarily. 'I came to see you and was told you went to the stream. Then I waited and waited but ... O-o-o – who is making her cry? Who is making her cry again? Did they say that if one has children one should not have a moment's rest. Bring her to me.' The weeping girl was brought to Ajanupu by one of her children. 'Who has been making you cry?' Ajanupu asked fondly. The little child pointed at one of her brothers and tried to say in a child's language that her brother wanted to take her yam from her. 'Never mind Ifeanyi. Yes, I know him. He tried to take your yam from you. Never mind, clean your eyes I shall deal with him. Eat your yam.'

The child stopped crying and began to eat what was left. She did not eat for long when she fell asleep.

'Who is there?' Ajanupu called. Ifeanyi answered.

'Ifeanyi, come and take your sister to the room, she has fallen asleep.' Ifeanyi came and carried his sister to bed. She was still holding the piece of yam in her hands. When Ifeanyi put her down on the mat and wanted to take the yam from her, she held it tight and showed her resentment by crying again.

'I know you want her piece of yam.' Ajanupu shouted. 'Leave her to sleep, Ifeanyi. When she is fast asleep, the yam will fall from her hand.'

'As I was saying,' Ajanupu said to Efuru, 'I came to see you yesterday and Ogea told me that you went to the stream. I want—'

'Mother, mother, you see what Nnoro is doing. You see what Nnoro is doing?'

'Oh, these children; what is Nnoro doing?'

'Nnoro is licking the soup in the pot.'

'Is that true, Nnoro?'

The child did not answer.

'Go and get me a good whip,' she told her son.

'As I was saying,' Ajanupu began again. 'Have you heard the voice of your husband?'

'No, I have heard nothing.'

'What do you intend to do?'

'I don't know yet. Honestly I do not know.'

'I hope you understand the part I am playing in this your marriage with Adizua. Ossai, your mother-in-law, is my younger sister. She is my only sister. If you leave things to her, nothing will be done. She does not seem to know her duty, that's why she says nothing to you. But she is very sorry, genuinely sorry. A young beautiful woman like you cannot sit down with folded hands and wait indefinitely for a husband who ran away with another woman; a husband who did not think it fit to come and bury an only child. This is six months' since Ogonim died, and about eight months since Adizua went to the Great River to trade. Tell me, what do you want to do?'

Efuru's eyes were filled with tears. She wanted to speak, but she was choked. She felt so dry inside. She battled and gained her self-control. 'My father called me the other day and asked me whether I have heard from Adizua. He then went on to tell me that he heard that he is at Ibeocha with the woman. He said he was going to send people with me to go in search of him or if I wanted he could send people to go and look for him. I have not decided on what to do yet. After the talk with my father, somebody told my mother-in-law and me that he saw Adizua with the woman at Ibeocha. He told him about the death of Ogonim. He was sorry and said he was coming home immediately. This happened about a month ago. I am glad that the message reached him. I am quite sure that that was not the first time that message reached him.'

'What do you want to do then?'

'I don't know. I have not made up my mind yet.'

'You know that I am proud of you. You are a good woman. There is no woman like you. Your mother-in-law knows this very well though she does not show it. It is a pity that this has befallen you. But don't worry, it will be all right. By the power of God it will be all right. Adizua has wronged you. You have been rough-handled, but don't worry. Give Adizua one year, just a year and if he does not come back to you and you have an offer of marriage from another man, with a good background and wealth, leave him and marry the man. Wait for a year, just a year. After a year and you marry again, nobody in this world will rise an accusing finger at you and say you have not done well.'

Efuru left Ajanupu's house that day feeling somewhat better. She would wait for a year and if Adizua did not come back to her then she would leave him. She went about her business as usual. Each time she remembered her dead daughter she locked herself up and wept.

One day she returned from the market, had her bath and just

as she was about to go to collect her debt from someone, Ogea told her that somebody had come to see her. Efuru came out and greeted the visitor in her usual, pleasant way. She had known him before, as they were in the same age-group. As young girls and boys, they had danced together. She remembered vividly one encounter she had with this man. Years ago, both the men's and the women's section of their age-group were invited by the head of the men's section to a dance and drinks. It was near their festival and they had been working hard rehearsing their dance. As they were going home from the party, someone walked up to her and seized her hand roughly and said: 'Why are you so proud? Why don't you greet people, don't you know you are a small girl?'

Efuru was afraid. She tried to free her hand from the strong grip of the rough boy. 'You can't get free. If you like you can struggle till tomorrow morning.'

There were other boys there and a few girls. The girls shouted at the rough boy to leave Efuru alone because she did not do him any wrong and because Efuru was a harmless girl. They could not do anything because they were afraid of the boy. Then just out of the blue, a rather tough boy emerged from the crowd and spoke roughly to the boy who held Efuru's hand.

'I say, leave or you will regret it,' the tough boy said.

'Learn to greet people, you proud girl,' the rough boy said. Before Efuru knew what was happening he had snatched her head tie from her head and run away.

Efuru wept bitterly. She begged the tough boy to run after him and get her head-tie, because if she went home without it, her mother would be so angry with her that she would not allow her to go to any more dances.

The tough boy ran after the boy and recovered Efuru's head-tie. He gave it to Efuru and she thanked him very much and went home. This tough boy was Efuru's visitor.

So when this man visited her that evening, the whole incident came to her mind's eye again. She hadn't seen the man for years because the man's parents decided to send him to school when he was over sixteen years old. So he could not join his age group to dance and to have their parties, because the Church frowned at such associations. The Church regarded it as pagan to continue dancing with your age-group when you were in school. When your parents sent you to school, you automatically became a Christian. Many parents would have been shocked to be told that some non-Christian parents in other lands specially requested the school authorities not to teach their children the articles of the faith and the Bible.

The boy read up to standard five but could not go farther for lack of funds. He had no influential relatives so it was not possible for him to secure a job in the township. So with the help of his parents and a handful of relatives, he got a few pounds and started a small trade. He started dealing in cigarettes and when he made headway, he soon owned a fairly large stall in the market. He was still unmarried which was strange.

Efuru brought kola-nuts and a bottle of home-made gin.

'Who will break the kola?' Efuru asked laughing.

'I will of course,' said Gilbert, for that was his name. He was baptized when he started school and was given this name. Nobody called him by his beautiful, 'pagan' name, which was Eneberi. He took offence when you called him Eneberi and if you were a friend he would tell you politely that his name was Gilbert and he wished to be called that.

'How old are you that you should break the kola?' Efuru asked still laughing.

'You are only a child of yesterday,' Gilbert said.

'I am older than you are.'

'Don't talk abomination. That we are in the same age-group does not mean that we are the same age. Besides I am a man and you cannot break kola in my presence.'

Gilbert was already breaking the kola as he said this. When he finished, he took one and passed the small plate to Efuru who took one. Then she brought out a small glass, Gilbert filled it and drank it in one gulp. 'This is a good gin,' he said. 'Who cooks it?'

'Nwabuzo cooks gin in the farm.'

'Nwabuzo Eneke?' Gilbert asked.

'Yes, Nwabuzo Eneke. Do you know her?'

'I don't know her in person, but I heard the police raided her hut in the farm but saw nothing.'

'Thank God, they did not see anything. These policemen want us to starve. Oh, I am happy they saw nothing, Nwabuzo owes me plenty of money and if the police had seen the gin, they would have seized everything and she wouldn't be able to pay me what she owes. But how do these policemen know the people who cook gin?'

'I don't really know. But I will tell you how Nwabuzo's hut was raided. Two men visited her on one Afo day. They asked her to sell gin to them, she agreed and got them a bottle. She cooked it only a day before. The two men drank a ganashi each, then two and three. Their behaviour was a bit odd to Nwabuzo who had never seen them before. So that night she got a canoe and with the help of neighbours she put all her gin in the canoe. All the stuff she could not remove she destroyed, and set for the town. If she had not acted quickly, she would have been caught, for the next day, the very next day, policemen raided her hut. She was not there and the police could not see anything.'

'Serves the police right,' Efuru said very happily. 'Why the Government does not allow us to drink our home-made gin, I do not know. The Government is strange. Does it know that it cannot stop us from cooking gin; that our people will continue to go to jail instead of giving it up completely. If they must stop us from cooking gin, then the white man's gin and his schnapps should be sold cheap. We sell our gin two shillings or sometimes two shillings and six pence a bottle, and they sell their gin and schnapps for many shillings.'

'It will not stop,' said Gilbert. 'Even those who are caught in the trade and go to jail often come back after their term of imprisonment determined to pursue the trade with all their might. Nothing stops them from trading in it.'

'You have not had some,' said Gilbert to Efuru. 'Here is the ganashi, have some.'

'No, I don't drink it. It is too strong for me. I only drink our palm wine, the very sweet one that is undiluted, that's the one I drink.'

Gilbert helped himself to another ganashi and got up. 'I am going, I just thought I should come and see you today.'

'Oh, so you are going. You sound very grown up. Do you remember your rascally ways when we were children?' Gilbert

86

laughed shyly. 'Thank you, Eneberi, you did well to come and see me today. All right, go well.'

When Gilbert left, Efuru saw that it was late to go to the woman who owed her some money so she went to see Ajanupu instead.

'I was just thinking of you now when you came,' Ajanupu said to Efuru.

Efuru smiled.

'Sit down here.' Ajanupu made room for her and she sat beside her on the mat.

'I have just returned from the market. You know Odikama is still owing me. The debt is more than two years old now.'

'How much does she owe you?' Ajanupu asked.

'She owes me five pounds. It was ten pounds, but she has paid five pounds.'

'What did she say today?'

'What will she say? She begged me as usual and said I should come next month when she shall have returned from Agbor. I would like to go to Agbor myself.'

'What trade is going on there now?' asked Ajanupu.

'I hear yam is good there. A couple returned last week and when they finished selling their yams they went again the next day. The problem now is that I have not got a good person to go with me. Can you recommend anybody?'

'Odikama is good. She is very serviceable. She does not know the trade but you want a companion – someone you will talk to and who will help you paddle the canoe. If you like, I shall ask her.'

When Efuru went home, Ajanupu could not help admiring her character. 'She is a woman among women. I like the way she is carrying her burden. She still loves that imbecile husband of hers and she is going in search of him.'

CHAPTER SIX

Efuru came back after a month and vowed that it was over with her and Adizua. She told herself that even if Adizua came back and begged her on his knees with a bag of money. She would not listen to him.

She did not only go to Agbor but Ndoni, Akiri and Ogwu in search of her husband, and nowhere did she learn anything about him except in Ogwu where she was told that Adizua was seen there only a week before.

A week after her return from Agbor she called her mother-in-law: 'Mother, I cannot stay any more. A man said that he had wept for the death that killed his friend, but he did not wish that death to kill him. I cannot wait indefinitely for Adizua, you can bear witness that I have tried my best. I am still young and would wish to marry again. It will be unfair both to you and your son if I begin to encourage men who would like to marry me while still in this house.'

Efuru's mother-in-law did not say anything to Efuru. Efuru then told Ajanupu and her father.

'My daughter,' Ajanupu said when Efuru finished. 'Adizua has treated you badly and you have borne it admirably. If your daughter were alive, one would have said don't go, stay for your daughter's sake. But Ogonim is no more and one does not know how to persuade you to stay. But I say, stay. I have no reason whatever for asking you to stay, but stay.'

'No, I will not stay,' Efuru said. 'I am sorry but I have to disappoint you. Adizua does not want me any more. It is so obvious. Do you want me to stay until he comes home and tells me to pack. That will be very shameful. You don't want this to happen to your daughter.' For once in her life, Ajanupu had nothing to say.

The next day, Efuru packed up all her things and took them from Adizua's house to her father's house. Her room was still empty. It was her mother's room. She swept it and rubbed it with red mud and charcoal. Then she rubbed the sitting-room floor and the walls. She used white clay for the walls and put in very beautiful designs typical of her people. Ogea was busy drawing water and grinding the white clay, the red mud and the charcoal. She wouldn't allow Ogea to rub the wall because she had not learnt how to do it properly. Charcoal was used for the floor, white mud for the walls and red mud for the mud-benches in the sitting-room. Then the designs were beautifully worked out with the three colours.

Efuru did not only beautify her own room but also her father's. She rubbed her father's room and his obi and scrubbed the Ofo, the Chi and many other things that needed scrubbing. Her father's walking-stick was scrubbed and the brass end was thoroughly scrubbed with the white sand of the stream.

Then she took all the cooking utensils to the stream and washed them. The mortar for pounding fufu was well scrubbed. Some people were surprised to see her in the stream and they talked in whispers. One of the women spoke out: 'Efuru, the daughter of Nwashike Ogene, welcome to your father's house. You did well, my daughter. We are sorry that your husband had rubbed charcoal on your face, but we are also glad that you have left him to come back to us. We women married to men of your village are very happy, and so when we see women of your village being ill-treated by their husbands we feel it very keenly. You have done well to come back. You are young, beautiful and of good parentage, so you will soon have a good husband.'

'You are right,' another woman took over. 'We are happy that you have left him. It is an ugly woman who looks for a husband. God will soon bless you with a good man who will look after you.'

Efuru was busy scrubbing her cooking utensils. The women drew their water and went home.

'Poor child, she has suffered,' one went on. 'I heard that her husband could not even afford the dowry.'

'Yes, so it happened,' the others said. 'He could not afford the dowry. Efuru had to work hard trading in so many things and when they got the money they went and paid the dowry. They were very happy together until Adizua went to Ndoni more than a year ago and refused to return.'

'O, was that what happened?'

'Yes, that was what happened. While he was away, their only child died, and he was sent for, and up till now, now that we are talking, he has not come back. Many people returned and said that he heard about the death of his child.'

'Ew o-o-o, is that true! This is an indirect way of asking a wife to go back to her father's house.'

Efuru began to swim after scrubbing. When she finished, she packed her things into a big basin, placed it on her head and walked home. 'Ew o-o-o, my daughter,' a woman stopped her.

'Did I hear that you have left your husband?'

'Yes, he has left me.'

'Don't say that, my daughter, don't say that. We say that a woman has left her husband, but never say that a husband has left his wife. Wives leave husbands not the other way round.'

Efuru began to laugh. 'It is the same thing to me.'

'No, it is not the same thing. Tell me what happened, my daughter.'

'It is a long story, mother.'

'All right, I shall come to see you at home. I am sorry.'

Efuru put her things in order in her father's house and went about her business as usual. Ogea was very useful to her. The little girl had grown to love her mistress. She regarded her as her mother and called her mother. She defended her anywhere she heard people say ill about her. She did all she was asked to do and respected and admired her mistress. She did remember her parents but only vaguely and once or twice Efuru had tried to persuade her to go and see her parents in the farm, but she had refused to go. She did remember those days at the farm when she and the other children went to swim in the river; she also remembered the time they went to fetch firewood in the bush and how they left their younger sisters behind crying because they wanted to go with them and they would not take them. How they frightened them by telling them that there were leopards and snakes in the bush. She also remembered how they went fishing with baskets, and the boys with small hooks. Then the fishes they caught and how they boiled them putting in salt and pepper and eating them up before their parents returned from the farm. She also remembered the huge fufu they ate in the farm, how they ate and ate until their tummies protruded and how they went about with bellies shining. It was a lazy life which they enjoyed, no doubt, but the life did not appeal to her now.

She did not like staying with Efuru at first, but Efuru had treated her so well that in spite of the fact that she worked more in Efuru's house than she did on the farm, she enjoyed staying with Efuru and disliked the idea of going back to the farm.

The harvest season came. Ogea's parents were late in harvesting their crops. Her father was ill and her mother was heavy with child, the children were too small to be of much use to them. So they had to send for relatives who with friends helped them with the yams. Ogea's mother was very busy. She had to cook for the men who had come to help them to harvest their yams. In the morning she boiled yam in a big pot for them and brought palm oil in which plenty of pepper and salt had been added, to the workers for breakfast. In the afternoon she pounded huge piles of fufu for them and as she prepared the fufu, her husband went to the river with his net to catch fish for the afternoon meal. Ogea's mother did this for several days until all the yams were harvested.

Packing the yams into the canoe was another difficult job for a man who had been ill for a long time. Nevertheless with the help of the children and some neighbours Ogea's parents managed to pack all their yams into their canoe and, the next day, they set out for the town with their children. Before it was dark they arrived in town after paddling upstream for several hours. Because it was late they could not carry the yams to their house. The carriers of the yams had all gone home. These carriers came to help the farmers carry their yams to their houses. They were given a few yams when they finished their work. The farmers teased them because they only came during harvest season and not during planting season when their services were needed most. So the farmers nicked-named them 'Those who come during harvest'.

The following morning 'Those who came during harvest' came in great numbers and they helped Ogea's parents with the yams. In the evening, they had stored all the yams in the back of the house and, by the time they had a bath and something to eat, it was very late, but Ogea's mother insisted on seeing Efuru that night.

When they arrived, Ogea was the first to see them. She greeted them and asked them to sit down while she went to call her mistress.

'Welcome, Nwosu, Ogbukea; Welcome Nwabata, Anamaa. Please sit down. What brings you here at this time of the night.'

'Well, we returned yesterday night and because there was nobody to help with the yams, I had to sleep in the canoe till this morning. We have our yams stored at the back of our house now and we felt we must come and pay our respects.'

'Oh, is that so? Welcome, welcome. Farm people, how is the farm?'

'The farm is there,' answered Ogea's mother. 'Just as we left it,' she added. 'We were almost the last people to leave. You heard of the illness of my husband?'

'Ew-o-o-o, I heard it, my sister. Pardon me. How are you now, Nwosu? Are you better?'

'I am much better now. Let's leave the rest to God. I have never been so ill before in my life. I could neither bend down nor stand up. I was all the time in bed. I am still feeling the pain, but it is milder now.

'Where exactly do you have the pain if I may ask?' asked Efuru feeling very sorry for Nwosu. If Ogea's mother had been a white woman, you would have seen her blush.

'If a disease does not hide itself, I won't hide it either,' said Ogea's father, and he continued, 'Efuru, the pain is below my navel,' and he tried to indicate the place. 'Sometimes it is swollen, some other times it is so painful I can hardly sit down or stand up.'

'Ogea, please bring kola for your parents.'

'Please leave kola this night. Night has taken kola. Don't you know that saying?' Ogea's mother said.

'I know the saying,' Efuru said laughing and showing her white teeth made whiter by the night. 'Night takes kola only when one has no kola.' They all laughed and Ogea brought the kola in the kola dish and placed it in front of her father.

'Thank you, my daughter,' Ogea's father said. 'Ogea has grown so tall,' he remarked.

'Yes, she has grown very tall,' Ogea's mother said.

Nwosu broke the kola, took a piece and passed it to his wife who took one piece but said she would not chew it because it would keep her awake all night.

'Kola does nothing to me,' Efuru said.

'Nor to me,' said Ogea's father.

Efuru then went into the room and brought out a bottle of gin and a ganashi. She gave the bottle and the ganashi to Nwosu. He filled it up and drank it in a gulp. He gave the ganashi back to Efuru who gave it to Ogea's mother. She filled it with the gin, took a sip, made a grimace and handed the ganashi back to her husband. He drank it in one gulp and gave the ganashi to Efuru.

'Do you want another?' asked Efuru.

'Won't you drink?' Nwosu asked Efuru.

'No, I don't drink it. It is too strong for me. It is meant for men not women.' And as she said this she poured another and gave Nwosu to drink. He drank it all in one gulp again.

'Please don't give him any more,' pleaded Ogea's mother. 'He will soon be drunk. Ogea, please take the bottle in, your father will soon be drunk if the bottle is left here.'

'Let's hear something,' Nwosu said. 'If I get drunk you will have to take me home.' They laughed.

'Do you know Omozere?' Efuru asked.

'Which Omozere? The drunkard?'

'Yes, the drunkard. He was a pleasant man and when he died it was a great loss for all children in those days. When he was drunk, and this happened every day, he came to us, and if we were eating, he would eat with us. If we were playing, he would play with us. Sometimes he went on all-fours and we mounted on his back and had a good ride. He taught us songs, he sang like a young boy. When we heard the voice of his wife we would all run away and watch them from a distance. "Foolish man, an overgrown child. Stupid man. A man who has children and cannot afford to feed them, but drinks every day and plays with children." She would drag him home and he surprisingly enough went meekly with her. Then we children followed. At home, he would ask his wife to bring food for he was hungry.

' "There is no food," the wife would shout.

' "Cook food then," he said, not perturbed.

' "Cook food indeed. Cook food indeed. So you want me to

93

cook food, will I cook my hand? Eh, the drunkard will I cook my hand? The bastard, will I steal to cook for you?'' As she said this, Omozere would fall asleep on the mud-bench in the sitting-room. This happened nearly every day and we children wondered whether his wife ever cooked a meal for him.'

'People should drink with moderation. I know of farmers who wash their mouths every morning with a ganashi of gin.'

'That is bad!' Efuru and Ogea's mother agreed.

After a long time during which they talked generally, Nwosu cleared his throat and said: 'Efuru we heard what happened. It is a long time now and we don't want to refresh your memory, but if one does not refer to it, one would be misunderstood. Nobody owns this world. Our people call their children. "Onwuamaegbu" – Death does not know how to kill, and "Onwuzurigbo" – Death is universal. So take heart, my daughter.'

'Thank you,' Efuru said.

'Then, just before we returned, we heard that you have left Adizua. We don't know why you have taken this decision, nor are we here as judges. But a man whose only child died and who could not come home to bury his only child and console his wife must be a very bad man. It showed that he hates his wife. So you have done well in leaving him. You are young, so the day is just breaking for you, other suitors will come. Just have patience.'

Efuru again thanked them.

'The night is very dark,' Ogea's father remarked. 'We are going. Thank you very much, Efuru; Ogea, let day break.'

There was no answer. 'Ogea,' Efuru called. The child was fast asleep.

'Children! how they sleep so easily. I wish I could sleep like that,' Nwosu said.

In the few days that followed, Nwabata, Ogea's mother, was busy selling the yams in the market. Occasionally, her husband would come to see how she was getting on. He came on Nkwo day to help his wife when he saw a very well-dressed woman in European dress. The woman selected ten fat yams and asked: 'How much?' in English. Ogea's mother did not of course understand. The woman asked again in English the second time. 'I say, how much?' and again Ogea's mother was at a loss what to say to her. When she said it the third time, Nwosu brushed his wife aside and said to the well-dressed woman in their language 'What do you mean by "hawu moch"? For months I toiled in the farm, morning and afternoon and now you come and say "hawu moch"; "hawu moch" your own too.'

It was then that it dawned on the woman that they did not understand what she said. She looked up and looked down again. There was nobody to help her, and so she picked up her basket and she and her maid went to another stall where she thought she would be understood.

Just before Nwabata finished selling the yams, her husband became ill. It was the usual trouble again. He had worked very hard of late and so this time the illness really knocked him down. For days he lay in the bamboo bed in their hut. It was difficult for him to get up. Nwabata who was heavy with child, nursed him. She went to a dibia who gave her some leaves to boil for her husband. When the pain grew worse, she went to Efuru and told her of her husband's illness. 'Nwosu is ill,' she told Efuru. 'He is very ill and I don't know whether he will recover.' As she said this, she began to cry.

'Wipe your tears,' Efuru said to her. 'What is the nature of the illness?'

'The usual one. The one he tried to explain to you when we came to you last time.'

'All right, I shall take him to see Dr Uzaru. I hear he will arrive from Onicha this evening.'

Nwabata thanked her and went home. That evening, Efuru bought a big fresh asa fish from the evening market. She made nsala soup with the asa and pounded some fufu; then she put the soup and the fufu in her best dishes and gave them to Ogea on a tray to take to Nwosu. 'I am sure he has not had a good meal for a long time,' she thought. 'When he eats well, then one will know how ill he really is for hunger could play a major part in his illness.'

Efuru then went to see whether Dr Uzaru had come. He arrived a few minutes before Efuru came and she was told that he was busy. But when the doctor heard Efuru's voice he came out at once and embraced her. 'You are looking very beautiful,' he teased her.

'Welcome,' Efuru managed to say. They went into the consulting-room.

95

'I heard you have left your husband?'

'No, he has left me. It is about two months now since I left his house.'

'But is he back yet?'

'No, he is not back. I think he has gone for good. I hope your wife and children are well?'

'Oh, they are very well, it is hunger only.' Efuru laughed and showed her set of white teeth.

'No, Difu. If you talk about hunger what do you expect us to do?' Efuru remembered the doctor when he was only a boy. She lived with his mother. The doctor's mother who was now dead was a very respectable woman. She was among a handful of girls who went to school when fathers frowned at sending their daughters to school. She was the only one who had insisted on obtaining her standard six certificate known in her day as 'As amended'. She was going to the little Church one Sunday when she saw a little girl run to her and embrace her. The little girl called her her friend and told her that she would like to live with her. Every time she passed that village, and if the little girl was playing with other children, she would run to her and embrace and ask her to take her home.

So one day the doctor's mother inquired about her and her parents were approached. Thus Efuru came to live with the doctor's mother. The doctor and Efuru grew up together and when Efuru was about fifteen years old, she went back to her parents' house. She learnt cooking, baking and sewing from the doctor's mother. The doctor asked about her immediately he returned from Yaba Higher College and he was told that she was already married.

'What are you going to do now that you have left your husband?' the doctor asked sympathetically.

'Nothing. Just stay in my father's house and continue with my trade.'

'Will you marry again?'

'I shall think twice this time.'

'That's a good girl. You think you were a little hasty before.'

'Well, maybe I was. But the success of a marriage does not depend on that. Marriage is like picking a parcel from numerous parcels. If you are lucky you pick a valuable one. It does not depend at all on the length of the courtship.'

'You are right. That's why some men dread it.'

'And some women too,' added Efuru.

'I don't think so. Women don't dread it. It is only we men who are scared of it, for we don't want to be roped in by you women.'

'Perhaps you are right. It is a necessary evil for us. You know our people's saying "Di bu mma ogori", so you can understand. Well I have come to see you. My maid's father is ill and I would like you to examine him.'

'What is the nature of the illness?'

'Some swellings.'

'All right bring him to see me when the sun goes down tomorrow. But remember I am on holiday. I don't want to do any work so don't tell people I am home.'

The next day at the appointed time Efuru and Nwosu arrived at the doctor's house. Efuru introduced Nwosu and left the room. 'Where does it ail you?' the doctor asked sympathetically. It was the tone of his voice, his sympathy and kindness more than his medicine that endeared him to his patients.

'Here,' Nwosu said, and pointed to the part he meant.

'Remove your clothes and lie on the bed.' The doctor examined him thoroughly. 'Get up and wear your clothes. When you finish come to the next room. I am going to give you an injection now,' the doctor told him, 'but it is just to help you for now. You will have to come to my hospital at Onicha for an operation. Unless you are operated upon, you won't be well. Don't worry, it is going to be an easy operation. There is nothing to fear.'

Efuru was called in and the doctor told her that Nwosu needed an operation. 'What kind of illness is this doctor?' Nwosu asked, very worried.

'You are lucky to have it detected now,' the doctor told him. 'It is something to do with the male organ.'

'Male organ? Our ancestors forbid. Nobody in my family has ever suffered from the disease of the male organ.'

'That may be true, but you have it and we want to help you. Don't worry, it is nothing. The operation won't be long and you will be in the hospital for a week or two depending on how you respond to my treatment.'

97

Nwosu went away more worried than he was before he saw the doctor. He told his wife what the doctor said and she burst into tears. Nwosu sat down on the bare floor, his hand on his chin, looking very miserable.

'You won't have this operation,' Nwabata wept. 'I say, you will not have it. I don't trust these doctors. Think of it. They will first of all "kill" you, then they do the operation, and after, if they know they cannot cure you, they give you poison. Who will look after me and my children? No, no, you won't be operated on. Ew-o-o. My world is very bad. I have come to suffer in the world. My ancestors please help me. Please fight against my enemies. Nwabata wept on and on.

'Don't take it so badly, my wife. I don't think it is as bad as you think.'

'What are you saying? Eh, what are you saying? You want to die and leave me? Let's see how you will die and leave me with these children to look after. Already we have pawned our first daughter and I see now that we shall use all our children this way. Which is a shame, which is a shame Nwosu, and you know it, you know. And now you want to be operated on, so that you will die and leave me a widow with six children to look after. Nwosu, you are wicked. Nwosu Madukaibeya you are wicked.'

'Woman, stop your nonsense. If you don't stop this nonsense now and I raise my hand and descend it on you, you will not know yourself for days!'

'Beat me. You beat me. You try and beat me. Beat a pregnant woman, and when I die the police will accuse you of murder and hang you. Beat me. If you don't beat me now, shame on you, shame on you.'

Nwosu looked at his wife. Looked at her lean body, her protruding belly, hissed and went to his room and locked himself up.

'Coward, coward. You are running away from a woman. You come and beat me,' Nwabata said banging at the door.

The next day Nwosu and his wife went to see Efuru. Anybody seeing them then would not think that they were near blows the night before. When they got there, Efuru and Ogea were in a very happy mood. They were laughing, and there was a boy about seven years old on the floor who was crying.

'All right, Emeka go well,' Efuru said still laughing.

'What is the matter?' Nwabata asked interested in the cheerfulness of her daughter and Efuru.

'Emeka wants to go,' Efuru said.

'And when he told us he wanted to go home, we said, all right, Emeka, go well, greet your mother and your brothers and sisters. But he started crying,' Ogea said and continued laughing.

Nwosu and Nwabata did not understand the joke at all.

'I will tell you the whole story,' Ogea volunteered. 'Emeka came here when we were just about to start cooking. He played with the children and occasionally he would come to the kitchen, survey the place and go out again to play. Then the last time he came, the food was ready. I was actually dishing it out when he ran in and said: "Mama, I am going", Mama was busy and did not hear him, so he said again, 'Mama, I'm going', Mama of course knew what the little boy was after; he wanted to have a formal invitation to lunch. So mama said, "All right, Emeka, go well." Then Emeka burst out crying.' Nwosu and Nwabata understood and began to laugh with Efuru and Ogea.

'Children,' Nwabata said, 'there is no end to their tricks, and it is most interesting to see how they think they could take you for a ride.'

Ogea had already dished out Emeka's food. So she called him and asked him to eat. Emeka wiped his eyes quickly and fell to.

'Welcome,' Efuru said to Ogea's parents. 'Emeke did not allow me to welcome you properly. Children! How clever they think they are. Ogea, please bring a better mat from the mud wardrobe for your parents and remove that one.' When Ogea brought the mat, Efuru asked her to bring it nearer to her. 'Spread it there,' she said. 'That's good. All right, Nwosu and Nwabata sit here and eat with me. You think well of us, that's why you always meet us eating or about to eat. It's only a friend and well-wishers who meet one eating.'

'Oh, thank you very much,' Nwabata said. 'We ate before we came, just before we came.'

'Come and eat again. Why do you always refuse to eat here? I don't like it. We are all one.'

But Nwabata and Nwosu were not persuaded. They still insisted that they had had lunch.

So Ogea's parents waited as Efuru slowly ate her lunch. As she was eating, one of Ajanupu's children came in. She greeted everybody one after the other: 'Nwosu, Ogbukea, Anamma,' she turned to Ogea's mother. 'Nwaononaku,' she greeted Efuru.

'That's very good,' Nwabata observed. 'Ajanupu is giving you very good training. Children should greet their elders when they see them.'

'Adiewere, come this way and eat with me. Ogea, bring another plate.'

'Thank you, Efuru,'

'What did you say?' Efuru asked in astonishment. 'You are a fool not to want to eat here. Didn't your mother tell you the relationship between us. Or did she tell you not to eat in my house I am joking,' she said quickly. 'Ajanupu will never tell you not to eat in my house So wash your hands and eat.' Adiewere still refused to eat. Efuru called Ogea and asked her to get a plate; when she brought it, she picked some fish from her dish and gave Adiewere to eat. Adiewere could not refuse that. So she took it and began to eat.

As Adiewere and Efuru were eating, a troop of children with shining tummies in front of them were seen approaching. 'These children are just in time. The way they time themselves is admirable. If you have a late lunch, they are sure to be there to have it with you. If you have an early lunch, it suits them best. Ogea,' she called, 'bring enamel plates for the children, bring more soup from the pot also.'

The children were seated, five of them. It seems as if they had a special invitation to lunch. 'Now, wash your hands properly here, and don't fight,' Ogea nagged. She did not like these children at all.

'We washed our hands at home before coming,' one of them said.

Efuru and the others laughed.

'Silly child, so if you washed your hands at home you won't wash them again before you eat. Here is some water in a basin. Wash your hands well,' Efuru said to all of them.

The children washed their hands in the basin and the water became very dirty. 'Now wait,' Efuru said. 'Don't eat yet. Ogea, please get another basin of water.'

Ogea threw the dirty one away, and brought fresh water.

'Now, wash again,' Efuru commanded. They all washed again and even this time the water was still dirty. Then they began to eat. After some time, one of them got up and went to Efuru.

'You see, you see, Oputa does not want me to eat. He is asking me to go home.'

'Oputa, why don't you want him to eat?'

Oputa got up. 'Wait for us,' he told the other children and went to Efuru. 'Yesterday, we went to his sister,' Oputa said. 'His sister gave us oranges and ground-nuts, but he refused to give me.'

'Is it true?' Efuru asked.

'Yes,' said the boy looking down.

'Now don't do it again, go and eat.'

When the children had finished eating, they left and it was then that Nwosu and Nwabata had a chance to tell Efuru the purpose of their visit.

'My husband told me that the doctor wants to operate on him. Since he came back yesterday, I have not been able to eat. I have been so upset that I was useless to myself. I am afraid of operations. Can't anything be done for him? Can't the doctor continue giving him injections?'

Ogea's father said nothing. He was in favour of the operation. Somehow, he trusted the doctor immediately he saw him. But he dreaded his wife.

'I have heard what you have said,' Efuru said at last. 'I don't want to persuade your husband to go. But I don't think you are doing the right thing by persuading your husband not to have the operation. In any case, if you change your mind and want to go for the operation, let me know so that I can send a word to the doctor.'

In a fortnight, Nwosu came back this time alone. That was the first time he had come to Efuru without his wife. 'I must go to the doctor,' he said to Efuru urgently. 'I must go. If I remain here I shall die. When can the doctor see me?'

'Go back again and discuss this with your wife, and then come to me,' Efuru said.

It was with great difficulty that Nwabata was convinced about the operation. Ogea went with her father to Onicha. The operation was successful and Nwosu remained there for a fortnight. By the time he came back, he was a changed man. He looked fresh and healthier. Nwabata could not believe her eyes when she saw her husband. She quite forgot that she had been firmly against the operation that had brought life back to her husband. She embraced him many times. 'So there is so much life in you, my husband. These white people are great, they are deep. Welcome home, my husband.'

Neighbours were equally glad to see Nwosu looking so healthy. They greeted him warmly. They also went to Efuru and thanked her for saving Nwosu's life.

The town was in a festive mood when Nwosu returned. It was the feast of the new yam – the time of plenty. It did not matter whether a farmer had paid for the money borrowed for his farm or not. All that mattered was that the year's work had come to an end and it was time for feasting.

So Nwosu called his age-group. He bought a bottle of schnapps and about three bottles of home-made gin. Then he bought several kegs of palm wine. His wife was in a festive mood too and for a while they forgot that Efuru's money was to be paid. Nwosu's age-group came and danced and drank wine.

After this, he killed a white cock for his chi and his wife also killed a cock for her own chi. Their chi had saved them from death and, therefore, they were grateful.

The children played an important part at this time. The moon was full. They organized themselves in groups and sang from door to door. Their song went like this:

'If you give us yam,
    Igbemgbele, Ocho-ockwuoo, Igbemgbele, we
        shall take.
    Igbemgbele, Ocho-okwuoo, Igbemgbele.

If you give us fish,
    Igbemgbele, Ocho-okwuoo, Igbemgbele,
        we shall take.
    Igbemgbele, Ocho-okwuoo, Igbemgbele.

Let a male born live,
    Igbemgbele, Ocho-okwuoo, Igbemgbele.
Let a female born live,
    Igbemgbele, Ocho-okwuoo, Igbemgbele.'

Women gave the children yams and fish, pepper, salt and vegetables. When they were given any of these things the children would then say: 'Thank you, very much. Let what you have given us be replaced a hundred-fold. You will give birth to one baby (implying that she would not have twins) at a time until your house is filled with babies.'

When the children were tired, all that they had collected was given to the eldest among them to keep. The next day they had a feast. Plenty was left over which was thrown away.

Nwosu and Nwabata were in a festive mood. When the children came round singing their song, Nwosu was slightly tipsy after taking some home-made gin. Immediately he heard the singing of the children, he came out from the room and began to dance. It was great fun for the children as this dance was for children only and men did not feature in 'Igbemgbele'.

Nwabata was worried because there was no yam at hand to give the children, and the young things did not want to be kept waiting.

'If you give us yam, fish, pepper, we shall take.
    Igbemgbele, Ocho-okwuoo, Igbemgbele.'

They sang this again and again and nothing was given them.

We have spirits behind us,
    Igbemgbele, Ocho-okwuoo, Igbemgbele.'

Nothing came out.

'Our throats are dry,
    Igbemgbele, ocho-okwuoo, Igbemgbele.
We are losing our voices,
    Igbemgbele, Ocho-okwuoo, Igbemgbele.'

Nwosu stopped dancing, went into the room and came out with two shillings. The children shouted with joy and thanked him. 'Thank you very much. Your wife will give birth to a baby boy,' they said.

Nwosu and Nwabata were both at home on the day Ogea paid them a visit. Her brothers and sisters came to welcome her. 'What have you brought for us?' they asked her. She gave them some ground-nuts.

Ogea went into the room, saw a pot of soup in the mud

wardrobe and asked one of the children to make some gari for her. 'Let the children pound yam for you,' her mother told her. 'I wonder how you can swallow that stuff. I cannot get it through my throat.'

'You are right, mother. Efuru does not eat it She says it scratches her throat. But I like it because it is easy to prepare. You make the fire, boil some water and make gari, whereas if you want yam fufu, you wait for the yam to be cooked, then you pound it. It wastes so much time.'

'You are lazy, that's all. You children of nowadays are lazy. Left to me, gari wouldn't be sold in the market.'

Ogea ate her gari and while she was eating, she asked her mother whether they had seen Efuru about the money they borrowed from her. Her mother's heart missed a beat.

'Did she say anything?'

'No, but don't tell me you have not seen her again. And by the way, did you take yams to her?'

'Nwosu, come and hear what your daughter is saying! Ogea, my daughter, I have been telling your father about this ever since we returned from the farm. He has been postponing it, and now we have not got yams that are worth giving to somebody like Efuru. Ogea, I nagged and nagged and when it was too much and I did not want any quarrel, I put my mouth in a bag and sewed it up. I don't want to be accused of being a "male woman". Nwosu, we are now ingrates in the sight of Efuru and many others because we have eaten the parcel and the thanks. And now what . . .'

'Woman, keep your mouth shut this instant. Are you drunk? When things go wrong you always blame others and don't blame yourself. Keep quiet I say.'

Nwabata surprisingly enough kept quiet.

CHAPTER SEVEN

It was full moon. Efuru had finished her evening meal. She asked Ogea to bring out a mat for her to lie on, so that she could enjoy the full moon. Ogea brought out the mat, she spread it for her mistress and sat down near her.

One of the women of the compound brought another mat and sat down beside her. 'The moon is very bright,' she remarked.

'Yes, the moon is very bright. When there is moon, one likes to walk about.'

'My children hurried over their food and rushed out to play. You can hear them playing.'

'And do you blame them? We did the same when we were children. Who can see such a moon and go to bed? So let the children enjoy themselves. I want to hear a good story, I wonder whether Eneke is around. Ogea, go and find out whether Eneke is in. Ask him to come if he is in.'

'Oh, Eneke. I enjoy his stories,' the woman said.

'He tells his stories beautifully. It is not only the story that is so absorbing, but the way he tells it. And he has such a beautiful voice too.'

They waited for Eneke. The clouds were moving.

'Who says the moon does not move,' said the woman.

'It moves of course,' agreed Efuru. Suddenly, Efuru was reminded of her life with Adizua; of that fateful moonlit night when she slipped out to meet Adizua and came back very late. Then she thought of the many meetings afterwards, all on nights when the moon shone.

'If it has been . . .' she did not finish. 'What is the use?' she asked. Then she saw Ogea coming from a distance. 'Is he coming, Ogea?'

'Yes, he is eating. After eating, he will come.'

On her way, Ogea had told some of the children playing that Eneke was coming to tell them stories. Some children followed her but others went on with their play.

'Ahaa, Eneke you have come,' the children said. Some of them took his hand, others stared at him.

'I am here now, what story am I going to tell you?'

'Tell us about the woman whose daughter disobeyed her and as a result was married to a spirit.'

'All right. Now keep still. Don't move.'

'Mbadee,' the children responded, 'de', 'Mbadee', 'de'.

'One day in the land of Idu-na-oba (Benin) there lived a woman and her daughter. This woman was very rich, but she had only one child, a very beautiful daughter. She was as beautiful as fire. She twinkled like the stars. She had very long hair which her mother plaited for her. Her mother bought beads for her which she wore round her waist. She was so beautiful that she was tired of being beautiful.

'Her mother did not allow her to go out for fear that she might be kidnapped, sold or beheaded. So anywhere she wanted to go, she was accompanied by a maid.

'One market day, the woman prepared for market, and told her daughter not to leave the house. To keep her away from mischief, she gave her plenty of work to do. "My daughter," the woman said softly to her only daughter. "I am going to the market. There is water in the water-pot. Sweep the floor and rub it, wash the plates. When you finish, stay indoors and wait for me."

'The girl agreed and her mother went to the market. Before her mother could reach from here to the stream, other girls from the village came to her. "Come let us go and pick some udara fruits," they told her.

' "No, I won't go with you," the girl said softly. "My mother has gone to the market and has asked me to sweep the floor, rub it and wash the plates. I am afraid I cannot go with you." "Oh, never mind that, we shall help you do the work."

'In the twinkling of an eye, the girls had finished all the work and the girl went with them to pick udara fruits. The udara tree was very far away and many people in the village dreaded it. Many mothers had warned their girls not to go there, but the girls gave deaf ears to their mothers' warnings.

'When they got to the udara tree, the girl did not pick any fruit while all her mates picked many fruits. She was sad. Then

106

just out of the blue a ripe udara fruit fell from the tree at the girl's feet. The girl picked it up and said:

"My good udara, my good udara."

The spirit of the udara tree and the owner of it shouted:

"My good wife, my good wife."

The spirit pursued her. The girls ran into the girl's house and entered one of the rooms and locked the door. The spirit waited outside.

'The girl's mother returned from the market and saw the spirit. She threw away her basket. She beat her chest. "I am dead. My daughter has disobeyed me. What am I going to do? A bad daughter has killed me."

'Immediately the spirit saw the woman, he began to sing through his nose, for as you know spirits speak through their noses:

"Woman, give me my wife,
    Shara.

Woman, give me my wife,
    Shara.

My wife dyed her body in front,
    Shara.

My wife dyed her body at the back,
    Shara.

When my wife comes out,
    She is like lightning."

'The woman went into the room and saw the girls. She dyed the body of one of the girls and brought her out for the spirit. The spirit shook his head, and began to sing again:

She is not my wife,
    Shara.

She is not my wife,
    Shara.

My wife dyed her body in front,
    Shara.

My wife dyed her body at the back,
   Shara.

When my wife comes out,
   She is like lightning."

'The woman went in, dyed another girl's body and brought
her out again. The spirit sang the same song. She brought out all
the girls and there were eight of them. When the spirit refused
them all, she went in, dyed her daughter's body beautifully,
dressed her gorgeously and presented her to the spirit.

"That's my wife,
   Shara.

That's my wife,
   Shara.

My wife dyed her body in front,
   Shara.

My wife dyed her body at the back,
   Shara.

When my wife comes out,
   She is like lightning."

'The spirit took the girl away to the spirit world, but before
they set out the girl suggested to the spirit that they should go
to her sisters and say good-bye to them before she went away
to the spirit world with him. The spirit agreed.

'Now the names of her sisters were Eke, Orie, Afo and Nkwo.
Eke was the eldest, then Orie, then Afo. Nkwo was the youngest and the kindest of them all. When the girl and the spirit
reached Eke's house, she began to sing:

"Eke, my sister,
Eke, my sister,
Mgbam mgba na obara kirida mgbam mgba.

Eke, my sister,
Eke, my sister,
Mgbam mgba na obara kirida mgbam mgba.

The ancestors who use human heads for roofs
   Mgbam mgba na obara kirida mgbam mgba.

The ancestors who use human blood for the floor
  Mgbam mgba na obara kirida mgbam mgba.

I am lost, I am lost
  Mgbam mgba na obara kirida mgbam mgba."

'Eke came out and saw her sister and said: "Serves you right. Do you remember the day I came to borrow salt from mother and you refused to give me?" and with this, she banged the door in her face.

'The girl went on to her next sister, Orie. She sang the same song to her. Orie treated her as Eke: "Do you remember the day I came to borrow pepper from mother and you refused to give me?' She banged her door in her face.

'Afo did the same to her reminding her that she refused to give her the pestle on the day she came to borrow it. When she came to her sister Nkwo, she sang as she had never sung before. She knew that this was her last chance. If Nkwo did not take her in, she was lost for ever. So she began to sing, her voice shivering and there were tears in her eyes:

"Nkwo, my sister,
  Nkwo, my sister
  Mgbam mgba no obara kirida mgbam mgba

Nkwo, my sister
  Nkwo, my sister
  Mgbam mgba no obara kirida mgbam mgba

The ancestors who use human heads for the roof
  Mgbam mgba no obara kirida mgbam mgba.

The ancestors who use human blood for the floor
  Mgbam mgba no obara kirida mgbam mgba.

I am lost, I am lost,
  Mgbam mgba no obara kirida mgbam mgba.

I am lost, I am lost,
  Mgbam mgba no obara kirida mgbam mgba."

'Nkwo jumped out and embraced her sister. But when she saw the spirit, she shuddered. "My brother-in-law", she addressed the spirit. "She is my sister and before a woman marries in our world, she must pay visits to her relatives to say good-bye. So come in and stay for the night." The spirit was suspicious, but he agreed and went in.

'Nkwo ordered that food should be prepared for her sister and her husband. When the fufu was pounded, Nkwo asked the spirit to bring the fish for the soup. The spirit got up and beat his right ear and maggots filled the floor. He beat the left ear and again maggots filled the floor. "Use that for the soup," he said pointing at the maggots.

'Nkwo used the maggots to cook for the spirit. When the food was ready, she set it before her sister and the spirit, but she made sure that the oil lamp was carried away. She then brought her sister some anara fruits which sound as maggots when they are chewed.'

The children made faces, some spat on the ground. And the storyteller continued:

'The spirit found the food delicious. He ate the maggots with relish. Occasionally he would ask his wife if she enjoyed it. The wife would say she did. But in actual fact she was not eating the soup. She dipped the food in the soup, threw it behind her and chewed her anara fruits.

'It was time for bed,' Eneke continued. 'Nkwo had prepared the room for her sister and her spirit husband. In bed, the spirit embraced her and held her tight. But she waited patiently. She had told her sister that her spirit husband snored terribly and that when she heard him snoring heavily, she would know that he was not quite asleep. But when he snored softly, he was fast asleep. So when Nko heard the soft snoring, she got up, woke her entire household and with their help, she removed all their valuable property from the house. When everything had been removed, she got some banana leaves. Then she went to the room where her sister and the spirit were sleeping. Her sister got up immediately she saw her. Then Nkwo used the banana leaves, putting them on the feet of the spirit, so that he would think that his wife was still lying beside him. Then they left the room.

'Nkwo brought a tin of kerosene. She poured it on the roof and set the house on fire. The house burnt to ashes, and thus the spirit was killed.'

'Serves him right,' the children rejoiced, 'to think that he could marry such a beautiful girl.'

'But that's not the end of the story,' Eneke continued. 'The ashes of the burnt body of the spirit were in a heap and as Okirikpa was passing by, he saw the heap of ashes. "What a fine snuff," he said. So he collected some, and with his thumb he put some in his two nostrils, and went home. When he got home, he began to enlarge and to enlarge and to enlarge until he was too big for his house, and finally he burst and died.'

'Ew-o-o-o,' the women and the children exclaimed.

'That was all I saw in the land of Idu-na-oba,' continued Eneke, 'and I said to myself – I must come home to my people for I have journeyed far.'

'Mbadee,' and the women and the children answered 'de'. Eneke got up to go.

'Please don't go, tell us another story,' the children begged.

'I shall tell you another story tomorrow, I must go now to my age-group. We are going to drink somewhere,' and before the children could get hold of his cloth or his hand, he escaped.

'Ogea,' Efuru called. But there was no answer. Efuru called again. The children helped her to arouse Ogea who was fast asleep on the floor. Ogea got up still feeling sleepy.

'What happened to the girl?' she asked. The children laughed at her.

'You are erofo,' they teased her.

'Are you Umutogwuma people who sleep early?' one of the children asked.

'We sleep early so that we can count our wealth,' a child from Umutogwuma village said humorously. The others laughed.

Ogea folded the mat and went to the room. The children heard other children playing and so they went to join them. Efuru was about to go to the room when she saw somebody approaching and recognized Gilbert.

Gilbert had not called again since that first visit. Sometimes she wondered why he had not come, but she did not give it much thought.

'Welcome,' Efuru said to him. 'So this is your eyes? Let the eyes I have used in seeing you not desert me. Where have you been all these years?' Efuru exaggerated.

'I went to Onicha to buy provisions for my stall in the market. Whilst there, I learnt that the yam trade was good so I plunged into it and made a good profit. You have to paddle upstream along the Great River. After paddling for four days, you get to the place. The natives don't know what to do with yams. Some yams are so big that two men cannot lift one. In the mornings when you see wives pounding fufu for their husbands and children, you would think that they are inviting a whole village to feast. It is so in the afternoon and at night also. They don't eat cassava though they have plenty of it. If a woman takes cassava to the market and she does not sell it, she leaves it in the market, because it is a great trouble carrying it back to her home when they have plenty at home. I did about five trips and made quite a profit. Many people don't know about this. Next year I am going again.'

'How lucky you are! And we are here messing around. Our debtors won't pay us. When you go to collect your debt it seems as if you have brought poison to the house.'

Gilbert laughed. 'What do you expect? They have no money. Trade is bad in this town. You know what, I was nearly robbed of all my money in Onicha market. The god of my fathers is awake.'

'Tell me. How did it happen?' Efuru asked sitting up.

'Immediately I returned, I told my mother and she sacrificed to our ancestors.'

'How is that, you go to Church?'

'What about that? I shall give the pastor some money to thank God for it.'

'I see. I can never understand you Churchgoers. All right, go on.'

'Foolishly enough, I put all my money in my pocket – over forty pounds. I went to the market to buy provisions for my stall. I noticed that I was being followed by a man. I stopped in one stall and began to price things there. This man stopped at a distance and pretended to be busy buying things. When I walked away, he too walked away. I watched him out of the corner of my eye. I stopped again and he stopped. Then he came and stood behind me. I pretended as if I did not see him and went on buying. Then I felt a hand going into my pocket, I turned and gave the man a slap – a big slap that he will never forget in his life. "Thief," I shouted. "Pickpocket." He would have been killed, but for a policeman who came to his rescue.'

'You are lucky,' Efuru said. 'When I go to Onicha market I make sure I put my money on a string tied round my waist. Even when I want to buy something, I don't mind untying it there. One day one woman laughed at me. "You Ugwuta women," she said, "why do you tie your money round your waist?" I laughed at her. She did not know what she was saying.'

'Onicha market is a terrible place. A market where you can see all sorts and conditions of men. There is nothing under the sun that is not sold there. I am sure that if one looks for a human head, one can easily find it in that market.'

'You know I was looking for uziza the other day,' Efuru said, 'and I only asked a woman from whom I had bought some pears and she told me at once where to get it. I went straight there and got it. Another day, I was looking for akpukpo akabo and the fat of a python. I asked somebody and he took me to where I got them. But what puzzles me is the cheapness of the things in that market.'

Gilbert laughed. 'Most of the things you buy there are not genuine. One must be very careful before one buys anything from that market, especially medicines and cosmetics.'

'You are right,' said Efuru. 'You know I bought a tin of powder the other day and when I opened it I saw that it was starch.'

'Since buying M &B tablets from the market and discovering that they were white chalk, I don't buy medicines or powder from the market,' said Gilbert.

For some time they did not talk. In the distance they could hear the children playing and laughing.

'What a bright moon,' Efuru remarked.

'Yes, how bright it is. The wonderful work of nature. A piece of yam that is sufficient for all the world. How I enjoy these children. I feel like playing with them. Did you play a lot in the moonlight when you were young?'

'Of course I did. When there was moonlight we children did nothing for our mothers. We did not even have our evening meals. We had a very influential aunt. She was very good at organizing our play. The night she was not there, our play flopped. Immediately she arrived, everybody became lively again. But she was a difficult aunt and queer in her ways. For no reason at all, she would decide not to take part in moonlight play and she wouldn't allow we children to enjoy ourselves. If you opposed her, she showed you that without her the play could not go on.

'Once I wanted to show her that without her we could organize something. She was only five years older. So, one night, the moon was shining very brightly. I gathered all the children in the compound and we began to play. It was not very interesting, but it was better than nothing. I managed to keep the children together. When my aunt came, she was angry. She felt that I had no right whatever to organize anything without her permission, and so she tried to break up the small party of children.

'She did it in a most interesting way. First she called one of the children and sent him on an errand. Before the child was back she called another, "Sa, sa, look, your mother wants you. Your father has just returned from fishing in the moonlight and has caught a big asa and echim and your mother wants you to help her. If you don't help her she won't give you some tomorrow." To another child she said, "Look, what are you doing? Your mother will beat you, don't you hear your little sister crying?"

'She continued in this way until she completely disorganized the little band of children. I was very angry and she laughed at me. "I told you that without me there won't be any market." We all laughed. If she was in her good mood and wanted to play, she would rally round the children and in no time we had very good play. She was such an influence on we children in those days. She took us everywhere, to the stream, to fetch wood and to steal guava from the white man's garden, whose dog was a great terror to us. Even when we ate, we showed her the amount of food we took before we dipped it into the soup. We had to take some off and sometimes we received cracks on the head for being greedy.'

'She must have been a great influence,' Gilbert agreed. 'And where is she now?'

'She is married and is living in Onicha with her husband. She is as calm as a lamb now.'

Efuru and Gilbert were quiet again. They heard the children singing in their play:

114

'Kpeturu Kpeturu fenato
Fenato na mgashi mee.
Mgashi mee uwa bia ero
Uwa bia ero.
Tiringo ringo, tingongo – iyo!'

'You played that, didn't you?' Efuru asked.

'Yes, of course, we played that. But do you know what the words mean?'

'No, I don't, do you?'

'I don't know.'

'We children liked the rhythm of it, that's all.'

'But do the words mean anything?'

'No, the words don't mean anything. It is one of these collections of meaningless words which children use for their plays. It means nothing in our language and I don't think it means anything in any other language.'

The 'mother' who led the children in this play had given the children names for the purpose of the play. So she began to 'build houses' for her children in the sand. Calling them by their new names:

'Ngaji Ona, dewu uno yi o-o, Nwa oma.
Akpationa, dewu uno yi o-o, Nwa oma.
Udene nwa Okworinga, dewu uno yi o—o
Tufia, Tufia, Tufia.'

'This is not nonsense,' Efuru said. 'It means: "Silver spoon, here is your house, good child. Golden box, here is your house, good child. Vulture, here is your house." '

The vulture is an unclean bird that eats decayed things and even decayed human flesh. It should not live with human beings and so the children were horrified when it was mentioned and showed their horror and disgust by saying; 'Tufia, Tufia, Tufia.'

The children continued with their play. Gilbert and Efuru listened. The 'mother', after building the houses for the children went on a long journey carrying an imaginary small canoe on her head and singing as she went:

'Ugbo ose o-o
Chamanche

115

Ugbo akai
Chamanche.

Ugbo ose o-o
Chamanche

Ugbo akai
Chamanche.'

When she came back home, the children disappeared.

'Where are my children?' she asked. 'Where are they?' she asked again and before she asked the question the second time, the children came flocking to her, pretending that they were helping her with her load.

'I am happy, my childhood did not just pass by,' Efuru remarked.

'Eneberi,' Efuru said. She could never bring herself to call him Gilbert. 'Eneberi, it is late, I am going to bed. Let day break.' As she said this, she began to fold the mat she was sitting on.

'Visit me tomorrow,' Gilbert said.

'No, I cannot come tomorrow. I am going somewhere.'

'All right, what about Nkwo, after market?'

'You talk as if you are a stranger in our town. How can a woman visit anybody on Nkwo day?'

'But I said after the market.'

'Yes, you said after the market. No woman in our town has time for any other thing except to buy and sell on Nkwo day. After the market, she goes to collect her debts. Nkwo is not a day to make social calls, it is a day of business.'

'Come on Eke day then.'

'No, I won't come. You come when you have time. I am going to sleep. Let day break.'

'I must marry her,' Gilbert kept on telling himself. All night he thought of nothing but Efuru and what a good match they would make. 'I must marry her,' he said again to himself throughout that night. 'She left her husband because he was unkind to her. I am going to look after her well. I am going to do all in my power to see that I marry her.'

Throughout the night Gilbert did not sleep. He thought of another woman he had wanted to marry. About five years ago he had seen a very beautiful girl whom he liked. He immediately told his mother who at once was so opposed to the girl that Gilbert suspected that there must be a misunderstanding between the girl's mother and his own mother. He could not soften his mother's heart. His mother said she was going to commit suicide if he married the girl, and she did not stop there. She went to the parents of the girl and threatened that if her son married their daughter, they were responsible for anything that might happen to their daughter.

The parents of the girl were furious and warned Gilbert not to come to their house. It was such an unhappy experience for Gilbert that when it was over, he did not have the heart to associate himself with any other woman. When the girl in question married, Gilbert forgot everything about marriage, and refused to think about it until he saw Efuru one day in the stream.

Efuru had gone to the stream to bathe and Gilbert was in the stream also, washing his shirt. He liked the look of Efuru and, when he asked about her, he was told that she had married but had left her husband.

The next night, Gilbert again went to see Efuru. The moon was still bright and the children were playing. Eneke was telling a story to a group of children and women. When he had finished and gone away, the children began to sing some songs, and when they heard the voice of other children, they went to play with them. Efuru and Gilbert were left alone.

'Since you prefer to come at night, the night has taken kola,' Efuru said.

'Don't worry about that. I have something very important to tell you.'

'Ewo-o-o, is that so? I hope it is well.'

'It is very well, Efuru. I have come to ask you to marry me. And I want you to give it very serious thought before you give me a reply. I believe that in a matter like this, since both of us are adults we should behave accordingly. I don't want the courtship to be prolonged. Think of it seriously and give me your answer on Eke day. In four days, I shall come to hear what you have to tell me.'

The children were still playing and as on the previous night, Efuru and Gilbert listened to their play in silence.

'If you go near the lake, you will think that a big festival is going on. There are many people there beating their drums and dancing. On the lake itself, you see fishermen throwing their nets in the deep and catching fish. I just wonder why we cannot have the moon always. It makes people so happy.'

'Well, everything must have its season so God made it to be.'

'Why do you always sit here and not go out; come let's go out,' Gilbert said lifting Efuru from the mat.

'Leave me, I am not going. Men and women don't go out at night.'

Gilbert left her and sat by her. 'Are you going to think seriously of what I have told you this evening? Promise me that you will give it serious thought.'

'I shall give it serious thought, don't worry.'

'I am going then. Come and see me off to the gate.'

Efuru got up and saw Gilbert off to the big gate of the compound.

'I am turning back. Let day break.'

'Already? See me off to that Iroko tree near the market,' Gilbert pleaded.

'No, I won't go as far this night.'

'But the moon is shining.'

'I know the moon is shining. There are witches on that tree. You can hear the owls now. They are no owls, they are witches.'

Gilbert laughed. 'You are superstitious,' he said.

'Say what you like, I cannot pass that tree this night.'

'All right, we won't pass that way, we shall go the other way.'

'No, I won't go. It is late.'

Gilbert stood at the gate. 'Come on!'

Efuru shook her head. Before she knew what Gilbert was doing, she felt his hand round her shoulders. She did not move away. 'You are pleasing to me. I shall see you again tomorrow night.' He was gone. Efuru stood at the gate and watched him until he was out of sight.

Gilbert knew that he was going to have another sleepless night, so he went to fish with one of the men in the village. Gilbert was a good fisherman. He had learnt to fish as a boy, and now he was almost an expert. There were not many professional fishermen in the town in spite of the fact that they had the lake to fish in. They also had the stream that flowed into the lake, and the river also that flowed into the lake. The life of a fishman was so precarious that the man combined fishing with farming, fishing with trading and so on. But it did seem that everybody born in that town knew how to fish and could always get some fish for a meal at least, if he bothered to take the trouble to fish in the lake or the stream or the river.

That night, Gilbert caught many fishes and he returned in the small hours of the morning just when the cock was crowing. He selected very big fish like asa, atuma and aja and sent them to Efuru first thing in the morning. Efuru was flattered when a little boy came to her carrying the fish in a basin.

She did not know what to do with all the fish. So she sent some to Ajanupu, and some to Adizua's mother. Then she dried some, and used some in cooking for her father.

Gilbert came earlier than usual that evening.

'Thank you for the fish,' she said to him. 'So you are a fisher-man.'

'Yes, I try to catch fish occasionally when I have the time.'

'Would you like to eat something?'

'Yes, have you anything for me?'

Efuru brought out some pounded yam and soup. That was the first time Gilbert ate food cooked by Efuru. It was delicious and, like all men, Gilbert did not play with his stomach. He ate up nearly everything on the plate, when he remembered that one did not eat everything on the plate. Etiquette demanded that a small fraction of the food must be left on the plate so that the children who cleared away the dishes did not grumble.

Ogea cleared the plates, giving Gilbert a very sweet smile.

'Is Efuru at home?' Gilbert and Efuru heard from the gate.

Efuru smiled. 'Who is that?' asked Gilbert.

'It is Ajanupu, do you know her?' Ajanupu came in and sat down.

'Idenu,' Gilbert greeted her.

'Who is that my brother, greeting me?'

'It's me, Eneberi Uberife.'

'Ew-o-o-o, my child. Is this your eye. It is a long time since I saw you last. How are you? How is your mother? When did you return from Onicha?'

'About a week ago,' Gilbert replied.

'Welcome, my child. I hear you made money in Onicha. Is it true?'

'How stories travel. Our trade was good, that's all.'

'That is good. It is good trade that we want.'

'Efuru, it is a long time since I saw you last. What is the matter?'

'Nothing, Ajanupu. I have been very busy.'

'How is your father?'

'He is quite well.'

'I have come to thank you for the fish you sent to me. Where did you buy such a fish?'

Efuru began to laugh, Gilbert kept a straight face. 'He sent them to me,' Efuru said pointing to Gilbert.

'Is that so, Eneberi? You caught that fish?'

'Yes.'

'Are you going to fish today?'

'No, today is Orie.'

'It is true. I talk as if I am a stranger. I forget that today is Orie day and that all worshippers of the woman of the lake go on special diet and eat plantain which is the favourite of the woman of the lake. Who sells your fish for you, Eneberi?' Ajanupu asked.

'I don't really fish always. It is only when I feel like it that I fish and, if I catch plenty of fish, I give some to friends. My mother sells some, and uses some in cooking for me.'

'Do you want to tell me that you are not married yet? It is strange. Why have you not been married?'

'I have not seen a nice woman yet.'

'Nonsense. You have not started to look for a wife yet, that's why you have not seen one. I am going to see your mother about it. Why should a grown-up man like you remain a bachelor. But come, I remember you were to marry somebody some time ago. What happened?'

'Her parents refused to let her marry me. It was a long time ago. About five years ago in fact.'

'Really, why did her parents refuse?'

'I don't know.'

'Or did your mother refuse, which is which?'

'I can't remember exactly.'

Ajanupu then turned to Efuru who was giggling all the time during the interrogation. 'Efuru,' Ajanupu began, 'Debtors don't pay their debts these days. I am knee-deep in debt myself. But my debors won't pay me. How is one going to survive the famine this year? By the way have Ogea's parents paid you yet?'

'They have not paid me. I have not gone to ask them either. I thought they would use their discretion.'

'Discretion indeed. Whoever uses his discretion when it comes to debts; if you don't go often to remind them, your money is lost. Didn't I hear that Ogea's father took a title about a month ago?'

'A title? But he has no money and he owes me so much.'

'That's what I am telling you. Unless you worry a debtor, he will never pay; when he has money he uses it for other things. Some of these people who are very good debtors come to you and buy a piece of cloth knowing that they won't have to pay you. If after two months you come for your money, they ask you to take your cloth. You ask where it is and you are told that it has been washed and is hanging outside. A woman did that to me years ago when I was dealing in cloth. She bought a piece of cloth from me and told me she would pay by instalments. Every Nkwo day, she was going to pay five shillings. The price of the cloth was three pounds. For eight Nkwos she did not pay anything, and one day I went to her. She begged me and told me to come after four Nkwos. When I got there, she said I could take my cloth. "Where is it?" I asked. "Outside," was all she told me and continued with what she was doing. I went outside and took my cloth. I gave it to one of my relatives. Debtors can be as bad as that. So go to Nwosu and ask him for your money otherwise you won't be given it and, moreover, the planting season is at hand.'

'Yes, that's it, the planting season. If they give me my money, what are they going to use for the planting season? Won't it amount to their borrowing from somewhere with exorbitant interest?'

'You are sorry for them; I can see.'

'What disturbs me is that they have not come to tell me

about the money. If they come I shall let them keep it for another season. After all, they are Ogea's parents and I am fond of Ogea.'

'If you like, leave your ten pounds with them. I am going. When your father comes, tell him I called. Eneberi, I shall see your mother. Let day break.'

'Let day break,' Efuru and Gilbert said together.

'What a woman, embarrassing me like that,' Gilbert said immediately Ajanupu was out of sight.

'I am fond of her. She talks too much, no doubt, but she is good. She has a good heart.'

Gilbert remained for a long time at Efuru's house that night. It was very late when he got up to go.

'Come and see me off to the gate,' Gilbert said rising. Efuru agreed. She went into the room and came out wearing her head-tie. 'Let's go.'

They went slowly to the gate. At the gate, Gilbert embraced her. 'Your behaviour is very pleasing to me. I shall do anything for you if you will be my wife. Think seriously before you give me a reply.'

Efuru said nothing. Gilbert embraced her again. He did not kiss her. The men did not kiss their women folk. They stood still in their embrace. 'I shall be the happiest man on earth if you agree to marry me. I shall make you happy. I shall be faithful to you and, if our God wills it, we shall be rich. Come on, see me off to the iroko tree. You refused to go there last night. Come along, don't be afraid.'

'It is so quiet,' Efuru remarked. 'Many people have gone to bed. It must be very late, and yet the moon is shining, so brightly.'

'Let's go to my house,' Gilbert suggested. 'I shall bring you back. Let's go.'

'No, I won't go. I am going back now, Eneberi. Let day break.'

And before Gilbert knew what was happening, Efuru had run back to the gate just in time, for an aged woman who was in charge of the gate was about to lock it.

'Where are you coming from, young woman, don't you know that the night is deep?'

'Oh, is that you Nnona? Ezeuri,' Efuru greeted her.

'Who is that my sister greeting me in this dead of the night?'

'It is me, Efuru, Efuru Ogene.'

'Efuru Ogene,' she repeated doubtfully.

'Yes, don't you remember me?'

'Ew-o-o, my daughter. Is this your eye? I have not seen you since you came back to us. I went to Akiri and returned only three days ago. I have not come out since because of my bad leg.'

'That leg of yours. So it still hurts you.'

'My daughter, it is still there. It will kill me. I have said it, this leg will kill me. Why it has not killed me all these years as a mystery to me.'

'Sorry. If you like I can take you to the hospital. The doctor will look at it and he can do something for you.'

'Is it true? If you do that, my daughter, God will bless you.'

'We shall see what we can do for you when the doctor comes to the town. I am going. Let day break.'

'Efuru, wait, don't go. Where are you coming from this night?'

'Oh, I saw somebody off. Didn't you see us when we passed?'

'I see. Well, we are old and we don't know what to say and you accuse us of not minding our business, but you should not be seen with that man.' Then she paused for some time, and said, 'I heard about your husband. Is he back now?'

'No, he is not back.'

'You mean that for more than two years he has not come back?'

'No, he has not come back.'

'Don't worry, my daughter. Keep cool. You are a beautiful woman, and good too. Husbands are difficult to get for only bad and ugly women, so don't worry. Our gods will bring a better husband. Good husband will meet you, my daughter. Go and sleep now, my daughter. Let day break.'

'Let day break,' Efuru said to the woman, and hurried to her house.

When Efuru got to her room, she undressed and went to bed. But she did not sleep. She thought of Gilbert and what he had told her that night. She thought of what life would be with Gilbert as her husband. 'I think he is pleasing to me,' she said to herself. 'He talks so responsibly. I think I shall marry him. But I shall first of all see Ajanupu about it, and hear what she has to say.'

In the morning. Efuru got up early and went to the stream to fetch water. She took extra care about her appearance. She wore a new wrappa and plaited her long black hair into four. When she came to the gate, she saw the old woman who was at the gate the night before.

'Have you risen from sleep?' the woman asked her.

'Oh, Nnona, Ezeuri, have you risen? I am going to the market.'

'Go well, my daughter.'

'Thank you,' Efuru said.

'Efuru, Efuru,' the woman called. Efuru turned and walked towards her. 'Remember what you said to me last night. I could not sleep last night for joy. When is the doctor coming?'

'Never mind, when he comes I shall take you to him.'

'All right, my daughter. You are a good child.'

Efuru was very happy. When she got to her stall that morning, she left her things with another woman who shared her stall and went home.

She cooked food for Gilbert. She put plenty of fish in the soup and pounded fufu that was enough for four hungry farmers. Then she went to her mother's mud wardrobe and brought out two big dishes which she had used for Adizua's food when they were newly married. She dished out the food and put it on a large tray. She covered it up with one of her head-ties and asked Ogea to carry it to Gilbert's house. Then she went back to the market.

Gilbert was very happy when he saw Ogea with the tray of food. He got up from where he was sitting with his friends and helped Ogea with the tray. 'Efuru said I should bring this to you,' Ogea said shyly.

'Where is she?' Gilbert asked. 'Did she not go to the market today?'

'She went to the market in the morning, then came back to cook the food.'

'So she is now in the market?'

'Yes, she is now in the market.'

Gilbert's friends cleared their throats mischievously. Gilbert brought a small table and set the food on it. When he uncovered the soup, the men swallowed their saliva.

'Did she ask you to wait and collect the dishes?' Gilbert asked Ogea.

'No, she did not say that but I shall wait and collect the dishes if you like.'

Gilbert called his mother's maid to bring some water for washing their hands. They washed their hands and began to eat.

'If the woman who cooked this food put poison in it, I don't mind dying,' one of the men said. Others laughed.

'You chronic bachelor, you are enjoying the food cooked by a woman and yet you refuse to get married,' the only married one among them said.

'I hear she has left her husband,' one of the men said.

'Who has left her husband?' one of the men asked.

'So you don't know the woman who cooked the food you are eating?'

'No, I don't know her. Who is she?'

'Don't you know Efuru Ogene who married Adizua. Adizua deserted her for another woman and since three years he has not come back.'

'I know the husband very well. We men are fools sometimes. What didn't Efuru do for that man?'

'Has she agreed to marry you?' one of the men asked Gilbert.

Gilbert smiled and went on eating. Then he called the maid and asked her to get them some drinking water.

'If you want to marry her, marry her,' the married man among them said to Gilbert. 'She is a good woman. I have heard so much about her. She will look after you. Her hands make money. Anything she touches is money. If she begins to sell pepper in the market, she will make money out of it. If in salt, money will flow in; I say marry her.'

Gilbert was happy to hear this. He had known these qualities already in Efuru, but he was happy because others knew that Efuru was a good woman also. 'The woman who cooked this food must be a good woman,' one of the bachelors said. 'Think of it,' he went on. 'To marry a woman who does not know how to cook.'

'What will you do if you marry a woman who cannot cook?' one of the bachelors asked.

'I shall send her back to her mother,' another replied.

'It is easier said than done,' the married man said. 'Let me tell you, you will not do anything of that sort. You will think of the dowry and the trouble you took before you married her. I can tell you, you will not send her packing to her mother. A way out is to ask her to cook for you before you marry her. For instance, Gilbert knows Efuru can cook, without his marrying her. It is easy.'

The men finished eating and, as they were washing their hands, they were still talking about Efuru's cooking. 'The person who has cooked has cooked well, and the people who have eaten it have eaten it well, so goes the saying.'

The maid cleared the dishes and washed then and put them back on the tray. Gilbert gave Ogea a shilling and she went home.

Soon it was Eke. Gilbert went to Efuru's house and remained there for a long time. It was about midnight when he got up to go.

'Today is Eke, Efuru. Are you going to marry me? Have you thought of it seriously? Will you be my wife?'

For an answer, Efuru took Gilbert's hand and said softly and shyly: 'I will marry you. You are pleasing to me.'

CHAPTER EIGHT

A few weeks after, the doctor came home on a visit and Efuru went to see him. As usual the doctor was very happy to see her. He came out from his room and embraced her.

'Come in and tell me everything about yourself. Wait,' he said very warmly. 'I bought you a piece of cloth from Onicha. Let me go and fetch it.' The doctor came out with a piece of Dutch print and gave it to Efuru.

'Thank you very much,' Efuru said very shyly. 'Please what is your salutation name?'

'Adishiemea,' the doctor said laughing.

'Adishiemea,' Efuru said and bowed low.

'Come, tell me about yourself, what has happened to you since I saw you last?'

'Nothing has happened exactly. I have been living in my father's house. My trade is going well, and Adizua is yet not back from his journey.'

'Are you hoping that he may come home and ask for your forgiveness?' the doctor asked seriously.

'No, I have refused him. As far as I am concerned I am not his wife any more.'

'Has anybody come?'

For an answer Efuru began to laugh.

'Tell me,' the doctor teased.

'Yes, a suitor has come. He is pleasing to my eyes. I have agreed to marry him.'

'I am glad to hear this. Who is the man? Do I know him?'

'I don't know whether you know him or not. He is called Eneberi Uberife. He went to school and they call him Giribat.' The doctor laughed and Efuru laughed knowing that she did not pronounce the name well.

'Is that not what they call him? You who went to school know how to pronounce these names. I did not go to school with you.'

'I don't think I have heard that name before. What does he do?'

'He has a small stall in the market where he sells odd things. Sometimes he goes to Onicha and to the Great River buying yams and other things.'

'Has he been married before?' the doctor asked.

'No, he has not been married before.'

'He must be young then, for our people marry young.'

'Yes, he is quite young. We are in the same age-group and I knew him as a boy. He should be a few months older than I am.'

'And he has not married? Why has he not married?' asked the doctor.

'You forget that he went to school and that those who go to school do not marry early.'

'I am glad about Eneberi. Has he seen your father yet?'

'He has paid one or two visits to my father, but he has not told him that he wants to marry me.'

'And the dowry? Has he money to pay the dowry? A man who has no money to pay the dowry, and ours is very reasonable, is not serious at all when he says that he wants to marry a wife. Can he pay the dowry then?' the doctor finally asked.

'We have not talked about that, but I think he can pay the dowry. He is quite prosperous by our people's standards. I am sure that he can pay the dowry without feeling the pinch at all.'

'Adizua is a fool. You were a gift given to him. He could not appreciate what he had. He did not know the value of what he had. We men are like that sometimes. Tell me when Eneberi brings wine to your father. What about that man I operated on? How is he?'

'My maid's father? He is well. I have not seen him for some time now though. But there is nothing wrong, if there was anything wrong, he would have come to me. I have another case now. It is an old woman this time. She has a bad leg. Since I was a child, she has always had a dirty bandage on that leg.'

'I won't be staying long this time, so bring her to me tomorrow.'

Efuru and the doctor talked generally for a while and Efuru

got up to go. 'Thank you very much for the cloth. Adishiemea, thank you, you have done well.'

'Don't worry. Go well,' the doctor said.

The next day, Efuru brought Nnona to the doctor. Her leg was examined. 'It will take a long time to heal,' the doctor said to Efuru after the examination. 'She had a bad sore and she allowed it to eat into the bones. I shall send her to the hospital where she will have an operation. So bring her any time next week and we shall see what we can do for her.'

Nnona was overjoyed. She had a daughter who was married and had children. One of the children could go with her to the hospital because she would need someone to cook for her since the hospital did not provide food for its patients. It was arranged and Efuru had to buy them a few things they needed, like yams, fish, pepper and salt. She paid the fare to Onicha and gave Nnona a few shillings as pocket-money.

The leg took time to heal and they were in the hospital for over a month. One day, Efuru and Ogea came to see Nnona in the hospital. They brought her live oguna fish. Oguna fish take a long time to die. If you have them in a big basin full of water they live for as long as you wish them to live provided you change the water occasionally and the basin is large enough to give them ample space for swimming. Any time Nonona's grand-daughter wanted to cook for her grandmother, she would take two oguna fish, kill them and use them in cooking.

One day the girl went to the stream and, when she came back, she saw that the pot of soup she had cooked for her grandmother was gone. Somebody had come while she was away and took her pot of soup. She sat down and wept. She told her grandmother, who consoled her and begged her to go and cook another soup. The little girl cooked another pot of soup. In the morning, she went to the stream and, as she was coming back, she heard someone yelling. The person was in great pain. She walked very fast and by the time she got to the hospital, there was a crowd of people near the kitchen. The yelling had not stopped. 'What is the matter?' she asked as she put her water-pot down.

'Somebody was stealing your fish and God caught her red-handed. Please help us remove the head of the fish from her hand.'

'She has been justly punished,' said one of the male nurses from the hospital who came out when the woman yelled for help.

'Didn't I say that our gods are awake. Didn't I warn that nobody should steal my things because our gods will visit the thief. So I said, so I said and it has happened as I said.'

'Do something, little girl, don't you see that the woman is in agony,' one of the people in the crowd said.

'Our gods have fought for me today. The woman of our lake has fought for one of her daughters today. Where is the woman? Where is she? Give way, everybody.' The little girl held the woman's hand with one hand. She tapped the fish on the head, just a gentle tap and the fish dropped. The people were amazed.

'How did she do it?' they asked one another.

'Don't you see that there is a technique employed. We were pulling the fish, but she simply tapped the head of the little fish,' said one of the bright ones in the crowd.

'You will not steal again!' the male nurse told the woman as he took her to the hospital to give her first-aid. 'You will not steal again. When you come to this hospital you behave as if you have not seen food all your life. You steal pepper, you steal salt and you steal soup, soup cooked for another patient. Anywhere you see fresh fish, in future, you will remember today. Look at your mouth. Do you know how to eat fresh fish? Have you ever seen fresh fish in your home to come here and steal fresh fish?'

Nnona's grand-daughter remembered this incident all her life. She told it to everybody at home ten times over, adding that after the incident all the people in the hospital feared her. She could leave her wood, soup, meat, pepper, salt, anything at all in the kitchen and come back to find it where she had left it untouched.

They spent two months in the hospital and Nnona came home cured. She was looking very fit and went to see Efuru as soon as they arrived home. Efuru was out, but her father was in. 'Nwashike Ogene, are you home?' Nnona called.

'Who is that my sister, calling me?'

'It is Nnona. I am back. I have come to say thank you. Your daughter is a good woman. She has cured me. Come and see me,' she said. Efuru's father came out. Nnona bowed to him.

'Agundu,' she greeted.

'Ezeuri,' Efuru's father greeted her. 'Are you back? Did you go well?' he asked.

'I am back, our Nwashike, I am back. Your daughter has saved my life, I am well now. Your daughter is a good woman. A good husband will meet her. Good fortune will meet her. She will live long, nothing will happen to her. Her house will be filled with children.'

'Welcome, Nnona,' Efuru's father said again.

'Efuru is not in?'

'No, Efuru is not in,' he said. 'She has gone to collect money from her debtors. But wait, don't go yet. Let's have kola before you go.' Kola-nut was brought and Efuru's father broke it and took a piece and passed it on to Nnona.

'Tell me what happened,' Efuru's father said.

'Nwashike, the white men are little gods. I did not know what really happened. But I was told that I was going to be operated on. So one day, I was wheeled into a big room where I saw different kinds of instruments. I saw men and women in white clothes. They covered their mouths and noses with white cloth. They were all very busy and all their attention was on me. I was given something to inhale and when I inhaled it, I did not know what happened again. When I opened my eyes, I saw that I was in a large room. Please thank your daughter for me and the doctor also. He came every day to see me.'

'Welcome home. I shall thank Efuru when she comes back.'

The woman got up, greeted Efuru's father again and went away.

About a week after Nona had returned from the hospital, her daughter and her husband and her son and his wife came to thank Efuru for what she had done for Nnona. Efuru was in and Gilbert was there also. When they exchanged greetings, Efuru brought out kola and offered them. Then Nnona's son said:

'We have come to see you, Efuru, to thank you for what you have done for our mother. What you have done surprised everybody that we have no mouth to thank you. It is true that a person who has people is better off than a person who has money. Our hearts are glad and we have come to show you our appreciation. Thank you very much. Thank you.'

131

'Efuru,' Nnona's daughter said. 'Thank you very much. My brother has spoken for all of us but I want to say again that we are happy that you have helped our mother. You have done what only men are capable of doing and so you have done like a man. We have no words to thank you. Only God will thank you for what you have done for our mother. So thank you very much.'

'You have done well to come and thank me,' Efuru said shyly. 'I feel happy that I have made you and your mother happy. So please don't think I have done something very great.'

Ajanupu's voice was heard from a distance as Efuru's visitors were leaving. 'Our Nnona,' she called. 'Are you in?'

There was no answer. Nnona's daughter told her that she was not at home.

'Oh, is that you, my daughter. You are coming from Efuru.'

'Yes, we went to Efuru to thank her for what she did for our mother.'

'You did well to go, for we don't know tomorrow, tomorrow is pregnant as we say. Is she at home?'

'Yes, she is at home,' the woman said wondering what Ajanupu meant.

'Is Efuru at home?' Ajanupu asked before she got to Efuru's door.

'Oh, who is that, my sister? Is it Ajanupu?'

'Yes, it is Ajanupu.'

'Idenu,' Efuru greeted as she came out from the room.

'Nwaononaku,' Ajanupu greeted her.

'Idenu,' Gilbert said.

'Who is that?' Ajanupu asked.

'It is Eneberi.'

'Our Eneberi, is it you. Are you well?'

'It is well,' Gilbert answered.

'Did they say that you sent Nnona to the hospital?' Ajanupu asked Efuru.

'Yes, I sent her to the doctor.'

'That's why I talk good of you, Efuru.' When people hear me say good of you, they don't understand me. Is her leg healed now?'

'Yes, it is healed. She was in hospital for more than a month.'

'And you looked after her all that period?'

'Partly. Her daughters contributed too.'

'You are a good child. God will bless you, my daughter. And is that why her children have come to thank you?'

'Yes.'

'That's the way to behave. That's the way our people behave. My heart is glad. There is nothing as satisfying as showing appreciation when someone does something for you. There is nothing like that at all. And did Nwosu and Nwabta show all that gratitude?'

'Yes, they came and thanked me,' Efuru said.

'That was not enough. They should have sent people to help them thank you. Don't you see how Nnona is broadcasting the news? That's what should be done. In a short time everybody will know. That's how to show you are grateful for what has been done.'

'Eneberi,' Ajanupu went on, 'I did not see your mother the day I went to your house, but I heard the good news and so I came. I don't believe in hearsay. When I tell my own lies, I mention the name of the person who told me. Ojoru told me yesterday that Eneberi wants to marry you, Efuru. Is it true?'

Efuru began to laugh. She went into the room.

'Why are you laughing? Did I not hear well? If I did not hear well, tell me. Eh, Eneberi is it true?'

'Yes, it is true. I want to marry Efuru,' Gilbert said.

'It is not fair. Honestly it is not fair, Efuru; come out and be ashamed of yourself. Why did I hear this outside and not from you? Efuru this is very much unlike you. Why have you treated me in this way? Why? As if I don't count any more. Or is it because I am Adizua's mother's sister? Perhaps you thought I was going to tell her about it, or what, I don't know. This is bad. I am going.'

'Please, Ajanupu, don't go. Let me explain to you,' Efuru pleaded.

'All right, explain to me. Give me your reason for not telling me.'

'I finally agreed to marry Eneberi only about eight days ago. We have not made it public yet, and you know how people talk. Don't worry, Ajanupu. You know that you are my mother today. Before I do anything I must consult you.'

'Only that you did not consult me in this case. But never

mind. I am glad it is Eneberi. Eneberi, you have got a good wife. Look after her well and you can see that you are blessed. Efuru, Eneberi is a good man. He is very responsible and will take care of you. But Eneberi, have you told your mother about Efuru?'

'Yes, I have told her and she has no objections whatever,' Gilbert said.

'I am glad that she does not object. You know that I don't look at people when I talk to them. Eneberi, if I don't say it to you, I won't say it to anybody. Your mother is difficult to please. She is going to give Efuru trouble. I am sorry to say it, but it is true. You are going to help Efuru in seeing that your mother does not interfere too much in your affairs since you and your mother are going to live in the same compound.

'Efuru,' Ajanupu went on, 'I know you can live with the devil himself. You are going to follow your mother-in-law with sense. With sense, I say. You are not a child, so I trust you will be in control of everything. When your mother-in-law talks harshly to you, do not answer back. I am going. That's how I talk to my own.' But she did not go. She hissed and continued: 'Adizua, the broken one, he can die wherever he is with that worthless woman of his. A man who was asked to eat on a plate and he preferred to eat on the floor. Serves him right.'

She went at last. Gilbert and Efuru discussed the carrying of wine to Efuru's father and Efuru saw him off to the Iroko tree and came back. As she was coming back, she was stopped by a woman she did not know.

'The daughter of Nwashike Ogene, the family who cook goats with twenty pots, the family whose ancestors killed leopards with their bare hands. The daughter of a great man. Thank you for what you did for your sister, Nnona. Thank you, my daughter. That's how sisters should behave to sisters, thank you. Mbona, mmekea.'

'Thank you, mother,' Efuru said. She did not know her, but she had to pretend that she knew her otherwise she would be offended.

'Mother,' she said, 'are you well. Are the children well?'

'We are well, my daughter. It is hunger.'

'Let it be hunger and not ill-health. Ill-health is worse.'

'Yes, ill-health is worse, my daughter.'

That night, Gilbert and some members of his family went to

134

Efuru's father's house. They brought with them kola-nuts, palm wine, home-made gin and schnapps. Gilbert's people and Efuru's people filled the obi of Efuru's father. Gilbert's relatives told the people why they had come and Efuru was asked whether they should drink wine. Efuru asked them to drink. After the wine, the dowry was settled, and Gilbert paid in cash.

'You have done like a man,' Efuru's father said to him. 'Men of these days are not as responsible as we were in our days. They want to marry wives, but they don't sit down and count the cost. Appearances are sometimes deceptive, but as I can see, you look good and responsible. Look after my daughter well. Don't ill-treat her. Both of you are adults so one does not have to talk too much. She has had a bad and unhappy experience. Her former husband rough-handled her. Don't treat her like that. She is a good women. I don't say this because she is my daughter. I say it because it is true. So live in peace with her. Efuru, my daughter, come here.' Efuru came and knelt down in front of her father. 'You married Adizua without my consent. But I prayed our ancestors to make your marriage a success. We are forgiving in our family. This is your husband. Take care of him and he will take care of you. Don't speak harshly to him. If he annoys you, wait until you go to bed. Then ask him softly why he annoyed you. He will explain. Respect your husband and your husband's people. Always greet them well. It costs nothing to be courteous to people.

'Our people, thank you for coming. And my daughter's husband's people, thank you also for coming. You all have seen the dowry. It is twelve pounds and ten shillings. My son-in-law has done like a man. You know that my daughter married Adizua before, and he deserted her for another woman. My daughter has seen a husband and the custom is that the dowry is to be returned to Adizua's people. We shall wait for them according to the custom of our people. When his people come, we shall give them back their money.

'My daughter had one daughter from that marriage and, as the gods would have it, she died. When Adizua's people come, we shall give them their dowry, and nothing more will connect us with that family. So the gods have willed it, so will it be.'

'So it will be, so it will be,' the people said.

The people drank into the early hours of the morning. Efuru

took the jar to Gilbert's house. She spent that night there, and in the morning she returned home for the final preparation to go to her husband's house.

In the morning the news spread that Gilbert had taken a wife. When Gilbert's mother went to the stream that morning, people congratulated her. 'Well done!' they said to her. 'We hear your son has taken a wife. Well done. We shall come and see the new wife,' they said.

The first year of Efuru's second marriage was a happy one. Gilbert loved and respected her. Efuru on the other hand knew the duties of a wife. She did not for one moment slack in her duties. She did not only take good care of her husband, she was sweet to her mother-in-law. She did not for one day give her cause to be dissatisfied with her. She would go to the market and buy kola-nuts for her. She would wash her clothes when they were dirty. She would cook for her and if she went to the market or to collect her debts, she would ask Ogea to cook for her. Occasionally, she would make nni oka and cook ogbono soup and take them to her. When she and Gilbert went to Ndoni to buy some fish or ground-nuts for sale, and they made good profit, she would buy clothes for her.

So Gilbert's mother considered herself lucky to have Efuru as her daughter-in-law. She confided in her and treated her as her own daughter. Before Gilbert married Efuru, his mother had done nearly all the housework. Now with Efuru and Ogea in the house, she had more leisure which she needed in her old age. She no longer cooked, Efuru took care of that.

But what pleased Gilbert's mother most was the fact that since her son had married Efuru things had moved well for him. Any trade she put her hand to was profitable. Soon Gilbert began to contemplate building a house of his own and buying a canoe. Efuru told him that a canoe would be better at that stage. So they bought a canoe and gave it out on hire and this fetched money for them. In no time they bought another canoe which they also gave out on hire and when Efuru saw that they could afford to build a house they began the house. They were going to rebuild the father's house first and later on, they would build their own house in the new layout.

Gilbert was very happy with his wife. He was proud of her

and respected her. They were so much together that people admired them. They went to the stream together, there they swam together, they came back together, and ate together.

One day they went to the stream, and while they were swimming the people in the stream began to gossip.

'Husband and wife, they are swimming together,' one woman began.

'They come to the stream every day,' another said.

'Nonsense, why should they swim together? Are they the only happy couple in the town? I see them every time I come to the stream. It is disgusting. Can't anybody talk to them?'

'They are simply showing off. I bet they are not as happy as they look. You give them two years, and we shall see what will happen.'

'Seeing them together is not the important thing,' another said. 'The important thing is that nothing has happened since the happy marriage. We are not going to eat happy marriage. Marriage must be fruitful. Of what use is it if it is not fruitful. Of what use is it if your husband licks your body, worships you and buys everything in the market for you and you are not productive?'

'Are you not in a hurry?' said the only reasonable one among them.

'What hurry? Of course not. What are they waiting for?'

'But they have been married for only a year.'

'Hear what she is talking. How long does it take a woman to be pregnant? What are you talking about?'

At this stage, Efuru came up to the shore to take her water-pot. 'Did you come to the stream?' she asked them calling them by names one by one and greeting them.

'Yes, our Efuru, we came to the stream. How are you and your husband?'

'We are well.'

'And your mother-in-law?' one of the women asked.

'She is well.'

She took her water-pot and swam out to meet Gilbert. When they finished swimming, they came out, Gilbert greeted the women.

'Oh, Eneberi did you come to the stream with your wife?' asked one of the women.

'Yes.'

'Are you well? Is your mother well?'

'My mother is well.' Gilbert and Efuru changed and went home.

'Did you look at her body when she was changing?' one of the women asked.

'So you looked at her body. I watched her too. Nothing has happened. You can be sure of that, nothing has happened. And I am afraid, because Eneberi is the only son of his mother. His mother would love to take care of her grandchildren. Nonsense, I must see Eneberi's mother. A woman, a wife for that matter, should not look glamorous all the time, and not fulfil the important function she is made to fulfil.'

'Yes, you must go to her,' the others agreed. 'Go to her and find out what she thinks herself.'

The next day one of the gossips went to Gilbert's house to see his mother. 'Is Amede at home?' she asked from outside.

'Who is that my sister calling? I am in,' Gilbert's mother replied.

'Oh, is that you, Omirima? Welcome Nwadugwu,' Gilbert's mother greeted her visitor.

'Our Amede, Nwezebuona. How are you?' the woman asked.

'We are well. You have come to see us today?'

'Yes, I have come to see you today.'

'Is it well?'

'It is very well. I just said I should call on you today. It is very well.'

Gilbert's mother called someone who brought kola.

'I took some purgative medicine. I won't take kola.'

'Ew-o-o is that so? All right you can take the kola home, it is yours.'

'Thank you,' the woman said and put the kola in one of her wrappa and tied it very tightly.

'As you have taken some purgative medicine, is it well?'

'My stomach is dirty. So I took some purgative to clean it out.'

'What purgative medicine did you take?'

'Ojoru gave it to me. It grows at the back of her house. You pick the leaves and use it in cooking some nice yam pottage. Then eat it first thing in the morning.'

138

'Oh yes, I know it. I have taken it myself. It is very good.'

'Yes, it is much better than any of these purgative medicines sold in the market.'

'It is much better, are you feeling well now?'

'I am feeling much better. I have gone many times already. I feel clean inside. It is the purgative medicine I give my children when their stomachs are dirty.'

The two women rambled on until Omirima got up to go.

'Amede, I am going. I just said I should come and greet you today. Where is your son's wife? Has she gone to the market or somewhere?'

'She has gone to the stream with her husband. They returned from Ndoni today and they have gone to the stream to wash their clothes. Young couple. They remind me of my youth.'

'Why must they go to these places together? It is your fault for allowing them to be together always. Are they companions? Don't they know that a man and a woman should not be seen together often whether they are married or not. Amede, you must see to this. You behave as if you are not the one any more. What has come over you?'

Gilbert's mother did not say a word. The woman's objections came as a surprise to her because she had not thought of them before. She remembered when she was newly married to Gilbert's father. If they had to go to a place together, she allowed her husband to go in front while she walked behind him. But it was different now with her son and his wife.

'Young people of this generation are different,' she said.

'And has she told you anything yet?' the woman continued.

'No, she has not told me anything yet. But did you hear anything?'

'No, I have not heard anything, that's why I have come to you. It is a year since your son married. One year is enough for any woman who would have a baby to begin making one. Find out quickly and if she is barren start early to look for a black goat, because at night a black goat will be difficult to find. Besides, there are other girls you will like to have as daughters-in-law.'

'You are right, Omirima, you are right. I shall find out. My daughter-in-law should be productive. We are productive in our family.'

'All right, Amede, I am going. Thank you.'

'Thank you, my sister, go well.'

Gilbert's mother could not sleep at all that night. She was lost in thought. The only alternative, if Efuru was not product-ive was to marry another girl to Gilbert. She did not find it easy to discuss the matter with Efuru who was so good she did not want to upset her.

About a month after the woman's visit, Gilbert and Efuru went to the market at Ndoni. They went to buy some ground-nuts which they were told were abundant there at that time. They went in their canoe and a relative of Efuru followed them to be their cook. This trip took a long time. By the time they reached Ndoni, they saw that there were no ground-nuts at all there. They were told to go farther down the Great River. When they were tired of paddling they stopped in Ogwu and Efuru suggested that they should buy corn instead, since the price of corn was good. Gilbert did not like this suggestion. He wanted to go farther in search of ground-nuts.

'I am tired of paddling, Eneberi. Let's buy corn in Ogwu. We shall make some profit from it. You can see that we have left home for a long time, and we have not bought anything yet.'

'No, we originally set out to buy ground-nuts, let us go far-ther, we shall see ground-nuts eventually.'

'You will do all the paddling then. I told you I am not good at paddling. I prefer trading at home. It is more profitable for me than this tiresome paddling.'

'Lazy woman. You prefer to stay at home and do nothing.'

'You know I am not lazy. I am tired of paddling and nothing will make me go farther. Leave me here. I shall follow some of our people home.' She put the paddle on the floor of the canoe and folded her hands. Gilbert looked at her, shook his head and stepped out of the canoe. The sun had just gone down when Gilbert left. He did not come back until next morning. Efuru was awake all night. If she had known where to look for her husband, she would have done so but she did not know where to go. And so she stayed in the canoe afraid of what might be happening to her husband. 'Why has he behaved in this way?' she asked herself several times.

When Gilbert arrived in the morning, Efuru greeted him as if it was quite normal that he should leave her in a strange place all night. When it was time to eat, she brought the food and they ate.

'Are you ready to go this morning?' Gilbert asked. That was the first thing he said to her.

'Where, my husband?' Efuru asked sweetly.

'To where we can buy some ground-nuts,' Gilbert replied.

'I won't go farther, my husband. And if you like you can spend another night in Ogwu. We have been told that to get ground-nuts, at this time, we have to paddle very far into the Great River. I cannot paddle. But if you insist on going, I won't stop you; only leave me here.'

'When can we buy the corn then?' Gilbert asked.

'When you are ready,' Efuru replied, trying very hard to suppress her anger.

After breakfast they went to the market and bought some corn. All along Gilbert was not happy with the purchases but Efuru did not mind him. She went ahead, arranged for carriers to carry the bags to the canoe, and with their help, the bags were neatly packed.

'If you don't mind, we can leave this evening. You can see that the Great River is calm,' Efuru suggested.

'I am not leaving tonight,' Gilbert said.

'Oh, you want to spend another night in the town. I won't stop you. But remember that thieves could come at night and steal all the corn we have bought. Then we shall go home empty-handed. It will be your folly, and I shall tell mother how it happened.'

Gilbert did not say a word. When it was night, he went out. He came back at about midnight and they started the homeward journey.

Two years passed and Efuru was still not pregnant. Her mother-in-law could bear it no longer and so she called her one day to her bedroom.

'My daughter, doesn't your body tell you anything?' she asked Efuru. Efuru knew that this question must come eventually. She, on her part was afraid. She had thought of seeing the doctor who was the only person to help her. She did not want to go to a dibia. Somehow she did not trust them. The only one she trusted was dead.

'No, my body does not tell me anything, mother.'

'Wouldn't you like to do anything about it? It is two years now since you married my son and if you are not pregnant by now, there is something wrong and you should see a dibia.'

'I shall see a dibia.'

'You will do something about it,' her mother-in-law said.

'Yes, we shall do something about it. I shall see Eneberi first.'

Efuru and Gilbert talked at length how best to solve the problem. At last, they agreed that Efuru should see the doctor. She was not to wait for the doctor to come home. She was to go to Onicha where the doctor had his clinic.

CHAPTER NINE

Efuru went to see her father one evening. She had been having strange dreams of late and she thought that her father would be able to tell her the meanings of her dreams.

Her father was sitting in his obi when she arrived. 'Agundu,' she bent down and greeted him.

'O-oh, my daughter, Nwaononaku, are you well, my daughter? Come nearer and sit down by me.'

Efuru sat down near her father. One look at her father showed her that he was getting on in years.

'Are you well, my father? You don't look very well to me. Does Odikama cook regularly for you? If she does not, please let me know so that I can get someone else to cook for you.'

'Odikama cooks regularly for me. But she is not a good woman. This is just by the way. A bad woman can cook delicious meals.'

'You don't want her to continue cooking for you?'

'I want her to continue, but I don't trust her with money at all.'

Efuru and her father were having kola, an angry man entered and Nwashike Ogene welcomed him and asked him to sit down.

'I have something very important to tell you,' the man began.

'Wait, my son,' Efuru's father said. 'You are in a bad temper. I don't listen to people when they are in bad tempers. So keep cool, my son. Sit down first and have kola.' Kola was brought. The young man was still not composed. Efuru's father saw it and kept quiet. Kola was shared, the young man shook his head when it was brought to him.

'Nobody refuses kola in my house, my son,' Nwashike said to the young man. 'Take it and do anything you like with it, but you must take it.' The man took it, and murmured a thank you.

'Efuru, do you know this man?' Nwashike Ogene asked.

'No, I don't know him.'

'Look at him very closely.'

Efuru looked at him closely and confessed that she did not know him.

'I'll tell you. He is the last son of Nnona.'

'The last son of Nnona!' Efuru repeated. 'You don't look like your mother,' Efuru said to the young man.

'I look like my father,' the young man said without smiling.

'Please give us a bottle of gin and a ganashi,' Efuru's father addressed somebody within. The gin and the ganashi were brought. 'You drink some, my son, it will steady your nerves. It has a way of steadying one's nerves.'

The young man refused to have it. 'I don't drink gin,' he said.

'This is unheard of. What does a young man like you drink if he does not drink gin. Are you a woman? Only women don't drink. A man drinks palm wine, and gin. So drink, my son. Drink, for drink has a way of drowning one's sorrows. Drink, my son, it will do you good.'

The man could no longer refuse. It would have been an insult if he had said no again. So he took the ganashi from Efuru's father and drank it all in one gulp.

'Thank you, Agundu,' he greeted.

'You have something worrying you, isn't it true? Someone has provoked you. But when you come to tell me things like this, you have to be composed. If you lose your temper, I won't listen to you. Now tell me what it is all about.' Nwashike Ogene sipped his drink. He did not drink it in a gulp like most of the people.

'I returned from the farm this afternoon with some yams for my mother and my wife who is nursing a baby. I left the yams at the door and went to see my wife because she had her baby in her mother's house. But before I left, I asked Aniche's son to watch the yams for me. Nwashike Ogene, when I came back, goats were feasting on my yams, and Aniche's son was there, just opposite my house. I turned to the boy and scolded him. "You are wicked, Aniche's son. Why were you watching goats while they ate my yams after I had asked you to keep watch over them?" "Am I your servant to keep watch over your yams?" the impudent boy told me to my face. "Who are you talking to like that?" I asked the boy. "I am talking to you. What will you do to me? Who are you to do anything?" So I

144

went and held him by the hand. There was a piece of stick near, so I broke it on him and he ran out yelling and saying very nasty things about me and my mother. Said he, my mother was a witch, she bewitched his brothers and I have come from the farm to kill him. It was time my mother died so that children in the village will live and not die.

'Nwashike Ogene, I have never been so upset before. A little boy of only twelve. With my eyes I saw his mother when she was expecting him. In fact we all went to settle the dowry when our brother wanted to marry his mother. This thing filled my stomach like food. I did not know what to do, so I came to you. It is not so much the yams now as what that boy had the impudence to say. That's why I have come to you. You are the eldest in this family and the father of us all. I am leaving for the farm early tomorrow morning.'

'You did well, my son, to come to me. I don't know what is wrong with children of these days. I shall tell his father and scold him very well, too. You did well to come and tell me; that's what a good man should do. Don't worry; don't take it to heart. And don't have any grudge against the parents, for as you said, they were not there when it happened.'

'I have heard what you said, our father. Thank you, Agundu,' the young man greeted and left.

'Children have bad tongues,' Efuru said. Nwashike Ogene shook his head.

'Don't worry, my daughter. I can bet you that's not how it happened. He is merely exaggerating. There was a feud between the young man's father and Aniche, the father of the boy he flogged. That was what brought all these troubles. It is not good, my daughter, to tell your children what happened many years ago in the family, especially when you know that by telling them you are placing one member of the family against the other. When the young man's father was alive, none of his children would go to Aniche's house and get fire, let alone eat.'

'What exactly happened?' Efuru asked.

'Never mind, my daughter. We don't say things like that. You are children and should not hear such things. I have not seen your husband for some time now, is he well?'

'He is quite well. It is trade.'

145

'I am happy to hear it, live well with him. He strikes me as a good man. When he does anything bad, tell him quietly, don't tell anybody, don't tell me even. Any reasonable man can listen to a wife who does not tell other people how they live in their home. Has anything happened yet, my daughter?'

Efuru shook her head. 'I went to Onicha with Eneberi to see the doctor. He treated me and asked me to come again. I have not gone. We did not tell you because we were in a hurry. There were a lot of things we wanted to do at Onicha then.'

'But these doctors, what do they know about women. Our dibias know a lot.'

'Yes, that dibia I saw before I had Ogonim was very good. It is a pity he is dead.'

'He was good. But there are others. There is a very trust-worthy one but he is not in our town. If you want to see that one, I shall arrange for you to see him.'

'All right, father. Father I have come for another thing al-together. I told my husband and he asked me to come to you. I have been having peculiar dreams of late.'

'Dreams? What kind of dreams?' Efuru's father asked, very interested.

'I dream several nights of the lake and the woman of the lake. Two nights ago, the dream was very vivid. I was swim-ming in the lake, when a fish raised its head and asked me to follow it. Foolishly I swam out to follow it. It dived and I dived too. I got to the bottom of the lake and to my surprise, I saw an elegant woman, very beautiful, combing her long black hair with a golden comb. When she saw me, she stopped combing her hair and smiled at me and asked me to come in.

'I went in. She offered me kola, I refused to take, she laughed and did not persuade me. She beckoned to me to follow her. I followed her like a woman possessed. We went to the place she called her kitchen. She used different kinds of fish as fire wood, big fish like asa echim, aja and ifuru. Then she showed me all her riches. As I was about to leave her house under the water, I got up from my sleep. I told my husband. He could not under-stand the dream. So he asked me to come and tell you.

'What I have noticed so far each time I dreamt about the woman of the lake was that in the mornings when I went to the market I sold all the things I took to the market. Debtors came of their own accord to pay their debts.'

The old man laughed softly. 'Your dream is good. The woman of the lake, our Unhamiri, has chosen you to be one of her worshippers. You have to see a dibia first and he will tell you what to do.'

'Chosen me to be one of her worshippers!'

'Yes, my daughter.'

'Why?'

'I don't know, my daughter, your mother had similar dreams.'

'Is that so?'

'Yes, my daughter.'

'When can we see the dibia then?'

'We shall go on Afo day.'

'I shall come on Afo day, then. I am going. I have not cooked for my husband and it is getting dark. Let day break, father.'

'Let day break, my daughter, greet your husband and look after him well.'

That night, Efuru was deep in thought. She had heard, when she was a little girl about women who were called worshippers of Uhamiri, the goddess of the blue lake. They were dressed in white on the day they sacrificed to their goddess. One particular woman came vividly to her. It was when she was living with the doctor's mother. One morning as they were going to the stream they heard a woman shouting at the top of her voice. They put down their empty buckets and went to see the woman, but by the time they got there, the woman had broken into a song, a very pathetic song, but to the children of Efuru's age then, it all sounded fun. Efuru still remembered the song:

> 'Uhamiri please
> Uhamiri please
> Uhamiri the goddess, please
> Uhamiri the thunder, please
> Uhamiri the kind, please
> Uhamiri the beautiful, please.'

The woman was sitting on the bare floor with her legs crossed and was dressed in white from head to toe. She had rubbed white chalk on her body. To Efuru now, the figure seemed pathetic though it had amused her years back.

The woman sat in that position for days, singing and swaying from side to side; sometimes she would get up, take hold of one part of the thatched roof and shake it vigorously. She was truly possessed.

So, that night after seeing her father, she wondered as she remembered the woman: 'Am I going to behave like that woman? What exactly is going to happen to me? Will I rub white chalk, dress in white, sit on the floor and sing swaying from side to side? No, I am not going to behave like that.'

She was not going to be like that woman. She had known several women who worshipped the goddess but yet behaved normally.

Gilbert was late in coming home that night. She waited. When he came home, she gave him his food.

'My dear wife, the soup is very delicious, come and eat with me.'

'I have eaten. You are very cunning. When you stay out late and you know that I am angry with you, you come home praising my food. Don't praise my food.'

'Come, come, my wife. Women are complicated human beings. You would complain if I did not say anything. Yet you complain when I do say something. What do you want us men to do?'

But it was true that since Efuru and Gilbert returned from the Great River, the latter had been keeping late nights. She did not worry herself about this, because Gilbert's late nights were not yet as bad as Adizua's. Adizua would come back and refuse to say a word to anybody. But Gilbert was different. He always apologized for returning home late.

'I have see my father about that thing,' Efuru said not exactly to Gilbert.

'Did you say anything to me?' Gilbert asked.

'I said that I have seen my father about that thing, don't you hear?'

'I have heard, my wife, and what did he say, my wife.' He put his arm round her waist. 'You are becoming very beautiful every day, my wife. I am really taking good care of you, only don't finish all my money.'

148

'Eneberi leave me. I am talking about something very important and you come up with your jokes. You are still a boy.'

'And that's why you married me.'

'I have seen my father and we are going to see the dibia on Afo day.'

'I would have gone with you, but I won't be at home on Afo day.'

'Where will you go on that day?' Efuru snapped.

'I am going to fish.'

Efuru began to laugh.

'Why are you laughing?' Gilbert asked.

'You are laughing yourself.' Efuru said still laughing: 'Why don't you fish any more? Is it because there are no more moonlight nights?'

Gilbert smiled and went on eating: 'You were the cause of it. You made me fish that night, and you made me stop fishing afterwards.'

'How?' Efuru asked interested.

'Let it be so,' Gilbert said and continued eating. 'When do you say you are going to your father again?'

'On Afo day,' Efuru said.

'You must go. I have thought of it. You must go to the dibia. I want us to see the head and the tail of this.'

Efuru went to her father on Afo day. Her father was not very well. 'You have come, my daughter. I cannot go to the dibia today, so I have sent for him. He will soon be here. I cannot lift these two legs.'

Efuru got up to look at the legs. 'Are they swollen father?'

'They are not swollen. If they were swollen, I would have used shear-butter on them. They are so painful. They don't appear to be my legs.'

'We shall see what we can do, father, when doctor comes home. When will the dibia come?'

'He has been sent for. He will be here any time from now. Do you still have your dreams?'

'No, not so often as before.'

'You see, your mother had similar dreams. Now that you are here, I recall these dreams of your mother. Your mother prospered in her trade. She was so good that whatever she put her hand to money flowed in. When she sold pepper, she made huge profits; when she sold yams or fish, she made profits also. She was so rich that she became the head of her age-group. She spent a lot of money for her age-group. Then she took titles. She was about to take the title of "Ogbue-efi" when she died.' Nwashike Ogene hissed and shook his head.

'She was like you. Of all my wives, I loved her best. She never for one day annoyed me. Even when she did, she behaved in such a way that I forgave her before she asked for forgiveness. I wept and wept when she died. For days I refused to eat, for she cooked all my food. I did not hate my other wives, no, we don't do that in our family. I was fond of her not because of her beauty but because of her goodness. If I gave her one pound to buy things for me for my age-group, or things for my own use, she bought me things worth my money. If she was given any change even if it was only threepence, she returned it to me. But others? the others? They nearly killed me. They cheated me each time I gave them money to buy things for me. One of them, I won't mention her name, I gave some ogbono to sell and she cheated me. Your mother was not at home then. The ogbono was worth some ten pounds, so your mother told me. My wife took it to the market and sold it. She brought back six pounds. I was furious. She swore by all the gods and goddesses of our people that that was what she sold the ogbono for. I left her. Days after I heard from a reliable source that she sold the ogbono for twelve pounds. I said nothing to her.

'You are like your mother, my daughter, that's why I love you more than all my children. So when you ran away from my house, to your first husband, I was very upset. But never mind, my daughter. It is all right now. Our people's anger does not last long. Our people cannot refuse their children because of anger. It is not done in our family. I am happy with you now, especially as you have had another husband. So I am . . .

'It is the dibia,' Efuru's father said to her. 'He is very talkative.'

The dibia was seen emerging from behind one of the buildings on the compound. He swayed from side to side as he walked as if he was drunk, but he was not drunk. He had never been drunk in his life.

'Agundu,' he greeted Efuru's father as he got to his obi.

'Ogbu madu ubosi ndu na agu ya,' Nwashike Ogene saluted.

'That's it, Nwashike Ogene, that's my salutation name. That was my father's salutation name. Those days? They were terrible days. But we still retain that salutation name. Perhaps for prestige. I don't like to relive the life. It is very bad to do evil. That's why I won't do evil. My father and my father's father did evil. They were guilty of murder. I was very young then. One night, a man was beheaded in my grandfather's house. I saw with my own eyes when one of our young men was murdered in cold blood – a young man. He was from our village. I still remember that young man's face before he was cut down. His blood flowed like a young stream on the mud floor. But God is great. Fear Him. For ten years, no child cried in my father's house. My own mother had seven children, all boys. All died immediately they were born. I was the only one who refused to die. Until my father died, he was atoning for the crimes of his father. I am still atoning for the evils of my people.'

'That's what happened,' Nwashike Ogene said. 'But sit down and let's look for kola. You have been standing since you came, if you stand too long, you will cause strangers to come to us.'

'You are right,' the dibia said and sat down. 'Some days I feel like talking, today is one of the days. I became a dibia because I saw too much. I saw things that could blind the devil himself. I am a poor man now. But there is no day I don't eat. If I don't eat in the morning, I eat in the evening. If I want to sacrifice to my ancestors, I can always get a fowl.

'One woman came to me years ago and asked me to divine for her. I brought out my instruments. I called on our gods and the ancestors to help me. To my horror I saw that she was not clean. Her heart was evil. I stopped abruptly. I looked steadily at her, and she tried to hide her face. Then I bellowed at her! You dare come to me with an unclean heart and expect me to "see" anything for you. I don't do that. So I asked her to go home, when she was clean she could come to me. She was sorry. She asked me what she should do. I did not ask her what she did. It was not necessary. I asked her to buy a white fowl and sprinkle the blood on her husband's obi; then I asked her to ask for her husband's forgiveness if she had wronged him. Then I asked her to keep herself holy for four days beginning on an Orie day.

'That was what I told her, Nwashike Ogene. So my fathers taught me. I cannot "see" anything for a person who is evil. If a woman commits adultery and comes to me, I cannot do anything for her. Her sins blind me and nothing is revealed to me. Likewise if a man goes to a married woman and comes to me, I cannot "see" anything for him.

'So, Nwashike Ogene, I am here today because you are good and your daughter is good. I don't as a rule go to people's houses, but you are an exception. You are great. Your fathers were great. My fathers were great also, but they were guilty of murder. Guilty of murder I say, but, well, let it be. Where is your daughter? Is she the one sitting there? Don't mind me, my child, that's how I talk. Occasionally I feel like talking like this. Because you see I was . . .'

'Enesha Agorua,' Efuru's father called quietly. 'Don't talk any more. Let's go on with what we have sent you for.'

'Do you say I should not say anything more Nwashike Ogene? I won't say anything more then. You know all. You know what I am suffering. You know how the world has left my family. Let it be. I won't say any more.'

The dibia opened his dirty bag, took out a dirtier rag and wiped his eyes. Tears were beginning to cloud his eyes. It is pathetic to see an old man's tears. He fought back his tears and looked into space. He said no more.

His family had been large and prosperous years ago before the Europeans came. The men in that family were blessed with male children. Every year their wives had boys, they rarely had girls. Women liked to marry into the family because there were many men there.

They were also strong. When they went to the farm they worked hard, and they were rewarded with big fat yams. Those who took to fishing were even more successful. They took titles and really dominated the whole town because of their number and strength.

Then trouble arose in the village. The head of the family bungled, and as a result there was a feud between the families of the same village. It was most unfortunate. The two families were brothers. They sacrificed to the same ancestors. So it was childish for them to quarrel. Then just when the relationship of these two families was improving, a young man from the other side was waylaid by Enesha Agorua's family. He was brought to the head of the family, and without mercy, the young man was murdered in cold blood. The dibia was a boy then and witnessed it.

The family was now empty as the dibia refused to marry. He was atoning for his father's sins.

The sad story of the guilt and extinction of his family was the cause of his sadness. He always said that it was better to talk than to keep quiet. He respected Nwashike Ogene, and he too knew the story. So he was the only person to whom he could open his heart.

Kola was brought and as Nwashike Ogene was breaking it, he began to tell the dibia about his daughter. 'Enesha Agorua, it is about my daughter, Efuru. She has been having dreams and she wants to know the significance of the dream.'

'Ogbu madu ubosi ndu na agu ya,' Efuru saluted.

'Good, my child, good. That is my salutation name. I was about to warn you that before you start addressing me, you must salute me first. You already know that. I am glad you have not forgotten our customs.'

Efuru narrated some of her dreams and added that some mornings after these dreams she felt particularly happy.

'You are a great woman. Nwashike Ogene, your daughter is a great woman. The goddess of the lake has chosen her to be one of her worshippers. It is a great honour. She is going to protect you and shower riches on you. But you must keep her laws. Look round this town, nearly all the storey buildings you find are built by women who one time or another have been worshippers of Uhamiri. Many of them had dreams similar to yours, many of them came to me and asked me what to do. I helped them. Some of them remember me, some don't remember at all.

'Now, listen to me. Uhamiri is a great woman. She is our goddess and above all she is very kind to women. If you are to worship her, you must keep her taboos. Orie day is her great day. You are not to fish on this day. I know you don't fish, but you should persuade others not to fish. You are not to eat yams

153

on this day. You are not to sleep with your husband. You have to boil, roast or fry plantains on Orie days. Uhamiri likes plantains very much. You can even pound it if you like. When you go to bed, you must be in white on Orie nights. You can sacrifice a white fowl to Uhamiri on this day. When you feel particularly happy, or grateful, you should sacrifice a white sheep to her. Above all, you will keep yourself holy. When you do all these, then you will see for yourself what the woman of the lake would do for you.'

'Is that all I am to do?' Efuru asked.

'Oh, wait, that's not all. I have omitted the most important thing. Listen, my child. You are to buy an earthenware pot. Fill it with water from the lake, and put it at one corner of your room. Cover it with a white piece of cloth. That's all you have to do.'

'You have done well, Enesha Agorua. My daughter and I are happy. What is your charge?'

'My charge?' Enesha Agorua asked, surprised. 'My charge?' he asked again and shook his head.

'How can I take anything from you, Nwashike Ogene? How can I forget so soon. It is an insult to ask me to take anything from you. Ada, meaning Efuru, I am going.'

'But you must take something,' Efuru tried to persuade him.

'No, I won't take anything. Your father knows, Ada, that I cannot take anything. Of what use will ninepence be for me, for that is normally what I charge for outsiders.' He left, murmuring to himself.

'Tomorrow, very early, take a bottle of home-made gin, one head of tobacco and ninepence to him. He will not refuse them,' Efuru's father advised.

CHAPTER TEN

Efuru had just returned from the stream and was getting ready for the day's market when Ajanupu arrived.

'Is that Ajanupu?' Efuru asked from within. Ajanupu answered and she was asked to come into the bedroom.

'Is it well, as you have come so early?' Efuru asked.

'Adizua's mother is very ill. We don't know whether she will live. I spent last night with her. She had you in her lips all night.'

'Adizua's mother is ill? Why have you not told me earlier? I have been in town for the past eight days. You should have sent for me earlier. What is she now?'

'She is in her house. One of my children is with her.'

Efuru took her wrappa, tied it quickly, and she and Ajanupu went as fast as possible to see Adizua's mother.

She was lying on the floor of her dark room. The room was stuffy and one's eyes watered as one went in, for there was an open fire at one corner of the room and she was warming herself. It seemed as if there was no life in her. She lay there in a heap.

The sick woman raised her head when Efuru and Ajanupu came in. When she saw Efuru, she made a great effort to sit up.

'My daughter,' she began. 'My daughter, have you come to see me before I die? Ajanupu, didn't I tell you that my daughter will come to see me when she hears of my illness. I can die in peace now that you have come, my daughter. You are looking very well. I am all bones and no flesh. But you looked better when you were my son's wife. My son, he wronged you. Let's not talk about that. I am glad you are happy with your husband. Sit down here.'

Efuru sat by her side. 'The fire is quenching, mother, let me kindle it for you.' Efuru went near the fire and arranged the firewood properly. The fire was blazing again. 'Are you very cold?' she asked the sick woman.

'Yes,' she said nodding her head. 'You make me very happy,

my daughter. It is gratifying to see that you still care for me.'

'Where does it ail you, mother?'

'It started with loss of appetite. For days, I could not eat anything. I felt hungry, but when the food was brought, I was unable to eat it.' She paused for breath, and then continued more slowly: 'After a few days, I regained my appetite. But this did not last long. When I ate, I vomited everything out again. Even water could not stay in my stomach. I was very weak, and my body ached. There was nobody to help me. One day, a boy was passing when I was sitting by the door. I asked him to go and call Ajanupu for me. The boy did not come back to tell me whether he saw Ajanupu or not. Luckily for me, Ajanupu came. My daughter, blood is great. She had not seen me in the market for days, so she came to find out what was the matter. But for her, I would have died.'

'I wept the day I saw her,' Ajanupu took over. 'The room was in a mess. There was nobody to clean it. I went back to my house and brought my two children who fetched some water for me. I made the fire and boiled some water. Then I cleaned the room. Ossai was too weak to wash herself. So I washed her, and put clean clothes on her. She did not vomit again. The vomiting was not only due to the state of her stomach; it was due to the state of her room also. You know that my sister is a very clean person. Nasty things make her sick. So when all was clean, she stopped vomiting.

'When I had finished in the house, I consulted some people who recommended a cure. I was asked to get some leaves in the bush. These I boiled and gave her to drink. Luckily for us, she felt better after taking the medicine. But she became worse two days after. Last night, I thought that she was going to die. She had you in her lips all night, she must see you before she breathed her last, she said.'

'This is unlike you, Ajanupu. You yourself know the relationship between mother and myself. You know quite well that when I was Adizua's wife, I never for one day quarrelled with her. Such a relationship had never existed between mother-in-law and daughter-in-law. You know this very well. So if my mother-in-law took ill you should have come first to me. I am glad to have met you alive. What are we going to do, Ajanupu?'

'What you are to do?' Adizua's mother asked before Ajanupu had time to answer. 'What you are to do? You are not to
do anything, my daughter. You are to leave me to die. What
am I doing in the world? Many of the members of my age-
group have died. You want to live when there is something to
live for. My only son is lost. His wife has married again. What
am I living for? Please leave me to go back to my ancestors. I
have lost the willingness to live.'

Efuru and Ajanupu were quiet for some time. Then Ajanupu
broke the silence. 'Ossai, listen to me. I am older than you are.
If death kills old people first, then I shall die before you. You
have me. You have Efuru. You have my children, they are fond
of you. You know that very well. Adizua is not lost. Adizua
will be found.'

The sick woman allowed this to sink down for a few
seconds. Then she shook her head several times in protest.
'What are you deceiving yourselves for? You want me to live
that I may continue to suffer,' she said. Her voice sounded as if
she was very far away. 'My life has been one long suffering.
The bright part of it came when my son married Efuru. But
Adizua hated me. He hated me just as his father hated me. He
did not want me to be happy, and so denied me that happiness I
found in his marriage with Efuru. My son left his wife and ran
away with a worthless woman. My gods and ancestors, I have
not wronged you. I have been upright. I have never stolen in
my life. In all the long years I waited for my husband, I did not
commit adultery. But I have suffered as nobody has suffered
before. And you tell me to live. To live for what? What is the
purpose of living? I cannot live a purposeless life.'

The woman had never seen Adizua's mother in this
mood before. She had never talked to her sister like this
before.

'Help me get up,' she told Efuru. Efuru gave her a hand. She
went slowly to the back of the house. Efuru followed her.
When she finished she came back to the room and sat down on
the bed.

Efuru saw the sick woman better now. She saw how the
sickness had made great inroads into her health.

'We cannot take her to the hospital at Onicha, because she is
very weak and cannot sit on the back of a bicycle. We shall see

what the dibia here will do for her. Mother lie down again. Let me kindle the fire for you. Don't worry, all will be well.'

Efuru sent Ogea to Adizua's mother's house with yams and fish. 'Do whatever she asks you to do,' she instructed Ogea. 'If she wants anything bought, come for some money.'

When Gilbert returned, Efuru told him of Adizua's mother's illness.

'What have you done for her?' he asked.

'Ajanupu and I want to take her to a dibia. She is too weak to go to the doctor at Onicha.'

'That's good. But mind you, don't behave in a way that will give people cause to gossip.'

'I see what you mean,' she said slowly and thoughtfully. 'I won't give them cause to gossip,' she repeated, and smiled her sweet smile.

Efuru and Ajanupu went to see the dibia. He was in. He asked them to go, for he would catch them up. By the time they arrived at Adizua's mother's house, the dibia was already there. 'I took a short cut.' There was no short cut as both the women knew.

The dibia looked at the sick woman who was in a heap near the fire and was shivering with cold, though the room was stuffy. She did not say anything to the dibia nor to Efuru and Ajanupu. She simply lay there and refused to talk.

'She will live. She won't die until she has seen her son. Her son is not dead. Her son is alive. Until she sees him, she won't die.'

Adizua's mother's eyes sparkled when her son was mentioned. 'Will he come to me before I die?' she asked. The dibia did not answer. He went on:

'It is the absence of her only child that makes her ill.' The dibia went on, talking to Efuru and Ajanupu and ignoring the sick woman. 'I will not give her medicine. No medicine will cure her. She will have to sacrifice to the ancestors and to the gods, so that they will turn the heart of her son towards home. So you are to buy an egg, a bottle of palm oil and a new earthenware pot. When the cock crows, she is to get up and wash her face and hands. She will put the egg in the pot and add some oil. The oil will cover the egg properly. Then she will take the pot to a cross road and break the contents of the pot there.

158

She will then hurry home. She must do this herself,' the dibia said.

'But she is not very strong. Can't I do it for her?'

'She must do it herself. So I am told. It won't be effective if she does not do it herself. After this, she will sacrifice to the woman of the lake. The woman of the lake will approach the Great River and the Great River in turn will soften the heart of Adizua, and he will come home to his mother.'

'Is Adizua in one of the towns on the banks of the Great River then?' Efuru asked.

'Yes, he is in one of the towns, but I don't know the town. My ancestors have not revealed the town to me yet. I shall have to fast and make some sacrifices before they are disposed to reveal the place to me. Adizua is not happy where he is. He is wretched. The woman has left him for another man, so my ancestors tell me.'

Efuru and Ajanupu thanked him and paid his fee which was one shilling. He got up and left, muttering to himself as he was going with his dirty bag hung loosely on one shoulder.

Adizua's mother looked happy. This sudden change of mood was due to the mention of her son and the possibility of seeing him before she died. The sacrifice was performed and she felt better. Efuru got a maid for her. She went every day to see and to console her.

One evening, Omirima came to see Gilbert's mother. 'Are you in Amede?' Omirima asked from outside.

'I am in. Is that Omiria? Nwadiugwu,' she greeted from within. 'Come in and sit down, I am coming.'

'Oh, my sister, Nwaezebona,' Omirima greeted and sat down.

'Welcome,' Gilbert's mother greeted as she came out. 'I have not seen you for a long time.'

'Yes, I go about very much these days, what can one do? One must eat and feed one's children. I am so tired. This world is so full of suffering,' she hissed and shook her head.

'That's it, my sister, what can one do? That's how the world is, the day God calls one, one will have to go. It will be a peaceful end to this wretched life.'

'You know Mgbokwaro?' Omirima suddenly asked.

'Of Umuenemanya village?'

'Exactly, of Umuenemanya village.'

'What happened to her?' Gilbert's mother asked.

For an answer Omirima hissed and shook her head again. 'It is not what one can relate, my sister. It is sad. Children of these days think they know better than their parents, let it be. I don't want to say anything more.'

'Tell me. I know the mother very well. What has happened?' Gilbert's mother asked, getting more and more interested.

'That's what we have been saying. You advise these children not to marry a particular woman, they refuse saying that they will die if they don't marry her. You leave them to do what is in their minds, in a short time something goes wrong. The whole family suffers; children of these days!' she shook her head several times.

'What happened exactly?' Gilbert's mother insisted, a little irritated.

'When Irona wanted to marry that woman, his mother refused. "Don't marry her," the mother said. "Please don't marry her, her mother is not a good woman, she is a woman who ate all she had without thinking of tomorrow. If she went to the market and had a little gain, it went into her stomach. She did not mind starving the next day with her children." But Irona refused to give up the woman. The mother could do nothing. So they were married. Since that marriage, one misfortune after another has befallen them. Money did not flow in as it used to flow in. Amede, my sister, some women drive away riches when they are married.'

'Some bring in riches also,' Amede said.

'Yes, you are right, but that is not what I am saying at the moment. Last year Irona loaded some bags of kernel in a canoe to be sent to Abonema. One night, the watchman knocked him out of bed and asked him to come quickly with him. Irona ran to the stream; the canoe in which were loaded hundreds of bags of palm kernel had capsized. He called his people that night and they helped him get them from the water. Of course the kernel was wet. He was in serious trouble. The white people nearly put him in jail, but he was a strong man and had money to defend himself.

'This happened last year. All our people were in sympathy with him. He collected the little money that was left, and started trading again. His hands make money, you know. In no time he made plenty of money, then just a fortnight ago, the wife took fifty pounds to Onicha to buy some yams. Fifty pounds, my sister, fifty pounds at this time when money is so scarce. She came back to say that thieves waylaid her and robbed her of all the money. Have you ever heard of such a thing in your life? Thieves robbing a woman of all her money – the money tied round her waist – for no woman from our town will put such an amount of money anywhere else other than round her waist. I did not believe a word of it.'

'When did this happen?' Gilbert's mother asked quietly.

'Yesterday, only yesterday she came back with this incredible story.'

'Ewo-o,' Gilbert's mother shouted and clapped her hands. 'What are you telling me today, Omirima. Fifty pounds! Are you sure it is not fifty shillings? Ewo-o, what kind of thing is this? How did it happen?'

'Foolish woman. She only knows how it happened. She had the money round her waist. She said she went to urinate. Two men walked up to her, held her and asked her to surrender all she had. They stripped her naked and got all the money.'

'Where did this happen?'

'Onicha, it happened in Onicha.'

'This is very sad.'

'Very sad indeed; these children will never hear when you talk to them. Serves Irona right. He has married a beautiful woman. I said to myself when I saw her weeping this afternoon. Why are you shedding crocodile tears. You know what happened to the money. Tell the truth to your husband.'

'Was her husband there when you went this afternoon?'

'He was there all right. "Please tell her not to cry any more," he said to sympathizers. That was all he said. I was angry. I bit my lip. If he were my son, I would have taught him the way to behave on such an occasion.'

'What will he do?'

'What will he do? Is that what you are asking; what will he do? You have a son, what will you do if his wife loses so much money? Tell me what you will do. Amede, you don't behave as you used to. They must have bought you over. Well, Irona did not do a thing, the imbecile. And I hear,' she lowered her voice,

'I hear his mother-in-law bought him over with some medicine. He does whatever his wife tells him to do.'

'That is bad.'

'It is their own talk, I have nothing to do with it. You warn the ear, the ear will not hear. You cut the head, the ear goes with the head. He was warned. He refused to listen. Young people of nowadays have ears only for decoration, not for hearing. Let's talk about other things, my sister. How is your daughter-in-law?'

'She is quite well,' Gilbert's mother answered.

'Do I hear that she now has Uhamiri in her bedroom?' Omirima sneered.

'That's what I hear. She and her husband plunged into it. I was not consulted.'

'She has spoilt everything. This is bad. How many women in this town who worship Uhamiri have children? Answer me Amede, how many? All right let's count them: Ogini Azogu,' she counted off one finger, 'she had a son before she became a worshipper of Uhamiri. Since then she has not got another child. Two, Nwanyafor Ojimba, she has no child at all. Three, Uzoechi Negenege, no child. They are all over the place. Why do we bother ourselves counting them. Your daughter-in-law must be a foolish woman to go into that. Amede, you are to blame. Didn't you point out this to her? You are the mother, why didn't you point out this to her?'

'I was not consulted.'

'Where did you go? The house is yours, you should know everything and you say you are not consulted. Are you not ashamed to say that? There is nothing you can do about it now. You cannot mend a broken head. The chances of your daughter-in-law ever getting a baby are very remote now. You must marry a girl for your son whether he likes it or not. If you like take my advice. It is said she makes money, she makes money, are you going to eat money? I am going. When I talk, they say I talk too much, but how can I see things like this and shut my mouth? How can I? I will be failing in my duty to you. I am going. You and your son know why you have not looked for another wife all these years. Efuru must have bought you over with medicine. Any woman who worships Uhamiri must frequent the dibia. I am going.' She got up at last, but she did not

162

go. She sat down again. She lowered her voice and said 'Does your daughter-in-law want to go back to her former husband?'

Gilbert's mother's blood ran cold. She did not expect this question. Truly she had not liked Efuru before, but now she had grown to like her very much. Efuru had won her over completely not with medicine, as Omirima suspected, but by sheer goodness of heart. One could not help liking Efuru after one had any close association with her. The fact that she had failed to give her son any child was not enough reason not to like her. So Gilbert's mother was genuinely upset when Omirima asked her this question.

'Why do you ask that? What did you hear?' her voice was shaking.

'It is not true then, I am happy it is not true. Didn't I tell them it was not true. Please don't mind them.'

'No. Tell me what you heard. I would like to know.'

'There is no point telling you what I heard since it is not true,' Omirima said, disappointed that things were not going according to her plan.

'Well, if you don't want to tell me, don't worry. People must talk. But who put that idea into their heads in the first place? Efuru's former mother-in-law was ill. There was nobody to look after her, so Efuru cared for her. And now you ask me this impertinent question.'

'So it is true that she has been paying her visits?' Omirima went on, strengthened by this information. 'That's it, they saw something before they started talking. Did I say they must have seen something. It is your fault for allowing her to visit her former mother-in-law. That's how it begins. I won't be surprised to see her go back to her husband when he comes back from his wanderings. For, our fathers said that old friends are like the heads of yams that grow and don't die. You are the cause of the gossip, Amede. You have yourself to blame. But, all right I am going. Don't worry. It is nothing. It is not late at all. Look for a young girl for your son. He cannot remain childless. His fathers were not childless. So it is not in the family. Your daughter-in-law is good, but she is childless. She is beautiful but we cannot eat beauty. She is wealthy but riches cannot go on errands for us. As for the gossip about going back to her former husband, don't worry. If she had a child there living, I would have said that she could go back. I am going. Look to your house. You are slacking very much now.' She was gone at last.

'I wonder when the doctor will return,' Efuru said.

'Where did he go?' Ajanupu asked.

'He went to the country of the white people.'

'To do what again?'

'To learn book.'

'You mean he has not finished learning book?'

'My sister, do they ever finish learning book?'

'When did he go?'

'About nine months ago.'

'Nine months in that cold country. I hear it is so cold that they have fire in their bedrooms. So the white people warm themselves like us?'

'Yes, so the doctor said. It is so cold that you cannot leave your doors and windows open. When you go to bed, you sleep with four blankets.'

'Why is the doctor there again? God forbid. God will not agree that I should go to the country of the white people. God, don't allow me to go!'

'God has already answered your prayer. You cannot go, I cannot go. We do not know book,' Efuru said laughing.

'That's it, you are right,' Ajanupu said laughing. 'How is your mother-in-law?'

Efuru sensed something in this dramatic change of topic. 'Why do you ask?'

'I just wanted to know.' Ajanupu preferred plain talk. She could never go about anything in a subtle way, for she believed in speaking her mind at all times. 'Hasn't she said anything to you yet?'

'Like what?' Efuru said without offering any help whatever.

'Efuru,' she said at last, 'it is about you and your husband. Don't you think you will begin now to look for a young girl for him? It will be better if you suggest this to your husband. He will at least know that you want him to marry another wife and have children. If you leave it to him and his mother, his mother might get someone that will over-ride you. You will have no control over her and it will be difficult for you. One day they will tell you, you have no children and therefore no right to be in the house, your wealth notwithstanding.

'Mind you,' Ajanupu went on, 'I don't say that you won't ever have children. You will have children. I have known women live ten years with their husbands without having children and on the eleventh year God opened their wombs. So don't worry about that.'

Efuru went home that night with a heavy heart. It was not the thought of another wife for Gilbert that made her heart so heavy. It was the fact that she was considered barren. It was a curse not to have children. Her people did not just take it as one of the numerous accidents of nature. It was regarded as a failure.

'But, thank God my womb carried a baby for nine months. Thank God I had this baby and she was a normal baby. It would had been dreadful if I had been denied the joy of motherhood. And now when mothers talk about their experiences in childbirth, I can share their happiness with them, though Ogonim is no more.'

All night she thought. She was sleeping alone in her bed. It was an Orie night, and she was in white. She had to keep Orie days holy for the woman of the lake whom she worshipped. She was therefore forbidden to sleep with her husband.

As she lay awake that night, she thought of Uhamiri. 'Perhaps she will visit me this night. Perhaps I shall dream one of those sweet dreams about her. She will show me her riches, trinkets, ornaments and big fishes she used for her firewood.'

Then suddenly it struck her that since she started to worship Uhamiri, she had never seen babies in her abode. 'Can she give me children?' she said aloud. If her husband were sleeping with her, he would have heard her and asked her what it was all about. 'She cannot give me children, because she has not got children herself.'

Efuru was growing logical in her reasoning. She thought it unusual for women to be logical. Usually intuition did their reasoning for them.

At last she slept. She dreamt she saw Uhamiri gorgeously dressed as if she was going to a feast. She had never seen her look so beautiful before. Her long hair was loose on her shoulders and she had a huge fan in her left hand. She was fanning herself underneath the deep blue lake.

CHAPTER ELEVEN

'What are we going to do?' Nwosu asked his wife one night.

'Do about what?' Nwabata replied very rudely.

'About going to the farm this year,' Nwosu replied, taking no notice of his wife's apparent rudeness.

'We shall do nothing. We are going to starve, that's all.'

Nwosu said nothing. He thought for a while, wanted to say something, thought again and preferred not to say it.

' "What can a woman do?" you say everyday. In the end, a woman does something and even then you still look down on women.'

'But listen to me, my wife. You don't understand and . . .'

'And what?' Nwabata almost shouted.

'And what? I told you didn't I? I told you not to take that title, didn't I? After the sale of those miserable-looking yams, I told you to take some money to Efuru, however small. You preferred to take a title. Now there is no money to clear the farm, let alone to buy the yams for planting. What do you want me to understand? To understand that it is better to take a title than to starve? Is that what you want me to understand?' she hissed. It was like the hissing of a snake. Then she turned her face to the wall and covered herself up. She did not go to sleep. How was sleep possible that night?'

'Woman, you are so unreasonable. How many times have I heard this? You know why I took the title. You know how much I was humiliated by the members of my age-group who took titles. You yourself were in support of it at the time. I consulted you. Why are you talking now as if I took it without your consent?'

'You did not consult me. You are lying. That's how you lie against me all the time. You had made up your mind before you told me about it, and I could not stop you. And let me tell you, I am not going to pawn my children again. I will rather starve with them than do that. We have pawned our first daughter already. If you have scraped your eyebrows, I have not scraped mine. I will not go to Efuru either. She is a woman like myself, and therefore I will find it more difficult to go down on my bended knees and beg for more money when we have not paid the debts we owe her. And, mind you, we are already so much indebted to her. She sent you to hospital and was responsible for your bills there.'

'My wife, this is not the way to solve the problem. Let's put our heads together and decide on what to do. This is not the time to blame me. You always blame me when things go wrong.'

'You make me blame you. You think that you know everything when you know nothing. So there is nothing I can do. What can a woman do after all? I have one pound which I changed into paper money. It is the only money I have. I shall use it to trade in cassava. Our second daughter will look after the children, and Idika will go with me.'

'And where do I fit in?' Nwosu asked.

'You fit in nowhere. I warned you not to take that title. You took it because some members of your age-group laughed at you. Are you richer now that you have taken the title? Is it a sin to be poor? Are the members of your age-group who laughed at you, your chi? Have they no poor people in their families?'

Nwosu saw that this would lead them nowhere. He appealed to his wife to see reason, and when it was all in vain, he fell asleep. When Nwabata saw that her husband was asleep, she was furious. Her first impulse was to wake him up to watch the night with her. But her good sense prevailed and she allowed him to sleep. Her life with Nwosu had never been different from what it was that night. Most of the time, they were so poor that they nearly starved. But miraculously enough, they had nearly always managed to solve their financial problems.

This was the fifteenth year of her married life and, when she looked back on those years, she saw that they made up one long suffering. She could not attribute their poverty to laziness. Her husband was not lazy. It was their chi that was responsible. Her husband had worked very hard in his farm and she too had contributed in her small way. But they were always in want. The sense of insecurity had aged her a great-deal.

But then what could she do? Her husband was good to her. He had never beaten her. In fact he had never been deliberately unkind to her. Her husband had no other wife, and her mother-in-law was dead years ago. So nobody molested her. What molested her was poverty.

Looking back on those fifteen years of her married life, she saw her husband in his youth when he was courting her. He had been a handsome man and she had loved him. She did not go to the farm with her parents, but remained at home with her aunt who traded in palm oil. She and others of her age-group went to the beach to collect oil. They made quite some money out of this and she was able in those early days to buy clothes for herself, and to look as beautiful as other girls of her age who collected oil from the beach.

Nwabata's eldest brother objected to Nwosu marrying his sister for no reason at all, or for reasons known only to himself. Nwabata was angry and threatened to elope if her brother did not see reason. Nwosu came to see her one moonlight night. Nwabata's brother together with his gang waylaid him, beat him up and tore his loin-cloth into pieces. This loin-cloth had been bought by Nwabata.

Nwabata wept when she learnt of this. She had an open quarrel with her brother. She told her brother in no uncertain terms that if he tore Nwosu's loin-cloth twenty times, she was going to replace it twenty times.

In the end, she had her way and married Nwosu. That was the beginning of her suffering. She had to go to the farm with him and she had to learn the hard way. She was able to endure it because of the tremendous love she had for her husband and her children.

Surprisingly enough, the following evening husband and wife found themselves going to Efuru's house. Efuru was in. As usual, Ogea brought kola for her parents and took her little brother to the kitchen.

'So these are your eyes?' Efuru asked Ogea's parents after the kola. 'You have not done well. Evil is not good. Since you returned from the hospital, Nwosu, this is the second time I am setting my eyes on you. Did I quarrel with you? Did you hear I said anything behind your back? Why do you behave so childishly? And Nwabata, you have not done well. You have the greater blame. You should correct your husband, for what do they know after all? What you have done is not good at all. And right I have said what I had in mind, and everything is cleared from my mind. Welcome again. Ogea, bring Idika to me.' Ogea brought the baby. 'You have grown my child. Children grow so rapidly. He is laughing, laugh again my child. Ewo-o, there is no tooth in your mouth. How old is he?'

'Four months.'

'Four months! That's too early. He cannot have his teeth now. If he has his teeth at this time, it won't trouble him though. No, let's see, those are two teeth I am seeing. That's right. Did you see them, Ogea?' Ogea shook her head and laughed mischievously.

'You have seen the child's teeth first. You owe him. You have to give him something for seeing his teeth first,' Ogea said still laughing. 'There you are, you saw the teeth first. I know how observant you are. You owe your brother, not me.' Ogea continued to laugh.

'Never mind, I shall do it for you,' Efuru continued. 'When your parents are going, give them one of the fowls in the kitchen to cook for Idika.'

'No, no, that's not it. That's not how it is done. We won't take it,' Nwosu and Nwabata protested.

'That's how and what is done. I saw the child's teeth first and I must give him something. So our fathers did in their days. A fowl is nothing,' Efuru added.

A fowl costs nothing in fact. Since she worshipped the woman of the lake, she had to sacrifice a fowl every Orie day, so she kept fowls. It was cheaper for her to do so.

'Did you hear of a baby born with two teeth in his mouth?' Nwabata asked.

'Ewo-o!,' exclaimed Efuru.

'The baby was born in the farm just after the planting season, a big baby boy. It was the first baby boy of the mother. She had three girls previously. The men in the farm were furious. "You have desecrated the land and the goddess of the land will not give us plenty this year," the men said to her. But the husband was strong. He sharpened his knife and dared anybody to come near and take their baby boy.'

'What happened in the end?' Efuru asked.

'Nobody troubled him. The child is living now.'

'And the harvest?'

'The abnormal boy was the cause of the poor harvest last year,' Nwosu said sadly. 'The goddess of the land was angry with us and we must appease her. So before we start tilling the soil this planting season, we shall sacrifice to the goddess of the land.'

'It is an abomination, our gods, our ancestors, forbid! And the mother of the baby?' Efuru asked.

'She is there, she was afraid, but her husband strengthened her.'

'He must be a remarkable man,' Efuru said. 'Very remarkable indeed.'

They went on talking about many things, then Nwosu asked. 'We heard that you have installed Uhamiri in your room.'

'So they said,' Efuru replied laughing.

'Well done,' Nwosu congratulated. 'We are glad. It befits you. You are a woman of note in our town today and if you don't do it, who else will do it?'

'That is right,' Efuru said of want of any other thing to say.

'Efuru, we have come to your house. My husband and I have come to your house,' Nwabata said unexpectedly. Nwosu was surprised but glad. At last the ice was broken. They had quarrelled last night, and this evening his wife had asked him to go to Efuru with her. He had obeyed. It surprised him to see that after all his wife's vehement protests about going to Efuru the night before, she was ready to go with him unsolicited. He attributed this again to the unpredictable nature of women.

'I don't know how to begin,' Nwabata went on. 'We owe you. And we are not even able to pay. We thought we could pay part of our debt after this harvest, but it was not possible. Our harvest was poor. Let me cut a long story short. It is planting season again and we have no money to hire labourers to clear the farm. We have no money to buy yams to plant. That is why we have come, Efuru. Please help us. There is nobody we can go to. You are the only person we can go to. You know us well and our nakedness.'

Efuru shook her head and hissed. 'You don't know the value of goodness,' she said sternly. 'Poverty does not affect the reasoning power or the innate goodness in human beings. Poor people do not behave foolishly. I gave you money last year without interest. You harvested your yams and did not bring me yams. You did not even come to tell me that you had sold your yams and could not pay me. Nwosu, you were ill and I sent you to the hospital. I paid for everything. When you returned you disappeared. What I heard next was that you had taken a title. It is planting season and you have come to me, hoping to get some money. Have I a tree that bears money as its fruits? Am I not a human being? Am I not free to be angry when I am provoked? Ogea's parents, you have not done well. Put yourselves in my position and see whether you would be pleased if someone did this to you. It is because of Ogea that I have the patience at all to listen to you. I am fond of her, otherwise, I would not have listened to you. How much do you want?' Efuru asked to the surprise of Ogea's parents. They had thought that after scolding them, she would send them away empty-handed. Nwosu looked at his wife, but she was not helpful.

'Whatever you give us, we shall take,' Nwosu said.

'Will ten pounds be enough for you then?' Efuru asked.

'Yes, ten pounds will be enough for us.'

'All right. It is late now, and my husband is not at home. When he returns, I shall tell him. So come on Nkwo evening.'

Nwosu and Nwabata went home. Husband and wife slept soundly that night.

After a short time, Nnona was seen coming from the gate of the compound. She was apparently sad. All day she had been muttering volcanically to herself. She had on two wrappas, one round her waist and the other round her chest. She greeted Efuru in a sad voice and sat down. 'What brings you here this night? Is it well?' For an answer, Nnona began to weep. 'Why are you weeping? Please don't weep in my house this night. What is the matter?'

Nnona wiped her eyes and said: 'Efuru, my daughter, I don't know what to do.' Tears filled her eyes again and she wiped her face with one side of her wrappa and continued: 'I don't know what to do. Everyday, I go to ferry people across the lake, I come home with one shilling, and some good days with one shilling and sixpence. I put the money in a cigarette-tin and put it in my box. Yesterday, I came home with only ninepence. It rained heavily and so we did not have passengers to ferry. I looked for the box, but it was gone. I ransacked everything in my house but it was nowhere to be found. My world is bad. My chi does not take care of me. My chi has left me. I have been saving this money with the hope that I can use it in buying an old canoe next year. And now the money is gone. A thief has stolen everything. Our ancestors please visit that thief. See that nothing good comes his way. See that a sudden death meets him on the way. See that he is inflicted with the white disease. See that that money . . .'

'That will do,' Efuru said quietly but firmly. 'Wipe your eyes. How much was in the tin?'

'Fifteen shillings, sixpence and halfpenny.'

'Ogea, bring me that small box near my bed.' Ogea brought the tin. Efuru opened it and brought out sixteen shillings. 'You take this. But if you want me to keep it for you, I shall do, so it is all yours.'

'Weo-o, my daughter, my daughter how can I thank you? Eh Ada Nwashike Ogene, how am I to thank you for this? Thank you, my daughter, thank you. Ogea, please thank her for me Nwaononaku, Mbona, my daughter.' She took the money and went away.

'If you continue giving people money in this way, they will take advantage of your generosity and worry you all the more.'

'I know it very well, but what can one do? It is difficult to deny these people anything. Come Ogea, unroll the mat; I want to go to bed now. What is keeping Eneberi from coming home again this night? The night is deep and people have gone to bed.'

'He said he was going for a dance and some drinks.'

'So he said. I am sure they are not dancing and drinking now.'

Efuru then went to bed. She had not been asleep long when she heard a knock on her door. She got up quickly and opened the door. Gilbert was standing at the door. He was not drunk but his mouth smelt of home-made gin and cigarettes. Efuru hated the smell of home-made gin and cigarettes. It made her sick. If Gilbert was drunk that night, she would have simply shut her door and refused him entry.

'I am sorry I could not come home in time. We went to drink in Okoroafor's house. One of our age-group's child died and we went to cheer him up. So Okoroafor, our group-leader, invited us to his house for drinks. We started dancing there. Then Anozie invited us to his house, we drank and danced there. Adiberi Izunne invited us also, and there we met our age-group women's branch, we joined them and danced till now.'

'And danced till now? Nobody told me there was a dance of our age-group tonight. And in any case, no woman in our age-group will continue dancing till this late hour. You know where you go every night. One day you will reveal yourself. I am old enough not to worry. Do you still want to have your supper?'

'Of course yes. I am very hungry.'

'I thought you were given food where you went.'

'No, my wife, I was not given food there. You know I enjoy your food very much. So I always look forward to eating your food. None of the women of our age-group can cook half as well as you. So I consider myself lucky in being your husband.'

Efuru laughed aloud. What woman was not susceptible to flattery. Especially if it comes from a man she loves.

While Gilbert was eating, he insisted on his wife sitting beside him and filling his glass with water. 'When I tell some of my age-group that I am greater than they are, they think that it is because I am prosperous. They don't know that is is because I am blessed with a good wife. My wife, this soup is very delicious. It is like the one you cooked for me when I was courting you and . . .'

Efuru laughed loud and long. 'The difference is that you did not kill the fish,' she said still laughing. Gilbert went on eating.

When he finished he washed his hands and relaxed in his chair. By the time Efuru finished clearing the plates, he was asleep.

'Eneberi, Eneberi,' Efuru called, but there was no answer. 'That is what you do every night. You come home late, eat and sleep. You and your wife cannot sit down like husband and wife to discuss important things that affect us. Tomorrow morning you go off and I don't see you again till night.' She sat down beside her husband. She was soon asleep.

The cock crew and she got up to start the day's work. She

was surprised to see herself in her husband's bedroom. She did not remember going there last night. She looked for the small hurricane lamp under the bed and lit it.

'The day has not broken,' Gilbert said sleepily.

'The cock has crowed.'

'Has it? You are very light you know, and a heavy sleeper too.'

'So you carried me to the room last night?'

'Yes, I did. What is today?'

'Nkwo.'

'Tomorrow I shall go to the Great River to buy some fish and crawfish.'

'Eneberi, I am thinking of getting a wife for you.'

'Why?' Gilbert asked surprised.

'You know why. This is the fourth year of our marriage and I have not had an issue for you. We have lived happily these four years. And I am worried. If we get another wife, a young girl, she will have children for you and I will love the children because they are your own children.'

'I may not like your choice,' Gilbert said.

'That is no problem. You are going to be shown several girls and you are to make your choice.'

'I don't quite like this arrangement. I don't care whether I have a child or not. And . . .'

'No, please be frank, you do care. Don't feel for me. All men care for children. If you don't like the method I want to use, say so. Perhaps you want me to leave it entirely in your own hands?'

'Not exactly that. Well, if you want it that way, I won't insist. But see my mother about it.'

'Yes, I shall see your mother about it. She is going to help too.'

'All right. It is settled then. Let's go to the stream.'

'I like them,' one woman said as Gilbert and Efuru were leaving the stream.

'When two people live like that, then the world is worth living in,' another added.

'What do you admire in the lives of those two?' Omirima asked contemptuously.

'Do you know what they went through last night? Don't be

174

carried away by the fact that they come to the stream together and swim and play in the deep.'

'You are right,' one of the women said.

'Have they children?' another asked.

'Children? You don't pluck children from a tree you know. You don't fight for them either. Money cannot buy them. Happiness cannot give you children. Children indeed, they have no children.'

'What is he doing? Foolish man. He sits down there and refuses to do anything. He doesn't see young girls all over the place to take one as a wife. It is their business not mine.'

'Hasn't the young man a mother?' one of the women asked.

'I went to the mother the other day. I said to her: "Did Efuru give you medicine that you have lost your senses? You see your only son married to a woman who is barren, this is the fourth year of the marriage, and you sit down and hope." '

'Why does she not allow her husband to marry another wife when she is barren?'

'But can't the husband do anything about it? He is to blame for letting a woman rule him. I am sorry for him. Please Ojiuzo help me with my water-pot. This news is like a fairytale, azigba – woo.'

Omirima finished her washing, and carried her pot on her head holding the cloth she had washed in one hand.

CHAPTER TWELVE

'Have you heard what I am hearing?' Ajanupu said excitedly to Efuru in her sitting-room, before Efuru had time to welcome her.

'What have you heard? Is it well?'

'Have you not heard that thieves broke into Nwosu's house last night and carried away everything? They carried everything, swept the house and left the dust on the front door.'

'Uhamiri forbid, our ancestors forbid. Last night?'

'Yes, last night, my sister, Efuru. Last night that broke into this morning. I am so afraid.'

'Have you gone to see them?'

'I have not gone. I went to Afagwu's house to collect some purgative medicine for my children. Three of them had frequent stools yesterday, and I want to give them purgative to clear their stomach of dirt. Afagwu told me as I was picking the leaves. So I left the leaves and came to tell you. Ewo-o! Thieves! What has Nwosu? What did thieves want in Nwosu's house?'

'I gave them ten pounds only a fortnight ago. Ewuu, the thieves have stolen it. Ogea, please get me my head-tie, I am going out now, I shall be back soon.'

The two women walked very briskly breaking into a run occasionally. 'Ewo-o,' a woman exclaimed as she saw Efuru and Ajanupu. 'Are you going to see them? Go and see them. It is very bad. They stole everything. What are we going to do about thieves in this town? The world is bad. In my youth, there was no stealing. If you stole you were sold as a slave. If your property was stolen, you simply went to one of the idols and prayed him to visit the thief. Before two or three days, you recovered your property. But these Church-goers have spoilt everything. They tell us our gods have no power, so our people continue to steal.'

By the time Ajanupu and Efuru reached Nwosu's house, only a few sympathizers were there. Nwabata was on the veranda.

She had her hands between her thighs. She did not say a word to anybody. She simply nodded as sympathizers came and went. Efuru and Ajanupu sat down and Ajanupu began: 'Nwabata, what are we hearing? What is the cause of this?'

Nwabata nodded. She had refused bluntly to say anything to the numerous sympathizers. For all she knew the thieves might be among them. When sympathizers came and blabbed, she merely looked at them, shook her head or nodded, according to what they said. She did not like them. She did not want anybody to sympathize with her for she believed that most of the women sympathizers who came to her feigned commiseration. But when she saw Efuru and Ajanupu, she made signs to them which meant that they should wait until the host of females had gone.

'Tell us how it happened,' Ajanupu finally said when she saw that the women had all departed.

Nwabata adjusted her wrappa, removed her hands from between her thighs and folded them on her chest. 'It is not a small thing,' she began. 'Yesterday, I had a feeling that something was going to happen. What it was, I did not know. But I knew that something bad was going to happen to me. When I started having that feeling, I went to the room and brought out my box which was in the mud wardrobe. The money Efuru gave us was there. I also had one pound there too. I brought all out and put it under my pillow. Nwosu was angry with me. "You women are very troublesome. Why are you bringing out that box from the mud wardrobe?" I said nothing to him, but before we went to bed, I went to the mud wardrobe again and brought out my empty money-bag. Nwosu nearly lost his temper for I disturbed his sleep. I put the money in the bag and tied it round my waist.

'I knew when the thieves entered the room, but I was afraid to shout. So I pretended to be asleep. They took everything. They even raised my pillow to look under it. There was nothing there.' Nwabata paused for some time, tears filled her eyes. She fought back her tears and went on: 'They stole everything. Even the ogbono soup and the nni oka I cooked last night were carried away by the thieves. I saw one eating the soup greedily.

'When they were satisfied that there was nothing more to be

stolen they left, leaving the door open. It was then I raised an alarm. Then Nwosu woke up and came out with his knife.

'Yes, it was then that my lord and master came out with his knife. Kill me, I said to him. I am the thief. He fooled around and went and sat down outside the gate. That's the man who is my husband. Women are nothing. He, my husband, was asleep when thieves came to the house. But I am only a woman. What can a woman do?

'Efuru, and Ajanupu, you see me here, able to talk because the money you, Efuru, gave us was not stolen. It was that money that they came for. I could see them, searching desperately in the nooks and corners of the room, opening tins and boxes. Thieves! I am greater than you are, because you will for ever continue to steal. I am greater because you steal my things; I am greater than you are because you work in darkness and I work in light. Sons of darkness, rogues and vagabonds; our gods will visit you. Utuosu, please visit them one by one.'

'It is enough, it is enough. You should be glad you did not raise an alarm when they were in the room. They would have killed you.' Ajanupu said.

'Raise an alarm? God forbid that I should fight against a thief. When they steal and leave me alone, I shall work and replace all that they have stolen.'

'I am so afraid of thieves,' Efuru said very timidly. 'I am not afraid of ghosts or such imaginary things, but thieves, oh no, I am afraid of them. What if you wake up suddenly at night and you see a thief in your bedroom, and he is somebody you know? He will simply kill you.'

'Of course, yes, he will kill you.' Ajanupu said and went on: 'When I had my first daughter, thieves came to our house. I had just fed my baby and she was asleep, I was about to sleep, when I heard some digging going on at the back-yard. I was afraid. The digging continued. It was then that it dawned on me that thieves were outside. My husband was not in. I said in a very clear voice: "You thieves who are digging at the back-yard, I am waiting for you. When you finish digging, come in. I will show you what a woman can do." "Haven't you slept, you witch?" one of them asked in a dialect that was not ours. "I have slept, come and steal, you lazy drone. Come in and steal. Come in and lick your blood."

178

'My brother-in-law was at home, luckily for me. He heard me and through his window he fired a gun. The thieves took to their heels. Till today, no thief dare come to our house. Cowards, thieves are cowards.'

'Efuru, keep the money for us. We don't know when we shall go to the farm. They have stolen all our pots, plates and children's clothes. Even our mortar is stolen. What are we going to use in the farm? My world is bad. What have I done to deserve this? It is high time I went to a dibia. Perhaps I have wronged our ancestors unknowingly. Perhaps I am being punished because of a guilt in the family?'

'Don't worry, Nwabata, that's how the world is. When trouble comes to you, everything goes wrong, even your fire does not kindle. That is life. We are going.'

'Thank you, go well.'

'I am so sorry for Nwosu and Nwabata.'

'I am sorry for them too but what can one do in this bad world? Come, Efuru so you gave them money again this year for their farm?'

'What do you want me to do, Ajanupu? They are Ogea's parents. If I don't give them, who will give them? I gave them ten pounds again. I was angry with them though and told them so.'

'You have money. I don't behave like that you know. If I lend you money you have to pay back what you owe. It is quite a different thing if I gave it to you as a present.'

'Who is that girl coming?' Efuru asked as they saw a girl coming from the opposite direction.

'Oh, her name is Nkoyeni Eneke. You know her, don't you? Her mother is your age-group,' Efuru said.

'It is true. She looks like her mother. She has grown so big.'

The girl greeted them in a casual manner and passed.

'Come, my daughter, why don't you greet people? Eh, Nkoyeni Eneke, why don't you greet your elders?' Ajanupu looked offended.

'Ewo-o, mother, I didn't know it was you.'

'You must greet your elders, my daughter. I know your mother very well. So when you see me next time, greet me. There is nothing in greeting. How is your mother?'

'She is well.'

'Greet her for me. Tell her Ajanupu sent greetings. All right go well. She is a beautiful girl.'

'Who knows whether she is engaged to be married?'

'It is easy to find out. She is beautiful and well behaved too. She will make a good wife for Eneberi.'

'But she looks like she is going to school, that will be a hindrance.'

'That is no hindrance. She will have to leave school if we decide to have her as Eneberi's wife.'

That evening, Efuru told her mother-in-law about Nkoyeni Eneke. When she finished, the woman shook her head: 'My daughter, Eneberi my son will not marry the daughter of Eneke. There is murder in that family. There is curse in that family. Eneke is not a good woman, how can a bad woman have a good daughter? We shall look somewhere else for a wife for Eneberi. There are many girls in town. Good girls are rare, as rare as a precious pearl, but one finds the precious pearl if one has patience.'

'All right, mother. Our people say that a stranger has eyes, but he does not see. I don't really know the girl's home background. Ajanupu and I saw her today and we thought we would recommend her for Eneberi. But since you say no, I won't insist. Have you anybody in mind for Eneberi?'

'You are taking keen interest, my daughter, in getting a wife for your husband. It is good. I am happy.'

'I want my husband to have children. I am barren.'

'Don't say that, my daughter, please don't say that. You are not barren. God will open your womb, in his own good time. Do you know Nwanzuruahu Nwanegbo? She is the only daughter of Nwasobi of Umuosuma village.'

'Is she Nwasobi the singer? She is a very beautiful woman. She is dark in complexion, and has a beautiful set of teeth?'

'Yes, that's the one. Her daughter is as beautiful as she is. She has pleasant manners; if she sees you twenty times in a day, she greets you twenty times. She is very gentle. She does not open her mouth. She is just like her mother. We shall make inquiries about her. Ajanupu will be of help.'

'I don't know the family at all. What is her father like?' Efuru asked.

'Her father is dead, and her mother has married again. But it is a respectable family.'

'We shall make inquiries. It is always safe to make inquiries in a matter like this. I am going out, mother. I shall be back soon.'

'Ogea,' Efuru's mother-in-law called. She called many times before the girl answered. 'Your ears are not for hearing, but for decoration. Go and bring the clothes you washed for me today.' Ogea brought them. She examined them. 'Look, there is soap in this one, and in this also. A big girl like you cannot wash properly. Get out of my sight.'

'Who is making you angry?' Amede turned round and saw her friend Omirima.

'Omirima, welcome, sit down. What about your children?'

'They are well. Who has been annoying you?'

'It is that silly girl, Ogea. She washed my wrappas and all of them will have to be washed again because there is still black soap on all of them. How is it that a grown-up girl like that is not able to wash clothes properly? How can she live in a man's house?'

'That's what I keep on saying, children of these days are no good. How men of today marry them is what I cannot understand.'

'Let me bring you kola.'

'No, I had an injection yesterday.'

'Injection yesterday? Did the doctor come?'

'Yes, the doctor came yesterday. You know I have been suffering from "bad blood". So I went to the doctor and had an injection. I am feeling much better now.'

'That's good. I am glad to hear it. When next the doctor comes, I shall go and have an injection. This my waist is not mine.'

'Your daughter-in-law will take you to the doctor when next he comes.'

'No, I won't wait for Efuru. She will take me to Doctor Uzaru who never gives me injections.'

'What does that mean?'

'Don't mind him. No cure is effective without injections. It goes through your body, driving out to the surface the diseases in the body and curing many more. But medicines you just swallow them and they go to your stomach. Injection is better,' Gilbert's mother concluded.

'The doctor who came yesterday gave everybody injection, and he charged only seven shillings and sixpence.'

'That's very expensive. Did you not ask him to make any reductions?'

'Well, he started by saying that we should pay ten shillings. Some of the people began to leave. When he saw this, he called them back and cut it down to seven shillings and sixpence.'

'When he comes again please come for me.'

'All right, when he comes again.'

'You don't want anything at all, Omirima, not even a little alligator pepper? Shall I give you some?'

'Please don't worry. By the way how are you getting on with your daughter-in-law? Have you and your son decided to leave her to do as she pleases?'

'Meaning what?' Gilbert's mother asked. Omirima was not disturbed by this question.

'I mean that your son should marry another girl who will bear children for us. I mean that Efuru is barren and therefore cannot reproduce. Have you understood me now?'

'Why are you so vehement about this, Omirima?'

'In other words you are saying that I have no right to discuss it. You talk like a child. You forget our relationship. You forget that my great grandfather and your grandmother had the same father. So Eneberi is my son, as well as yours.'

'It is true, Omirima, it is true. But you know marriage and what it involves. I won't say more. My son and his wife are now looking for a wife.'

'That's better. That's what I want to hear. I can now be truly alive. And, have you anybody in mind for him?'

'Yes, we are thinking of Nwanzuruahu Nwanegbo, do you know her?'

'Know her? I know her too well. Don't you know her? Our Uhamiri forbid that our Eneberi should marry such a girl. Don't you know her mother and her father?'

'Her father is dead.'

'Yes, her father is dead. But do you know what killed him?'

'He died of small-pox.'

'You don't know. What a pity. He did not die of small-pox. You were deceived. Arushi killed him. He stole and swore by Arushi – a very fearful one to be exact. Before the month was out, he died. So he was thrown into the evil forest. He was not buried.

'I don't know the girl. But I know her parents and that is more important. She is the daughter of Nwasobi the singer of Umuosuma village. The woman who does not sleep on a mat. Amede, there must be something wrong with you these days. I am afraid something is influencing you.'

'Really? I did not know all this. It is true what our people say, that a traveller who asks for directions never misses his way.'

'The father was a thief. If Eneberi marries her, their children will be thieves. If a child does not take to his father, he must take to his mother. And, as you know, children copy bad things more easily.'

'It is a pity. The girl is beautiful. Look at her set of teeth and her complexion.'

'Are you going to eat beauty, Amede? What has come over you?'

'Are you sure these things you say are true of the parents of the girl? I think I will have to investigate.'

'Do what you like. I have told you what I know.'

While Omirima was there, one of Ajanupu's children came. Ogea had gone to the stream and Efuru was out. The child greeted Amede and Omirima. 'Where is Efuru?' She asked.

'She has gone out.'

'Will she be long in coming back?'

'I don't know.'

'What about Ogea?'

'Ogea went to the stream.'

'I am going.'

'Come back, don't go. Why are you so much in a hurry?'

'My mother said I should come home quickly. That she will beat me if I didn't come home quickly.'

'Did she not tell you to leave a message?'

'She said if I did not see Efuru or Ogea, I should not give anybody the message.'

'All right, my child, go well.'

'Amede, so you put up with this nonsense. What is wrong with you?'

Amede did not say a word. But she did not encourage Omirima.

'Ajanupu has many children.'

'Yes, she has so many children,' Amede said.

'She is blessed. She has several boys and girls. That's good. What is annoying is when some women have about six children and all of them are girls. What one will do with six girls I don't know.'

'But it is nobody's fault. When God gives you a girl, you don't throw it away.'

'You are right. It is nobody's fault. Did you hear of Onukwume Uzoechi?'

'Yes, she had her seventh girl two years ago and her husband's relatives were angry with her.'

'That is not all the story, my sister, let me tell you. She had a boy last year.'

'A boy last year?'

'Yes, a boy, a bouncing baby boy. The strange thing is that boy looks like Onukwume's husband.'

'What is strange in that? That's as it should be.'

Omirima laughed. 'Onukwume knows the owner of the child. Her husband is not the father.'

'What are you saying?' Amede asked in surprise.

'Onukwume herself admits it. So don't ask me questions. She quarrelled with one of the relatives of her husband before she had the baby boy. This relative told her that she was nothing in the family until she had a baby boy. And she had a baby boy.'

'Then you conclude that her husband is not the father of the boy?' Amede asked quite astonished.

'I am telling you what happened.'

'And does the husband claim the child?'

'Of course he claims the child. There was a big celebration last month. As the guests were eating and drinking, some of them were making fun of him. You mean you did not hear it?'

'I did not hear. It is strange. Is the boy alive?'

'Very much alive. He will know when he grows up. I am sorry for him.'

While Omirima was still with Amede, Ogea returned from

the stream. Amede helped her with the big water-pot. 'I have told you not to carry this big water-pot. It is very big, and heavy loads will deter your growth. You will be so short that no man will marry you.' Ogea laughed. She showed Amede some fish she caught with a basket in the stream.

'What are you going to do with it?' Amede asked.

'I am going to show it to Efuru.'

'She is so late in coming home today, and it is getting dark.'

'Where did she go?' Omirima asked.

'She went to collect her debts,' Ogea replied. Ogea left to prepare the evening meal.

'She will do, you know,' Omirima said.

'Do for what?'

'Do for Eneberi as a wife. So that when Efuru spends so much on her parents in future it will be understandable.'

'How do you mean. I don't understand.'

'Have you not heard that Efuru gave twenty pounds to Nwosu and Nwabata, and that thieves stole the twenty pounds. And that she also gave them twenty pounds last year which they have not repaid. Don't you know that if Ogea marries Eneberi, the money Efuru is lavishing on Ogea's parents will not be totally a waste, but will be in the family somehow.'

'Ogea is a good girl. But it will be awkward for her and Efuru,' Gilbert's mother said.

'It will be awkward at first, but both will soon be used to the situation. Efuru must be very rich. It must be Uhamiri that gives her money. But why does she give Ogea's parents so much money?'

'Because they are Ogea's parents.'

'Is that all?'

'And Efuru is fond of Ogea.'

'Well, it is their business. It does not concern me at all. Amede, I think I must go now, it is getting dark and I shall cook for my children. Their father went to the farm. I wonder when he will come back.' She began to get up but with difficulty. 'It is this foot, Amede, this foot. When I sit down for a long time, I find it difficult to get up. Let day break, Nwaezebuoma.'

'Nwadigwu, let day break.'

CHAPTER THIRTEEN

When Gilbert returned from the Great River, he was told that his good friend Sunday Eneke was on leave. Gilbert was happy about this, and wanted to see his friend at once, but the fish and the ground-nuts bought from the Great River had to be sold before he was free to make social calls. It was therefore, a busy time for him. He came home each day from the market very tired, and slept as soon as his head touched the pillow. When the commodities were sold, he went to see his friend Sunday.

Sunday was in the army and had come home on leave for the first time since he was recruited. He and Gilbert attended the same elementary school and both left in the same year. Sunday had wanted to be a teacher, but when the war came he joined the army. He did not join the army voluntarily or out of any conviction whatever. It happened in a most dramatic way. A very impressive British Army Officer, he must have been a lieutenant, came to their school one afternoon. He had a brief talk with the headmaster, and Sunday together with four other huge boys joined the army. His parents wept the day he said good-bye to them. His mother could not get over it. She wept and nagged her husband who was as foolish as to send her son to school. If her son had been one of the simple illiterate boys in the village, he would not have gone to the army.

No soldier had ever returned to the little town since the war began, but they had heard fantastic stories about soldiers. Soldiers ate human flesh. If they were hungry and there was no food to eat and nobody to eat either, they cut their own flesh and ate it raw. If they were thirsty and there was no water to drink, they drank their urine. Sunday's mother heard these stories. So each time she remembered them, her blood ran cold.

Gilbert and Sunday were happy to see each other and they soon fell to talking about old times.

'Do you still play football?' Sunday asked.

'I don't play any more. When you leave school, you hardly

186

do any of the things you were doing when you were in school. Even if I had wanted to play people would have laughed at me. And some would even attribute it to irresponsibility.'

'I continued with my football in the army.'

'Your own case is understandable. I don't know how to play now. I would give anything to live that life again. Do you still remember that match we played against Amuku?' Both men began to laugh.

'What didn't we do to win?' Sunday asked.

'I still remember the night the captain and I went to see the dibia who gave us a talisman each for the team.'

'The talisman did not work, for we were beaten.'

'You remember our goal-keeper?'

'I remember,' Sunday replied.

'He complained that several times in the goal-mouth he saw over twenty balls without knowing which to catch. And of course he always caught the wrong one. And so we were beaten by, I think, four goals to one.'

'Yes, four goals to one. And you remember that we were all searched by the referee before we started the match.'

'The referee saw nothing for we buried the charm that the dibia gave us at night.'

'And where did we bury it? Can you remember?'

'In the centre of the field. The charm was to demoralize our opponents and confuse them.'

'Despite all this, we were beaten. Our supporters were very sad. Some of them attributed our defeat to the cry of a strange bird that flew past just before we started the match.'

'But our captain excelled himself that day. He was simply wonderful. He played as he had never played before. The gods were against us. We were not destined to win.'

'And where is he now?' Gilbert asked.

'Our captain, "Eric the field" so we nicknamed him in those days. He was a wonderful centre-half. His shots were terrific. No goal-keeper could stand them. He had a style all his own. He joined the army and now that the war is over he has a good job. I saw him when I was returning from Lagos. His wife cooked a most delicious lunch for me.'

'Who is his wife?'

'You remember that very beautiful girl called Agnes who was in standard four when we were in six? The girl who nearly always took the first position.'

'She is tall and fair,' Gilbert added.

'Yes, she is tall and fair. But don't mistake her for that big girl who was in standard four for four years,' Sunday said laughing.

'No, I know the one you mean. She was a member of the choir, and sang beautifully.'

'Exactly, that's the girl.'

'So, Eric married her at last. And you say they are happy?'

'They are very happy. It is a joy to be with them.'

'You remember that on many occasions Agnes's mother came to the school to report to the headmaster that Eric was a bad influence on her daughter, and begged the headmaster to use his influence in putting an end to the association of her daughter and Eric.'

'I remember very well. Agnes made it clear to her mother that she would rather commit suicide than live to be someone else's wife. In the end her mother gave in. I am happy that they are happy.'

Sunday's sister returned from the stream. She put down her water-pot and ran inside to change.

'Who is that?' Gilbert asked.

'Don't you know her? She is my youngest sister, Nkoyeni.'

'Your youngest sister? The little girl who usually helped you with your books when she saw you returning from school?'

'Yes, she is the one.'

'She has grown so big. Girls grow so rapidly these days. I wouldn't have recognized her in the street.'

Gilbert remembered the day Nkoyeni wept because he called her his wife. Sunday and Gilbert were outside doing their arithmetic homework when Nkoyeni returned from the stream carrying a very small water-pot. She was about nine years old at the time. She was beautiful and wore large red beads round her waist. Her body was very smooth for after swimming in the lake, she rubbed some coconut-oil and plunged into the lake again. The effect was remarkable – beautiful beads of water formed on her body. They had not all disappeared by the time she got home. Gilbert helped her with her miniature water-pot and was so indiscreet as to call her his wife.

Nkoyeni was upset. She threw away the cloth she used in balancing the water-pot on her head and wept, railing abuses on Gilbert who dared to call her his wife.

Gilbert and Sunday laughed and watched her mischievously.

'Oputa,' she called her brother, for that was Sunday's pagan name. 'Please tell that person not to call me his wife again. I am not his wife.'

'You are my wife whether you like it or not. I am going to pay the dowry today, this very day.'

The little girl began to cry all over again. She rolled herself on the ground and dirtied her beautiful smooth body. This angered her brother Sunday. 'Enough of it, you little fool. If you don't stop that nonsense I shall get a whip and break it on your body, do you hear? Look at her face. Won't you be glad to have somebody like Gilbert as your husband, you fool? You dare shout again.'

Nkoyeni kept quiet. She was fond of her eldest brother, and so did not want to annoy him. So she wiped her tears, and as she was entering the room, she eyed Gilbert in such a way that the two boys could not help laughing.

'Don't cry, my wife,' Gilbert teased again. 'And don't eye me like that. I have already told your mother. You must be my wife.'

Nkoyeni wanted to shout again but she looked at her brother, shot another ugly look at Gilbert and muttered: 'When my mother comes, I shall tell her that you called me your wife,' she said in between sobs.

Gilbert chuckled as he remembered this incident which happened some ten years ago.

'And what is she doing now?' Gilbert asked his friend, Sunday.

'She is in school. She is now in standard four. I shall send her to college if she does well.'

'That's good. I am happy to hear it.'

'Ahaa, what about Matthew? That very huge boy who was in school with us. Where is he now?'

'Matthew is in Onicha. He is a big trader now. He has three wives and lives in a big house with his family.'

'I am happy he is doing well. You remember that he was expelled by our headmaster because he wrote a love letter to one of the school mistresses.'

'Yes, and he was given twenty-four strokes of the cane before the expulsion.'

'And when he had the last stroke he turned round and asked the headmaster: 'Is it all? Have you finished?''

The two men laughed and shook their heads.

'A tough boy he was,' Gilbert said.

'Then the headmaster gave him his testimonial with unsatisfactory written in bold letters.'

'And he tore the testimonial to shreds,' the two men said almost simultaneously.

'He appeared so irresponsible in those days, but I knew he was a boy who knew his mind and knew what he wanted. He was the type of boy the authorities could not like.'

'And the headmaster? Where is he now?'

'The wicked soul! He is heading a school in a bush place. I heard from an unreliable source though that he flogged a boy so mercilessly that the boy's parents poisoned him and now his bottom is as big as a barrel.' The two men laughed. Obviously the story was not true, but then that was the only befitting end of the wicked headmaster.

'I hear you are married,' Sunday switched on to a more personal conversation.

'Yes, I am married. This is the fourth year.'

'Pity you did not marry that girl friend of yours. I hear she has been married to a very wealthy man who sent her overseas to learn dressmaking.'

'You mean Clara? We were too young then to think of marriage, remember. But I was very fond of her.'

'How many children have you?' Sunday asked innocently.

'I have a boy, but he is not the son of my wife. My wife has no child.'

'I am sorry. And does your wife know about the boy?'

'I haven't told her about the boy.'

'You haven't told her. Why?'

'I haven't the courage. If she had a child it would be easy to confess to her. I am sure it is going to upset her. You see it is one of those things we men cannot avoid. I went to Ndoni, met this girl, and the result is a bouncing baby boy. I have not told my mother either, though I know she will be very glad.'

'If I were you, I would tell my wife. Don't give her the chance of hearing it from other people. How old is the boy?'

'He is nearly two years old.'

'And you say nobody knows about it in this small town?'

'Nobody knows about it. The mother of my son lives in Ndoni with her parents.'

'I see.'

'And you? When are you getting married?'

'As soon as I can pay the dowry. Ex-servicemen have made things difficult for us. Now a man who has four grown up daughters counts himself a very wealthy man. Each daughter will bring to the father at least a hundred pounds in cash, in raw cash.'

'You are right. But you must get married. It is not in our culture to remain unmarried. Have you anybody in mind?'

'What is the use having anybody in mind? I had one in mind for several years and before I came home, a fellow ex-serviceman snatched her from me. When I have the money I shall have one in mind.' Both men laughed. What was the use of having one in mind when there was no money to pay the dowry. Gilbert remembered the proverb which said that, however good a suitor might be, he was never given a bride for nothing.

Nkoyeni came out, greeted Gilbert shyly and told her brother that she was going to choir practice.

'Do you know me?' Gilbert asked.

'You are Sunday's friend and you are married to Efuru.'

'She knows you,' Sunday said laughing. Nkoyeni left them.

'It is a good thing you are sending her to school. But it is a waste sending them to school you know.'

'I don't understand,' Sunday said in surprise.

'Well, I mean really that boys should be given the preference if it comes to that. If you had a little brother for instance and there is just enough money for the training of one, you wouldn't train Nkoyeni and leave the boy.'

'You are right.'

'Sometimes these girls disappoint one, you know?'

'How?' asked Sunday.

'They get married before the end of their training and the money is wasted.'

'You are right. But it is the fault of us men. We should allow them to finish their schooling.'

'And where does it all end? In the kitchen,' Gilbert answered his own question.

'It does not always end in the kitchen, when the girl is allowed to finish, she can teach and thus bring money in that way.' Gilbert rose up to go.

'You are going very soon. Won't you stay a little longer?' Sunday began to plead.

'No, I must go now. I have been out for a long time. And you remember it is only three days since I returned from Ndoni. I have not had time with my wife since then. Come and see us sometime.'

CHAPTER FOURTEEN

Omirima's voice was heard from a distance and Ogea frowned.

'She is coming, the gossip,' Ogea said under her breath. 'She has never in her life said anything good about anybody. I wonder who is going to be her next victim. She is always running people down.'

'Is Amede in?' Omirima shouted a few yards away from the house.

'She is in,' Ogea answered without looking up.

'You rude girl. Why do you talk to me like that. Look at me. I say, look at me.' She got hold of Ogea's face in both hands and looked at it intently. She hissed and left her.

'Who is your father anyway?'

Ogea did not reply.

'You go and ask questions,' Omirima said.

'What is the matter?' Gilbert's mother asked from within.

'It is the daughter of Nwosu. That ignorant girl. But never mind I have dealt with her.'

'Sit down, and don't worry. She is only a child.'

'A child indeed. Does she not know when there is no salt in the soup? Does she put food in her nose?'

'Don't worry. Leave her. That's how they all behave. Are your children well?'

'They are very well, thank you. It's only my daughter-in-law. She went to school and so she thinks she knows everything. She is so lazy. Have you ever known a woman, brought up in our town who sleeps until the sun is up?'

'No, impossible. Who sleeps until the sun is up?' Amede asked unbelievingly.

'My daughter-in-law, Amede, my daughter-in-law. I have talked and talked, my son does not want to listen to me. Please help me to talk. Go there now, and you will be told by one of the numerous servants that she is in bed sleeping.'

'This is bad. She is unlike our women. Where did she learn

this foreign bad behaviour? I thank God my daughter-in-law does not sleep till sunrise.'

'She learnt it from the white woman. That's what I told her. I said to her, you are not an idle white woman. Women of our town are very industrious. They rise when the cock crows. Husbands of white woman are rich, so their wives can afford to be lazy. An idle woman is dangerous, so I told her to her face.'

'Yes, an idle woman is dangerous. I pity these white women you know. How can one sit down in a big house all by oneself and do nothing? It must be a difficult life,' Amede said.

'My daughter-in-law enjoys it. She does not need your pity. What she does is to keep her children apart. My youngest daughter came back from her house yesterday in tears saying that she drove her away from her house because she has yaws. I went straight to her. You can trust me to go straight to her. I asked her why she drove back my daughter from her house. Did she not know that she was married to my son, and therefore must treat my children and me with respect? Was my daughter suffering from leprosy to merit such a treatment? And what did she say? She said she sent back my daughter because yaws was so contagious and so she did not want her children to suffer from it. She said she would allow my daughter to come to the house only when the yaws was cured. I laughed at her ignorance. What a fool she was, I told her. This is the time for your children to suffer from yaws. You don't want them to suffer from it when they grow up. This is the time. Allow them to suffer from it now and they will be free in future. But what did she say to me? She laughed at me. She said I did not know what I was talking about; that her children will never suffer from yaws; that it was not inevitable that all children must suffer from yaws.'

'Our fathers suffered from it, so did our father's fathers. I have not seen a person, in this town, who has not suffered from yaws,' Amede said.

'Leave her to fool around. She will regret it. These children get on my nerves. What exactly are they taught in that school of theirs that they mock at us and oppose us in nearly everything?'

'That's it. The world is changing. It is now the world of the white people. We and our grandfathers don't seem to count these days. We are old; let me bring you palm wine, that's all I have today.'

'Is it nkwu or ngwo?'

'It is nkwu.'

'Good, bring it if it is not too strong.'

Ogea brought the palm wine in a jug and poured it into a very clean glass. She gave it to Omirima without looking at her. Omirima took it from her and drank it in one gulp.

'It is a good wine. It is like the wine I bought for my husband yesterday. There was not a drop of water in it – just straight from the tree.'

'Ogea bought the wine for me. She knows good wine.'

'Where is Ogea going?' Omirima asked as she saw Ogea with a basket used in catching fish. 'Surely she is not going to fish.'

'She is going to fish,' Amede said.

'Going to fish, Amede? You allow Ogea to fish today being Orie day. The day our Uhamiri says we should keep holy – a day when our women must not be disturbed. And your daughter-in-law is an ardent worshipper of our lake? Omirima, I am ashamed of you. That's why there are no fish in the lake. That's why our Uhamiri is angry with us. The children of these days have polluted the lake. I saw three girls – all school girls, on Orie day, going to fish. I scolded them. You are responsible for the poverty of this town, I told them. I took a cane and chased them. But did they listen to me? Of course, they did not. As I was returning from the market in the evening, I saw them returning from their fishing. That's what they learn in school – to disobey their elders.

'The last flood was no flood at all. And the one before it was worse for it came too early, and damaged the yams, the cassava and other crops. We have these Church-goers to blame. That reminds me. How is your new daughter-in-law?'

'Oh, she is well.'

'How is she getting on with Efuru?'

'Oh, very well. Efuru is such a good woman. She does not make any trouble. She is taking great care of my son and Nikoyeni.'

'That's what it should be in the beginning. You wait and see.'

'No, they won't quarrel. They are both good and sensible.'

'How did they settle that problem of Gilbert's son who came from Ndoni?'

'Problem of my son's son? Who told you?'

'It is repeated everywhere. Our town is a small one. Of course, everybody in this little town knows that Enerberi has a son at Ndoni. What many people do not know is the mother of the child. However, I am happy that you decided to send the boy back to Ndoni. That was thoughtful of you. But don't you think you should persuade your son to marry the mother of his son? A woman who gave birth to such a boy should be married. You don't know tomorrow. Nkoyeni won't be barren of course – she is pregnant already. But nobody knows whether she is going to have a girl or a boy. She might take the footsteps of her mother who had four girls and a boy.

'We also know that when the boy came, that Nkoyeni was furious. She refused to have anything to do with him, and she was actually responsible for sending the boy away. But we know why she was so angry. She thought she was going to have the first son for Eneberi. Serves her right. Didn't I tell you not to have anything to do with that girl, that her mother was not a good woman?'

Amede did not remember Omirima ever warning her about Nkoyeni. It was she herself who did not like Nkoyeni's mother. She wondered how the arrival of her son's son came to be known by Omirima. The little boy came with his uncle and they remained for three days at the end of which the boy left with his uncle, but Nkoyeni made so much fuss threatening to leave if the boy did not go away to his mother. But Efuru was happy to see the boy. She saw the clear resemblance between him and her husband and treated them very kindly. Of course, she was angry with Gilbert, not because he had an affair with another woman, but because Gilbert kept the whole thing a secret from her until the week the boy was actually coming to visit them.

As for Nkoyeni, she was furious, and did not hide her feelings. She viewed the whole thing with disgust. She argued that the boy was not Gilbert's son, and so she was not going to have a bastard child. So in the end, Gilbert had no alternative but to send the child away to his mother.

'But coming to look at it from Nkoyeni's point of view,'

Omirima went on, 'I don't blame her very much. The boy may be the son of someone else. It is sad to claim someone else's son.'

'No, he is my son's son. He looks exactly like my son. You did not see him, did you?'

'No, I did not see him. You know our people and the way they talk. I am glad the boy is your son's child. Why then did you allow him to go back to Ndoni?'

'I did not want to interfere; Nkoyeni was insistent on the boy going back to his mother.'

'Did you say you did not want to interfere? Amede, I am ashamed of you. Gilbert is your son, your flesh and blood, and so all his problems are yours. You can never interfere in his affairs, because his problems are your own problems too.'

'She threatened to leave us if the boy remained.'

'That is nonsense. Why did you not let her go? There are so many girls in town who will gladly be your son's wife. This is nothing but weakness.'

'What do you expect me to do, Omirima, I am getting old. I am feeling every strain of my old age. And besides, Nkoyeni is pregnant.'

'So what? Is she the only woman pregnant this season? It is expected that she should have a baby before the year is out. If no baby comes in the first year, it is our duty to probe her girlhood, and find out why. I am going. I am wasting my time talking to you, and besides, I am going to Akiri tomorrow morning. Let day break.'

'Go well, let day break.'

CHAPTER FIFTEEN

'Nwabata, I had a very bad dream last night,' Nwosu told his wife when he woke up in the morning.

'A bad dream? Tell me the dream.'

'I saw Nwashike Ogene dressed very gorgeously as if he was going to a dance, his fan in his hand. I have never seen him look so well before.'

'Was his staff in his hand?'

'Yes, his staff of office was in his hand. He looked so handsome.'

'If Nwashike Ogene is not dead, then he is seriously ill; or one of his children is seriously ill. Our gods forbid.'

'I must go to the town, Nwabata. There is no point sitting here thinking.'

Boom! Boom! Boom!

'The cannon, Nwosu, your dream has come true. Nwashike Ogene is dead. But, was he ill?'

'Yes, he had been ill for some time now. A great thing has happened today.'

'Have you heard the cannon?' one man asked Nwosu.

'We have heard it. A great man has gone. Are you going to town?' Nwosu asked.

'Let's go,' the man said.

'Nwabata, I must go now. When you finish the cassava, bring it along with the children. I want to go and help Efuru with the funeral.'

'There, there, it sounds again, like thunder rendering the quiet of the morning. Did you say it is Nwashike Ogene?' the man asked.

'You are right, he is dead then. When you see a man gorgeously dressed in a dream, know that he is dead or about to die; on the other hand, if you see a man in rags in a dream, then he is going to live very long.'

'We must go, Nwabata. Bring the children to town by road. I am going with Igwe. Igwe, you go for your canoe.'

Both men carried their small portable canoes on their heads to the Great River. They got into them, balanced well and off they paddled to town.

'Did you hear the owl crying last night?' Igwe asked.

'I heard it.'

'It is a bad omen. But let's go on, perhaps it is not as bad as we think.'

Boom! boom! boom! The cannon began again to tear the stillness of the Great River. Nwosu and Igwe paddled on in silence. The only sound that was heard for a long time was that made by the men's paddles when the canoe came down on the Great River so rhythmically and reverently. Occasionally, the birds would make a noise among the woods on the other side of the Great River. Then fishes would come up and disappear again into the deep. At one time, one was very near Nwosu's canoe.

'It is ifuru,' Igwe, who was a fisherman, said. 'That's how they behave. They would never enter into your canoe, they only come near to tease you. Oh, the cannon again. Our ancestors help us. A great man has left us. You don't fire cannons when an ordinary man dies. Cannons can be seen only in wealthy men's houses. Cannons are the sign of greatness.'

'Are you returning?' some people asked Nwosu and Igwe.

'Yes, we are returning. Is the town good?'

'We are not from the town. We are from our farm. We have heard the cannon, and we are going to collect a relative who is ill in another farm. When we collect him, we shall go to the town. A great man has departed from us.'

Nwosu and Igwe paddled on in silence. They sang the songs of their age-group – they sang in praise of their ancestors; in praise of their village warriors; in praise of themselves and their children. Then suddenly Boom! boom! boom! – the cannon again began to rend the air.

'Uhamiri shield us,' Nwosu cried out.

'Don't call her name here. Don't you know that she is not on speaking-terms with Okita, the owner of the Great River? If you call her again to our aid, Okita will be angry with us and capsize our canoes.'

'It is true. I talk as if I am a child or a stranger. Okita, please spare your children. Don't harm your children. It is not spite, it is not disrespect; it is mere ignorance, so spare your children.'

'How far it is today,' Igwe observed.

'You mean the town?'

'Yes, the town. It seems as if it is moving away from us. When shall we get there?'

'Perhaps, when the sun is overhead. It is very far you know.'

'Sometimes when I fish, I come as far as this place without realizing how far it is.'

'We are anxious to get to town: that's why it is so far.'

Just out of the blue, a bird began to sing. Nwosu and Igwe looked at each other in astonishment.

'This is strange,' said Igwe. The bird went on singing its beautiful song.

'Why is the bird singing at this time of day?' Nwosu asked in utter amazement.

'That bird sings when the sun is down, in actual fact – when people are eating their evening meals.'

'But hear it now, singing without stopping. It is a bad omen. Our ancestors, please protect us. Have we sinned against you? Have we failed to sacrifice to you? Has any of you, your children been guilty of murder, of rape, or of adultery?'

The bird went on singing, impervious to the men's fears. Then suddenly, it flew out from the woods, above the heads of the men and disappeared into the woods again. Both men nearly lost their balance in their small canoes in utter fright.

For a while the two did not say a word. They paddled on and on. The beautiful blue lake seemed to move farther and farther away from then. The Great River was still. It was the first time the two men had found it so quiet at that time of day.

They paddled on, Boom! boom! boom! The cannon again! 'How many times now since morning?' they asked. It must have sounded six or seven times. It was the death of a great man. No poor man could afford to fire seven rounds of a cannon in a day. Nwosu and the fisherman could now vaguely remember the story of the cannons told them by their fathers. The white slave dealers gave the people the cannons in exchange for slaves. The white slave dealers were the Portuguese, the Dutch, the English or the French. The people regarded them as white men, their nationality did not make any difference, they were all the same. The white slave dealers gave them the cannons, the guns and the hot drinks. The hot drinks did what the Indian hemp is doing in politics today. The only difference is that the hot drinks were legal and the Indian hemp illegal, but both performed the same function.

The cannons were owned by very distinguished families who themselves took part actively in slave dealing. They were distinguished because they were privileged to have had contact with the slave dealers. Nwosu and the fisherman could not recollect what havoc the cannons and the guns and the hot drinks did for their people. All that happened, happened when they were children. Now, the shooting of the cannon did not only announce the death of a great man, but also announced that the great man's ancestors had dealings with the white men, who dealt in slaves.

At last Nwosu and the fisherman saw the waters of the blue lake mingling beautifully, majestically, and calmly with the brown waters of the Great River. The spot could be very calm or very rough, depending on the mood of Uhamiri, the owner of the lake, and Okita, the owner of the Great River. The two were supposed to be husband and wife, but they governed different domains and nearly always quarrelled. Nobody knew the cause or nature of their constant quarrels.

'We have arrived, Ogbuide, Ezenwanyi,' the fisherman greeted Uhamiri the owner of the lake. And as he said this, he took some water with his hand, washed his face, and drank again and again.

'Uhmiri, the most beautiful of women, your children have arrived safely, we are grateful to you,' Nwosu said as he washed his face and drank some water. They paddled on with more vigour now that they were reaching home.

'By the time the sun is here,' Nwosu said and pointing upwards to indicate where he meant, 'we shall get home.' They had no clock to read the time, but they had the sun and the sun to them was more accurate than the clock which was made by man. The sun rose every day and set every day. The people could easily tell the time, or make appointments by merely looking up at the sky.

'Uhamiri is also deserted,' the fisherman observed.

'Everybody has gone to the funeral, that's why Uhamiri is deserted. My dream has come true, I am sure now that it is Nwashike Ogene who has died,' Nwosu said.

'Don't say that, or else the gods will hear you. Don't say it again. It is not Nwashike Ogene who is dead. It is his enemy.'

'Yes, it is his enemy.'

There were some white people swimming. Some of them were fishing in their noisy boats. Nwosu and the fisherman stared at them for a long time, shook their heads, and paddled on.

'Are they not a queer lot? To come all the way to swim and fish here.'

'They are strange people. They come every time to fish, but they catch nothing.'

'How can they catch anything when they do not observe the rules of the woman of the lake. And look at their boats, how can they catch anything in such noisy boats. Fish swim away from them, and besides they disturb the woman of the lake with their boats.'

'It is a wonder she does not capsize their offensive boats and drown them all,' said the fisherman in annoyance.

'You forget, my friend, that our woman of the lake is the kindest of women, kinder to strangers than to her own people. She is very understanding. She knows that the white people are strangers to our land, that's why she is lenient with them. We, her people, dare not be so disrespectful.'

'Why do the white women wear tight dresses for swimming? Why don't they use wrappas as our women do? They have no shame; they do not know that they are naked.'

'You are right. But what beats me is their idleness. How can they leave the comfort of their homes in the big towns and come to swim all day in the lake?'

The two men paddled on. They reached the shrine of the woman of the lake. 'We have returned, the great woman of the lake; the most beautiful of women; the kindest of women; your children have returned safely.' Having thus paid their respects, they moved on.

'Nwosu, welcome, Igwe, welcome. You have heard the bad news – Nwashike Ogene has left us. He has not done well. Nwashike Ogene, the good one, friend of children, lover of peace and of truth. Nwashike Ogene has left us to mourn his loss. Who will replace Nwashike Ogene? Who will be like him in our great village? Death, you do not know how to kill. Death, why do you not kill the wicked ones first? Go along, you will see him lying in state, with his staff of office beside him. You won't know he is dead. You will think he is only asleep. All last night, his daughter, Efuru, cried at his bedside; this morning she lost her voice. She is so upset. Efuru was in the market when she was sent for. By the time she arrived, he was dead – a most peaceful death. That's what it should be. Nwashike Ogene deserved a peaceful death, he was so good.'

Boom! boom! boom! The cannon again. Years ago, they might have signified war between the peaceful town and a war-like neighbour, the people firing their cannons to frighten away the enemies, the crude enemies, who did not have contact with the white people. It was not so today, there was no war. The town was at peace with their neighbours and their gods, god-desses and ancestors. The booming of the cannons was an-nouncing the departure of a great son, the last of the generation that had direct contact with the white people who exchanged their cannons, hot drinks and cheap ornaments for black slaves.

CHAPTER SIXTEEN

'Efuru, listen to me. Your father lived well, and died well. He was a great man, and he died great. Luckily for him, he had a daughter like you to bury him. Why are you so sad about his departure? How many of his age-group members are alive today? I don't mean just alive, I mean really alive in the right sense of the word. What if you were not in a position to perform all the ceremonies? Or are you worried about Eneberi?'

Efuru hissed when Ajanupu mentioned Gilbert. She did not want to discuss it. She was very sad. Gilbert was not at the burial of Efuru's father. He was not at home when the old man died. He was sent for, but he did not return. It was four weeks after the burial and Efuru's husband was not back. It was a disgrace and Efuru felt like killing herself. She cried as she had never cried before. But she did not altogether break down, as people thought. Ajanupu's coming that morning made things worse for her. She wanted to be left alone, entirely alone.

'Didn't Eneberi go to Ndoni?' she asked herself several times. 'Has anything happened to Eneberi?' Had he drowned in the Great River? Had he deserted her? No, that could not be possible. After all Nkoyeni was there and even if he had a mind to desert her, he could not desert his young wife who was expecting a baby.

'Hasn't he come yet?' Ajanupu asked almost in a whisper.

Efuru shook her head and hissed. 'Children of these days, did he not go to the Great River? But Efuru don't take it to heart. He will come back. He will. Some people are coming to see you.'

'Efuru, my daughter Efuru. This is very bad. It is really very bad. I only returned from the Great River this morning. Don't you see my clothes? I have not even changed. I said I must come straight and sympathize with you. Oh, a sad thing has happened. How many are we that death should kill such a great man? Nwashike Ogene, the great man? Nwashike Ogene, the great man of our time, so, death can reach you, even you. Efuru, my daughter, I am sorry. I am very sorry.' The woman sat down on a mat and looked round.

'Oh, is that you, Ajanupu?'

'It is me, Ojizo, how are you? Welcome from the Great River.'

'Your children, are they well?'

'They are very well, and yours?'

'We are there, it is hunger,' she replied. 'Did I know that Nwashike Ogene was ill? Death is bad. Death is wicked. Death is heartless. Nwashike Ogene the truthful, the tall handsome man, it is a great pity.'

Kola was brought and as they were having the kola, other sympathizers came and joined them. Some greeted Efuru and sat down to have their own share of kola or palm wine. Others said a few things in praise of the dead man.

They were gone at last and Efuru was left alone. She was about to go to the room when her mother-in-law, Gilbert's mother, came to her. 'Nkoyeni, it is Nkoyeni, she is in labour. Come and see her at once. She is in her room. I don't know how to do these things. Come quickly.'

Efuru followed her. Nkoyeni was on the floor of her room. She was rolling and shouting.

'No, no, my child. Wipe your tears. Wipe your tears, at once. If you shout this time, you are going to shout in all your subsequent labours. So wipe your tears and lie down on the floor. Ajanupu will soon be here.'

Nkoyeni did not hear. She shouted at the top of her voice: 'I am being burnt inside. It is here, right here. No, it is there, there. Ewo-o, I am dead, I cannot survive this. I cannot, mother I cannot.'

'You can, you can. Say you can. Or else the gods will hear you,' Efuru warned.

'I have heard, mother, I have heard. But it is very painful. It is very painful. Oh, mother, am I going to die? You think I am going to live?'

'You are not going to die, my child. You will live. You are not going to die. Here's Ajanupu.'

'Lie down properly on the floor, I say,' Ajanupu commanded. 'Ewoo, that's the head of the child, that's the head. When I say press you press very hard. If you don't press hard enough, you have yourself to blame. Press now, press – press . . .'

A bouncing baby boy emerged. It was like magic.

'Good girl. You are a wonderful girl. You are a strong girl.' The three women praised Nkoyeni.

'What is wrong with men these days?' Ajanupu complained to Gilbert's mother. 'You must send some people to go for your son. This is getting too much. A man like Nwashike Ogene died and Eneberi did not come home. Nearly everybody in this town came home at the time. And Eneberi, the husband of Efuru Ogene failed to return. This is four weeks since the death. And here again is Nkoyeni, who has given birth to such a bouncing baby boy, and Eneberi is not home. What kind of trade is that? What has come over young men these days. It is disgraceful. Absolutely disgraceful. You must do something. It is humiliating. Our people are talking. Imagine Omirima saying the other day that Efuru should go and consult the dibia who will tell her why her husband has run away from her.'

'Ajanupu, we have sent people. My son will come home. There must be something delaying him. Perhaps it is illness. Perhaps something dreadful has happened to him. But if he is alive, and I know he is alive, he will come back to us.'

Gilbert came home two months after the delivery of Nkoyeni's son. He did not look well. Efuru and Nkoyeni were shocked to see how unwell he looked. In the night, Efuru went to her husband's room: 'Eneberi, what is the matter? You don't look yourself? What happened to you when you went to the Great River? What could have happened to prevent you from coming to bury my father. I was humiliated. I did not think that you could do this to me. Many people who were in the Great River when my father died, returned. My husband whom I have married since five years did not return to bury my father.' Gilbert bowed his head, and said nothing. It was better to keep quiet than to lie, he thought. Efuru was genuinely afraid of the silence of her husband, for he was a warm-hearted lively and jovial man. She could not understand this silence. What she believed was that he was hiding something from her. What that thing was, she did not know.

'Go to Efuru's house and ask her to come immediately –

immediately. Here is your navel. If you don't come back quickly, your navel will disappear. Run.' Ajanupu's son ran like a devil. Luckily for him, he saw Efuru bathing the baby. Gilbert was not in. Nkoyeni was near, handing things to Efuru.

'Remind me to buy more powder tomorrow; this is nearly finished. Now, bring his clothes. My boy, how well you look. Eh, my boy you look so well. You eat so much that's why you look well. Ah, Difu, when did you come in?'

'My mother said you should come now.'

And before Efuru could ask why, the boy had dashed out of the house. He did not want his navel to disappear.

'Take him, Nkoyeni, give him breast. Remember, give him the two, not just one. They are all right. If you give him both each time you breast-feed him, your breasts won't swell. Ogea, is Ogea at home at all? This child, I wonder where she goes these days. One never sees her at home when one looks for her. Ogea!' she called; there was no answer. 'Please tell her to clear everything on the bed, fold the wrappas neatly and put them away in the box. Please Nkoyeni, give me that piece of kola in the saucer in the bedroom. Thank you. Look after the baby, don't let it cry. I am going.'

'Go well, mother.'

'What on earth does Ajanupu want now? Did she hear anything that she wants to tell me? Is it about my husband? Is it about Adizua? What can it be?'

By the time she asked these questions, she had reached Ajanupu's house. 'Good woman, you are here already. My son said you were bathing Nkoyeni's son, and I thought you won't be able to come now. Welcome, sit down. Let's bring you kola.'

'No, I don't want kola, I have one right here. See.'

'Yes, we have fresh palm wine. It is very sweet. Let me bring that.'

'All right.'

'Difu, bring the palm wine in the jar. It is the one in the small jar. I know you have your eyes on your forehead. It is behind the door and don't tell me you can't find it.'

Difu came out with a very big jar of wine. 'Mother, is it this?' He asked as he put the jar on the floor.

'Didn't I say that this eyes were in his forehead. He cannot see. I said, you good for nothing child, the small jar behind the door. And leave that jar there, you will break it. Nobody wants you to exhibit your strength here. Leave it there.'

'What is in it?' Efuru asked.

'Oh, it is the palm wine that I bought yesterday. It was left on the floor of the room, and so it became sour in no time. So, when I bought some today, I made sure I put the jar on a small stool. There it can stay a longer time without being sour. Difu, is the jar holding you there?'

Difu shouted back: 'Mother I cannot find it. It is not behind the box.'

'You silly, hopeless, careless, deaf child. Who told you it was behind the box. It is behind the door, the door, crocodile. Do you hear, behind the door. The crocodile even hears more than you do.'

The child brought the jar and placed it on the floor. The two women had a glass each.

'It is very sweet. If I take another glass, it will enter my eyes. What will you do with the palm wine in the other jar?' Efuru asked.

'Oh that, when my husband comes with his age-group, they will drink it. Men enjoy sour palm wine. Not me. I cannot taste it. Come to the bedroom.

'I heard something today. Sit down, on the bed. I heard something in the market today, which made my blood run cold.' Efuru's heart jumped into her mouth. Then hot tears began to roll down her cheeks. She was unable to utter a word.

'What is the matter, I have not said anything. Why are you crying? Are you a child? Wipe your tears. There is no problem in this world that cannot be solved.'

'But, Ajanupu, you have not told me anything yet. What is it?'

'And you, you are crying when I have not told you why I called you.'

'Tell me now, please. You have always liked me, and I respect you very much. You have been a mother to me. Tell me what it is. Is it about my husband?'

'I went to the market this morning and while I was buying some fish. I overheard a conversation which I did not like. So I lingered on in the fish stall to hear all of it. All I gathered was that Eneberi was jailed at Onicha for three months. What he did, I cannot tell, for the two women who were talking did not know.'

'It was a long time before Efuru could say a word. 'Eneberi jailed? What did he do?'

'That, we must find out. Because if he stole, it is very serious. But why should he steal? His father did not steal. His mother has never stolen. Whom then will he be like?'

Efuru was deep in thought. Everything was clear to her at last. The mystery of her husband's absence at her father's burial was now explained. He could not come, because he was in jail. She felt very sorry at first, then suddenly she was filled with fury. She was angry because her husband, with whom she had lived for nearly six years, could, at that stage of their married life, hide something from her. Angry because she had again loved in vain. She had deceived herself all these years, as she deceived herself when she was Adizua's wife. She was filled with hate and resentment, qualities that were foreign to her nature.

Her husband looked haggard and ill when he returned, and the way he kept quiet each time she interrogated him about his absence at her father's burial were enough to make her believe the story. Then, she thought of the wonderful time Gilbert had given her, his loving care and good humour, and she became softer. But this did not last long. Another thought intruded – for years, Gilbert hid from her the fact that he had a baby boy by another woman. She was overwhelmed and she gave way to uncontrollable tears. The older woman left her to weep. Weeping would do her a lot of good. After weeping, they would plan what to do.

Ajanupu brought water and a towel. Efuru washed her face and cleaned it. She looked ten years older than she really was.

'What are you going to do?' Ajanupu asked as she saw the far-away look on Efuru's face.

'I will find out the truth, this evening, this very evening and if Eneberi is not ready to tell me the truth, I shall leave him. He must tell me the truth, or I go.'

Gilbert had already gone to bed by the time Efuru returned. She knocked at the door and when it was opened, she went and sat on the bed.

'I was so tired after the day's work that I came straight to bed,' Gilbert said, Efuru swallowed. She wanted as much as possible to avoid open quarrel.

'You forget, Eneberi, that today is Orie day, and the lady of the lake forbids that I should sleep with any man.'

'It is true, my wife. I forgot, forgive me,' Gilbert said meekly.

'I have come to discuss something very important. I heard something very strange today. And all I want you to do is to tell me the truth, nothing but the truth. Were you jailed at Onicha for three months? If so, what was the nature of your crime?'

There was silence – an unusual silence between two people who have lived together for nearly six years.

'Tell me, Eneberi. Were you jailed at Onicha?' Efuru asked again, this time she was afraid. There was fear in her voice. She had thought that her husband would flare up and demand the source of the news and then swear that it was untrue.

'I went to jail, but I did not steal. I was foolish that's all, and I paid for my foolishness.'

Efuru breathed in and breathed out again. She was greatly relieved. She still had implicit trust in her husband after all.

'You did not steal, thanks be to our ancestors and the woman of the lake. What happened, then, and why did you not tell me when you came back?'

'I was afraid that you would be upset. It was fear only, only fear, my wife. Fear that you would desert me.'

'Now that I have known the truth, I am not worried again. You did not steal, that's enough.'

Few women would be satisfied with this. But Efuru, good natured as she was, did not even find out what the foolish act was. Since her husband did not steal, she was at peace.

'Nkoyeni, what am I hearing. Did they say that your husband went to jail? What did he do? Eh, what did he do? What can Eneberi do to anybody? Eneberi who is very jovial and loving. This is very sad.'

It seemed as if cold water was poured on Nkoyeni's body during the harmattan. Her heart missed a beat. She stared at the woman who said these incomprehensible words.

'What are you saying?' another woman said. 'You will die for saying things you do not know. It is not Eneberi. Don't mind her, my daughter. She means Adiberi who was jailed some five months ago for stealing a fowl. Don't you know the difference between Adiberi and Eneberi? Take no notice of her, my dear daughter.'

It was the turn of the gossip to be surprised. She looked at Nkoyeni who was still lost, and then at her companion.

'My daughter,' she began, 'Please forgive me, I did not know. We old people do not know our right from our left. Please forgive me.'

'Ewo-o, what is this? This is not the way to sympathize, 'the gossip's companion said. 'You have caused a lot of trouble now. She is not a child. She is going to ask questions.'

'Ewo-o, poor girl, so she did not know. Wicked of them to hide it from her. It is really wicked. They should have told her. Does it mean that Efuru does not know about it?'

'She may know, or may not know,' her companion said. 'You should not have sympathized with her like that. You were merely giving her information.'

Nkoyeni was not a child. She demanded an explanation from Gilbert who flatly denied it all. 'Go and ask your mother, Efuru,' Gilbert told his wife. 'And don't annoy me any further.'

Nkoyeni was not satisfied when Efuru told her that the story was not true. She threatened to leave but Efuru tried to calm her down.

'Nkoyeni,' Efuru said one evening after a quarrel between Nkoyeni and Gilbert, 'Nkoyeni, listen to me. You are a child, a mere child. You do not understand. If our husband went to jail, will you leave him? If he committed murder today, will you desert him? Tell me frankly, will you? I have told you that the story is not true. Our Eneberi did not go to jail. Jail for what? Is our husband a thief? Was he a thief before you married him? If you knew he was a thief, why did you marry him? When we older people talk to you young people, try to weigh our words before you rebel. I know how you feel, but I have told you that it is not true. If you like you can go to Onicha and verify. Only before you go, leave my son behind for you won't take him there.'

Nkoyeni was not convinced. She made a lot of trouble and alluded to the scandal at the slightest provocation until Gilbert and Efuru were thoroughly disgusted with her.

'Who is sweeping at this time of the night?' Ajanupu's voice was heard. It was Ogea who was sweeping. She seemed to be nearly always doing wrong things when Ajanupu or Omirima came to see Efuru or Amede. 'Ogea, I know it must be you. Why are you sweeping at this time? Don't you know you are sweeping out the wealth in this house? You don't seem to know anything about our customs, and yet you did not go to school. Only school children are ignorant of our customs and traditions.'

Ogea of course stopped sweeping and stared at Ajanupu.

'Have you finished sweeping?' Ajanupu asked. Ogea nodded in assent. 'I have told you that we don't nod at night. Well, if you have finished, don't throw away the rubbish, leave it outside the door. In this way the wealth in the house will remain.'

Ogea obeyed.

'Sit down, Efuru will soon come,' Ogea said. 'She went to the back of the house.' Ajanupu went to Nkoyeni's room to see the baby.

'Ewo-o, have you grown so big. Bring him,' Ajanupu said.

Nkoyeni gave the baby to Ajanupu.

'That's a good boy. He does not cry.'

'He cries, especially at night,' Nkoyeni said smiling.

'That's how all of them behave. But he is a lovely boy. He looks very much like you.'

'So I said, but my mother, Efuru, said he looks like Gilbert.'

'Yes, there is something in Gilbert that he has taken, the smile and the nose.'

'You are right. I like the smile very much.'

'Ajanupu, Ogea has just told me you called. How are you?' Efuru said.

'We are well.' Both women exchanged greetings. Efuru took the boy and she and Ajanupu went to her sitting-room.

'Ogea,' Efuru called. 'Ogea,' she called again, but there was no reply.

'But I saw Ogea a moment ago, where has she gone? Ajanupu

I am worried about this girl. She goes out so often these days. It seems as if she has got an attraction somewhere.'

'Girls of these days grow up very quickly. Watch her. If she becomes pregnant, you are in for trouble. You are going to be responsible for everything. So watch out,' Ajanupu warned.

'Please bring me something heavier for my son. It is rather chilly this evening.'

'Do you know? Omirima nearly had good luck yesterday.'

'Really, why did she not have it?' Efuru said very interested.

'Foolishness, that's all, foolishness.'

'On whose part?'

'On the part of her daughter. She was foolish and slow, otherwise they should have bagged some thirty pounds.'

'What happened then?'

'You know that last year Omirima started trading in palm oil and palm kernel. She made very rapid progress and in no time, she was able to pay off all the debts she owed to several people. Just two days ago, she asked her daughter to take her voucher to the Company to be paid. When she got there, she presented her voucher. The cashier overpaid her by thirty pounds. Instead of the foolish girl taking the money, she told the cashier that she was overpaid. The cashier was very happy and gave her two pounds only.'

'That is foolish indeed and what did her mother do?'

'Poor Omirima, she was dumbfounded. Her chi gave her the thirty pounds, and now that she had rejected the money which her chi gave her, her chi is sure to be angry with her and make her poor because of it. You don't reject what your chi has given you. It is not done. I hope her chi is not angry with her. If he is, then she will never smell that sum again. I saw Omirima yesterday and I asked her about it. She said she was going to kill a white hen for her daughter's chi.'

'That is the right thing to do. She must kill a hen for her chi. Is that you Ogea? Where did you go?'

'I did not go anywhere.'

'You were not in when I called.'

'I went to get some fire from Anamadi's kitchen.'

'From where?' Efuru asked not believing her ears. Ogea kept quiet.

'How many times have I told you not to go for fire at An-amadi's house? Eh, Ogea, how many times?' Ogea stared at her. 'Ajanupu, I am tired of saying one thing over and over again. There is nobody in this compound that I have wilfully wronged. But since I came to Eneberi's house, Anamadi has hated me for no reason at all. She has told her children not to eat in my house, she has told them not to take fire from my kitchen. But Ogea constantly goes there to take fire. Ogea, it is high time you left this house. You are a grown-up girl now, and it does not seem as if you like to stay any more with me.' Ogea did not say a word in her own defence. Instead she began to cry.

'Keep quiet, you silly girl. Why are you crying? If I were Efuru I would have flogged you and afterwards put pepper in your eyes. What have you kept in Anamadi's house? Eh, what have you there?'

'Go and make the fire quickly and come and take some fish to Eneberi's mother.'

'Is she cooking her own food now?' Anjanupu asked.

'Yes, she is. I told Eneberi that it would be better for her to cook her own meals, but he refused. It did not work. So she is now cooking for herself.

'We want to marry again,' Efuru said laughing.

'Really, why?'

'Eneberi wants to marry another wife, and I think it is the right thing to do. Nkoyeni is giving us trouble. She heard about that jail sentence and she believes that our husband stole or did something very shameful. So she makes a lot of trouble. She quarrels and calls Eneberi all sorts of names during these quarrels. We must get another wife who will compete with her. She thinks she can do what she likes in this house. So we are looking around.'

'Ogea has grown you know. I think she will do.'

'I thought of it some time ago, you know. I think she will do. She is a lovely girl and has lived with me for so long. We know her parents very well. They are respectable but poor. That should not matter at all. If Eneberi agrees, we shall marry her. Never mind her childish ways. Basically she is a good girl.'

'And if you don't marry her now, suitors will begin to pour in.'

'Exactly. I shall discuss it with Eneberi this night. We shall send for Nwosu and Nwabata at once. Nwosu did very well when I lost my father. Immediately he heard the cannons, he came straight home. He helped me with serving the numerous guests.'

'Nwosu is a good man, his fault is poverty. He and his wife, Nwabata, will be very pleased if they hear that you want to marry Ogea to Eneberi.'

Gilbert was perfectly happy when Efuru told him about Ogea. Ogea was happy with the whole arrangement, and even said so to Efuru.

Before the final arrangements were made for the marriage between Ogea and Gilbert a sad thing happened. Efuru suddenly took ill. For three days, she was unable to get up from her bed. The illness was so sudden that everybody was afraid. Many dibias were contacted and all of them gave different diagnosis. Some said she was going to have a baby, others said the gods were angry with her, for what, they could not tell. When Gilbert's mother was tired of the contradictory dibias she went to a village a few miles away from the town. The dibia was a renowned one. His father and his father's father were all dibias. They cured the sick and gave people charms for health and wealth. This dibia specialized on women and their problems. Gilbert's mother reached the dibia's house. She gave her name and address. In a few minutes, a messenger came to her:

'The great dibia says that Efuru, the daughter of the great Nwashike Ogene, will not die. She has offended the woman of the lake by neglecting her. So she must appease the woman of the lake with a white hen, that is laying eggs. The eggs of the hen must be thrown into a pot containing palm oil. Unripe plantains, very big ones should be cut into pieces and put in the pot. The pot must be an earthenware pot. The great dibia says that his fee is elevenpence – all in pennies.'

Gilbert's mother paid the fee and the man disappeared. The sacrifice was performed, but Efuru was not better, rather she grew worse. Her condition was a puzzle to everyone. Then one day Omirima came.

'Amede, your daughter-in-law will die. She is guilty of adultery. Let her confess and the sickness will leave her. She has wronged the goddess of the land and she is being punished

215

accordingly. She must confess otherwise our ancestors will kill her. I am warning you. It is better for her to confess than to die.' She was gone before Amede recovered from her shock. Ogea was at home when Omirima came. She was filled with hate when she heard what she said.

'My mother cannot be guilty of adultery,' she said to Gilbert's mother. 'I don't believe a word of it.'

Efuru was not in a position to understand the plight that she was in. All Amede did was to go to another dibia who confirmed the guilt of adultery. 'She will surely die if she does not confess,' the dibia said.

Amede told her son Gilbert, who was of course incredulous at first, but when Efuru's condition grew worse and it was obvious to the little town that Efuru was guilty of adultery, Gilbert spoke to his wife: 'Efuru, my wife, the gods are angry with you because you are guilty of adultery, and unless you confess, you will die. So you should confess to me and live. I won't ostracise you, you will still be my wife, and I won't allow anybody to molest you. So confess and live.'

The sick woman heard, but had no energy to reply. It was a rude shock. She did not say a word. She called Ogea who was always near her. 'Go and ask Ajanupu to come now,' she said slowly. She motioned to Gilbert to sit down. In no time Ajanupu was in the room. She had been very worried about Efuru's condition. 'What is the matter Efuru, is it well? What has happened? Is it very serious now?'

Efuru was only able to point to Gilbert who was sitting at a corner.

'Eneberi, what is it? Did you send for me?'

'Ajanupu, this is what I am hearing. I don't know whether you have heard. My wife is guilty of adultery. The gods are angry with her and will kill her if she does not confess. So . . .'

'Eneberi, nothing will be good for you henceforth. Eneberi, Ajanupu, the daughter of Uberife Nkemjika of Umuosume village, says that from henceforth nothing good will come your way. Our ancestors will punish you. Our Uhamiri will drown you in the lake. Our Okita will drown you in the Great River. From henceforth evil will continue to visit you. What did you say? My god, what did you say? That Efuru, the daughter of Nwashike Ogene, the good, is an adulterous woman. Ewo-o, I am afraid, my people, I am afraid. Eneberi, who are you? Who is your father, who is your mother? What have you got to be proud of? You went to school. Eh? If your own brand of education is the only brand, then I am glad I did not go to school. Eneberi what happened at Onicha? Tell me what happened at Onicha? You don't know that we know that you were jailed. And here you are accusing Efuru, the daughter of Nwashike Ogene of adultery. You . . .'

Gilbert gave Ajanupu a slap which made her fall down. She got up quickly for she was a strong woman, got hold of a mortar pestle and broke it on Gilbert's head. Blood filled Gilbert's eyes.

CHAPTER SEVENTEEN

'Difu, welcome. Adishiemea welcome. When did you return?'
Efuru asked.

'I returned last month, but did not want to come home
straightaway. You look so haggard. What is the matter? Are
you not well? You used to look so cheerful. Is everything all
right?'

Efuru wiped her tears with her bare hands.

'You are crying. There must be something wrong then. Tell
me, what is it?'

Efuru wiped her tears again. But she was still unable to say
anything.

'Come on, Efuru, tell me. Can you hide anything from me
after so many years?' the doctor pleaded.

'I have left Eneberi.'

'You have left Eneberi. Why?' Efuru said nothing. 'Tell me,
why did you leave your husband? Did he beat you?' Efuru
shook her head like a child. 'Why then did you leave him?' the
doctor insisted.

'It is a long story, but I will tell you.'

'Come and sit down in the chair. Nwankwo, please give us
something to drink. I think schnapps will be all right for you,'
Efuru nodded. 'Bring schnapps and two glasses, Nwankwo,' the
doctor said. When it was brought, the doctor served Efuru and
poured himself two short drinks, then he sat down, quite relaxed. 'You may leave us now,' he said to Nwankwo who was
still waiting. 'Yes, tell me, why did you leave your husband?'

'It is about four months today since I left Eneberi. When my
father died, Eneberi did not come home to bury him.'

'Wait, Efuru, I don't mean to interrupt you, but do you mean
that your husband did not return for the burial of your father?'

'I mean, Difu, that my husband came home four months
after the death of my father,' Efuru emphasized.

'Where did he go?'

'He went to Onicha.'

'Onicha?'

'Yes, Onicha, Difu, he went to Onicha.'

'Go on, Efuru.'

'He returned four months after my father's death. It was a great humiliation. Our people gossiped. My friends were sorry for me; my enemies laughed at me. When he returned, he looked sick and miserable. We were concerned, Nkoyeni and I. Nkoyeni is Eneberi's wife.'

'I see, go on,' the doctor said.

'He was miserable. He did not tell us anything, about those four unspeakable months, and I did not want to press him. I was instead only happy that he had come home safely.

'Then one day Ajanupu sent for me. I went to see her. She told me that she heard Eneberi went to jail.'

'Jail?'

'Yes, jail. He was jailed at Onicha. Ajanupu said I should be calm and ask my husband to tell me the truth. To say that I was upset is to put it very mildly. I was afraid. Eneberi cannot steal, I said to myself several times that day. Why should he steal? His father did not steal; his mother is not a thief; if you are not like your mother then you must be like your father. But since neither is a thief, it is impossible for him to be a thief. However, I asked him. He denied it. He told me he went to jail through his own foolishness. He did not steal. As foolish as I was I believed him. I did not as much as press him to tell me the foolish act. Later on, a woman saw Nkoyeni on the way and began to sympathize with her for Eneberi's imprisonment. You know how our people sympathize. The poor girl was apprehensive. She nagged the two of us every day. I stood by my husband. I tried, used all my resources at persuasion to convince Nkoyeni that it was false, that our husband did not go to jail. She was not convinced. She threatened to leave us.

'Then, I became ill. Where the illness came from, nobody knew. Everybody thought I was going to die. Many dibias were consulted and we were asked to sacrifice to the gods, our ancestors and the woman of the lake. All was in vain. I was worse. Then a rumour went round that I was guilty of adultery – that I, Efuru, the daughter of Nwashike Ogene was guilty of adultery. My mother was not an adulterous woman, neither was her mother, why should I be different? Was it possible to learn to be left-handed at old age? Then, my husband, Eneberi, had the nerve to ask me to confess so as to live. Eneberi, my husband, of all people, asked me to confess that I am an adulterous woman. Ajanupu saved me. I was too weak to do anything. But Ajanupu said a few home truths to Eneberi. I hear he is in hospital on account of the injury given him by Ajanupu.

'She took me to a doctor in Aba. I was cured. I came back only a month ago. I went to my husband's house and collected all my belongings. Then I called my age-group and told them formally what I was accused of. According to the custom of our people, selected members of my age-group followed me to the shrine of our goddess – Utuosu. There I swore by the name of Utuosu, she should kill me if I committed adultery. She should kill me if since I married Eneberi any man in our town, in Onicha, Ndoni, Akiri, or anywhere I had been, had seen my thighs.

'I remained for seven Nkwos and now I am absolved. Utuosu did not kill me. I am still alive. That means that I am not an adulterous woman. So here I am. I have ended where I began – in my father's house. The difference is that now my father is dead. But I have nothing to say to Eneberi. He will for ever regret his act. It is the will of our gods and my chi that such a misfortune should befall me.'

The doctor was silent when Efuru ended her story. Then he asked: 'You will not go back to him?'

'I thought you were my friend, Difu?' Efuru said horrified.

'I am your friend. I have always been your friend.'

'If you are my friend, why then do you want me to go back to the man who accused me of adultery. You don't know the seriousness of the offence.'

'What will you do now?'

'What have I been doing before?'

'But, you are still young, and men will continue to seek you. If I were you, I would make up with Eneberi.'

'You might as well ask me to make up with Adizua, my first husband,' Efuru said laughing.

'Yes, where is Adizua. Any news about him?'

'I have heard nothing about him. To me, he has been dead years ago.'

'So he did not return?'

'No, he did not return.'

The doctor shook his head.

'Difu, I have not asked, how is your wife?'

'Oh, she is well. I left her in the country of the white people.'

'All alone?'

'She lives with an elderly woman who takes great care of her and our two sons.'

'That is good. I think I should be going,' Efuru said, standing up.

'I think you should consider going back to your husband.'

'Difu, it is not possible. Let day break.'

'Let day break, Efuru.'

Efuru slept soundly that night. She dreamt of the woman of the lake, her beauty, her long hair and her riches. She had lived for ages at the bottom of the lake. She was as old as the lake itself. She was happy, she was wealthy. She was beautiful. She gave women beauty and wealth but she had no child. She had never experienced the joy of motherhood. Why then did the women worship her?